THE CROSSED

By T.J. Rao

For the One who holds the stars,

Thank you for making each day worth living.

"I wonder where I'm going to die,

Being neither white nor black?"

– Cross, Langston Hughes, 1926

ISBN #: 978-0-578-72010-4
First paperback edition July 2020.
Edited by Kate Porch
Cover art by L1graphics
Layout by Marcy McGuire
TLSI Publishing, LLC.
651 N. Broad Street, Suite 206,
Middletown, DE 19709
tjrao.com

Contents

Chapter 1 *Hart*..4

Chapter 2 *Violetta*..19

Chapter 3 *Hart*...31

Chapter 4 *Violetta*..40

Chapter 5 *Hart*...51

Chapter 6 *Violetta*..58

Chapter 7 *Hart*...71

Chapter 8 *Violetta*..81

Chapter 9 *Hart*...91

Chapter 10 *Violetta*...102

Chapter 11 *Santiago*...111

Chapter 12 *Hart*...120

Chapter 13 *Violetta*...131

Chapter 14 *Santiago*...141

Chapter 15 *Hart*...148

Chapter 16 *Violetta*...161

Chapter 17 *Santiago*...171

Part II

Chapter 18 *Hart*...182

Chapter 19 *Violetta*...191

Chapter 20 *Santiago*...201

Chapter 21 *Hart*...213

Chapter 22 *Violetta*...221

Chapter 23 *Santiago*...229

Chapter 24 *Hart*...240

Chapter 25 *Violetta*...250

Chapter 26 *Santiago*...259

Chapter 27 *Hart*...274

Chapter 28 *Violetta*...285

Chapter 29 *Santiago*...296

Chapter 30 *Hart*...307

Chapter 31 *Violetta*...317

Chapter 32 *Santiago*...327

Chapter 33 *Hart*...339

Chapter 34 *Violetta*...353

Epilogue *Hart*...365

Authors Note...375

Acknowledgments...377

CHAPTER
1

Hart

Smile, Hart. You're on camera.

Chapter 1

I shamelessly flash my signature grin to the audience, hoping somehow my compliance will cause this event to end swiftly. My hand waves robotically to the crowd before coming to rest at my side. My father initiates his address to the thousands of citizens at our feet. The overwhelmingly strong scents of my mother's hairspray and layers of expensive Italian perfume are wafting over the elaborate dress she's adorned. She gazes at my father with a sense of admiration that seems so real that I almost believe the charade for a moment. Her look wouldn't be complete without her tightly upturned lips, and her hands all-too-delicately clasped in front of her. If I could roll my eyes without everyone noticing, I most certainly would.

"Not only have we completely repaired the homes from the last hurricane, but we also took the extra initiative and donated several thousand dollars in food to those affected. That's how resilient our city is and how well we are functioning under President Grey's administration." My father's voice booms out over the auditorium, and a thunder of cheers greets him back, which he receives gratefully with a contented nod.

After his speech closes, the security guards gesture for us to sit beside my father at a table. Dreadfully aware of the cost of my suit, I sit carefully, watching the MC as he begins to conduct a Q&A session with our city's beloved leader. This is about the time in the morning where I usually begin to tune out these useless questions from the people and fall asleep in my chair. If hearing my father's contrived speech didn't feel like punishment enough, I'm certain that this panel will. One by one, different faces step forward to greet my father and query him, though the answers they await could be found by running a simple Internet search. By the time I look down at my white leather watch, I can see that forty-five minutes have already passed. The Q&A should be ending soon, along with my veritable torture.

"One last question! Please step up to the mic, sir," the MC speaks charismatically to a man with a metallic card around his neck that reads, "PRESS."

"Governor Kang, I'm sure you're aware that the protests of the Crossed laws have been becoming more frequent in the past few years, especially in our city." My ears perk up at the mention of the taboo subject, and I sit upright in my seat. "The citizens of Briste are beginning to have concerns that these protesters will become violent. What will you do to stop them?"

A flash of something like panic reveals itself in my father's aging eyes, but he recovers in an instant and leans towards the man. "Thus far, they have not been a threat, but if it becomes an issue, be assured that I will personally see to taking care of the problem."

"Do you agree with the protesters, Governor Kang?" The man oversteps his right to the one-question limit, and the ghost of a smirk finds its way to my lips.

"My official position on the matter lines up with those of our lovely President Grey; I am in full support of the Crossed laws." He smiles at the reporter, but his tone drips with venom. "Thank you for your questions, but the Q&A session has now ended."

With that last remark, my father stands up and leads us off the stage. We wait silently as the tech team removes the clear microphones attached to our clothing. Not one word is spoken as Grey Guards form a protective wall around us, and we push past the congregation of citizens. We stride towards our limousine, waving at these strangers as if we are thankful for the lack of privacy. I briefly see several girls holding signs that say vaguely flattering things such as, "Marry me Hart!" and "Have my children Hart!" I shoot a wink towards them to keep up appearances, and their high-pitched screams meet my unwelcoming eardrums.

The very moment that we are seated on the premium seats of the limousine, my body slouches, and the feeling is so tranquil that it's almost indescribable. My hands are already unbuttoning the black fasteners on my ivory blazer, which had been attempting to suffocate me all morning. Glancing away from my parents proves as unsuccessful as the reporters earlier trying to get a genuine answer out of their fabricated governor. My father's charismatic smile turns downward into a scowl at my mother. She directs her attention to her manicured nails.

"Did you have to wear the pink dress, Hana? I told you that the blue pinstriped pencil skirt would have fit our image much better today." My father's low voice carries over to my mother, and she looks up at him from her fingertips.

"It would have given you too much satisfaction if I had, Luke."

He sighs at her in frustration and then turns his eyes to me. "Thank you, Hart, for being the only one to comply with my requests."

"Of course, Dad," I reply without missing a beat, gritting my teeth at how weak I've become. "I hate to request this, but could you have the limousine driver drop me off at home? I'd like to change before heading to my two o'clock class."

"Yes, consider it a reward for your impeccable behavior at the press conference."

I muster up the strength to nod with gratitude, though it nearly kills me. Although I lost all traces of my dignity a long time ago, I still wince sporadically in these moments where it must appear that I enjoy the presence of the people who "raised" me. The remainder of the ride to our estate is filled with silence, that is, besides the occasional rude comment that my father throws flagrantly at my mother. She seems completely unfazed. By the time they drop me off, I feel no remorse for running out of the limousine to the front doors of our home.

"Welcome home, sir. I've laid out a change of clothes for you in your room, packed your bag for Economics 101, and set the table for a quick lunch before you leave," one of our maids greets me. I pass by her, walking briskly to the stairs. I don't stop for anything these days, let alone the dread of exchanging pleasantries with my father's staff.

"I'll be down for my meal in twelve minutes, please have it fully prepared," I call down from the top of the stairs to the faceless maid.

Multitasking is a must when your father is the governor and you're being groomed to replace him. This is why I ask the virtual assistant installed in my room, Vara, to update me on headlines I missed this morning. As the tight ivory blazer slides down my arms, Vara tells me about another attack on the peaceful protesters of the Crossed laws. Five injured, and two dead. Two lives gone for opposing the law—a truly upsetting report to hear.

This subject of death is a topic that has bought a permanent place of residence in my mind as of late. It seems to me that we are all simply souls occupying mortal flesh while we spend time on earth, waiting for the imminent destruction of the outer vessel in which our spirits have been placed. Some, of course, believe in a higher being or cause for the explanation of our inner selves taking residence in these bodies. Others, like myself, can recognize that there is no reason for this scientific phenomenon other than the consciousness of our complex minds.

I've been told that eighteen years of age is too young to have such thoughts about the world and all that inhabit it, but I disagree. Though my thoughts run a mile a minute, each one is unique. I have trust in only the most correct things, the most logical. Some believe in religion, some in myth, and some in science. I personally stand to believe in reason; my mind is the only thing that has yet to let me down in any capacity.

Standing at six feet with dyed golden-blonde hair and dark brown eyes, it's only rational to assume that I am above average in looks. My features are as prominent as my intellect. My skin has rarely flared up. I carefully avoid ingesting anything that might cause harm to my overt appearance, and the team of styling professionals I have on call are diligent with my skincare.

Death *is* inevitable, and our only purpose on earth is to make living easier for generations to come, but that doesn't mean I should treat my body badly while I'm occupying it.

The general public watches my every move. I need to display a certain look to uphold my reputation.

Knowing how I appear to others comes in handy, too. Using common sense, I can see that as I am an attractive person, there will be opportunities to acquire the affections of a suitable partner. She must be as physically healthy as I am, as well as be able to engage in an intellectual conversation with me. She must be well-mannered, independent-thinking, and of Korean heritage, like myself. This way, when I am doomed to follow in the footsteps of my father, I will at least have an amiable wife whom the citizens can envy in their free time.

This train of thought fades as my focus is put to better use: listening to the celebrity portion of Vara's news recap and lingering on one intriguing story in particular that I'll have to remember for later. As she wraps up, each strand of my hair is carefully placed with my pure silver comb. The long-sleeved magenta shirt feels smooth on my skin, and the dark designer slacks slide on easily—at least my father's staff has taste. My stylist freshly dyed my hair again this morning, so my black roots don't show through. Golden hair looks fantastic with my skin tone, according to my parents. It's been this color ever since I can remember, and the public loves it. When I glance in the large mirror, I can't help but feel that something is missing. I should check on the latest trends this week with the remaining few minutes I have.

"Vara," I say, while staring at the screen installed into the upper right corner of my mirror. "What has been trending in fashion this week?"

"Top designers have been focused on small statement accessories in the past month," Vara's monotone voice speaks back, while displaying several images of notable people my age and their modest necklaces or handbags. Nothing sparks my interest until I see a photo of Stephen Grey, son of President Grey, wearing a sleek, silver bracelet.

If it's good enough for the president's son to wear, it must be more than suitable for the son of Governor Kang. Thankfully, I have just the item that will complete my ensemble. Decisively walking to my closet, I place my palm on the scanner and speak to Vara again.

"Please open drawer number fourteen, and unlock item two," I say to the closet, and the system immediately complies as it recognizes my handprint and voice.

The drawer slides open and the silver cuff-like bracelet my father gave me long ago is displayed before me. Reaching in and picking up the accessory, I slide the band onto my wrist. The metallic sheen suits the clothes that were laid out for me. Now I'm prepared if the paparazzi decide to follow me to school again. It's too bad my father gave it to me, or I would've thought to wear it sooner. After one last look in the mirror, I grab my clear backpack and head downstairs.

Racing down the winding staircase, I glance at my watch to see that it's been exactly 10 minutes since I told the maid to prepare my food. The head seat of the large dining table invites me over, and a butler slides a satin napkin over my lap before presenting me with my exquisite lunch. Per my usual request, he plays Vivaldi through the house speakers. I dine on the bowl of perfectly-portioned lobster bisque, a typical meal for the only child of the prestigious governor of Geal, who is adored by all.

After patting the excess soup off my lips, I glance out of the large glass archway to see my driver waiting for me beside the door of my private car.

My only class of the day is Economics 101 with Professor Arnay, and it is quite possibly one of the most mind-numbing classes known to man. My good friend, Ember, decided to take it with me though, and keeps me preoccupied for most of it with her antics. Having class with her during the week is one of the only things I look forward to nowadays.

"Already writing notes down before the class has even started? What a first-class student you are, Hart." Ember smirks in my direction as she sits down comfortably at the desk next to mine.

"I have to write my thoughts down now before I forget them," I glance in her direction, and she rolls her eyes at me for what must be the thousandth time.

"It sure seemed like you had a terrible memory when you got a 98 on the test last week."

"Well, not all of us can simply get by based off their looks like you can."

"Don't be envious, Hart. It's not a good color on you. That button-down though... that's another story." She winks at me with her long, royal blue painted lashes.

I chuckle at her before turning to the professor and jotting down everything he has to say, although I can't help but occasionally look in Ember's direction as I take notes. Her short, sapphire-colored hair is perfectly cut to complement her features, and her skin is unblemished as far as the eye can see. She taps her nails, painted light yellow, on the desk as she listens to the lecture.

She and I are quite compatible—this is a known fact. Since I was a young boy, her family has worked closely with mine. We share the same beliefs, culture, and connections to the political world. She has this individualistic kind of attitude that I can appreciate in a girl my age. Not to mention her appearance is more than suitable, and her clothing style is elegant. I sometimes wonder if we would be good together as a couple, but I want to enjoy my youth first.

As the professor makes his closing remarks, ending with an easily forgettable pun about economics, Ember looks my way and motions for me to follow her out the door. I quickly pack up my things and throw my sunglasses on, ready to face the bright sun of Geal. Soon enough, Ember and I are carrying on with our routine habit of sitting across from one another at the bookstore on campus as we study after class. Campus is the one place where I feel close to normal. I try to soak this up for as long as possible with her before heading back to the life where I'm constantly scrutinized.

"So, how was your date with Blaise Park?" I close my book slightly and lean in, grateful that Vara keeps me updated on tabloid stories.

She stares at me with eyes wide. "I didn't realize my personal life had to do with our economics homework."

"I was just surprised you wouldn't tell your alleged best friend," I gesture to myself, and she looks almost sympathetic for a beat. "Did you keep it quiet because you're embarrassed?"

"Why would I be embarrassed?" She takes a sip of coffee while keeping her eyes fixed on mine.

"Since he's *far* from the best-looking son of a government official that you know," I shrug at her, and she seems to almost spit out her hot drink.

She coughs slightly before collecting herself. "For your information, many people find Blaise to be charming."

"Ah, so his dazzling wit won you over?" I lean back into my chair while she checks her nails.

"We aren't dating, Kang," she says, still examining her nails in the light while holding a mug in the other hand. "I had dinner with him to discuss logistics for a charitable event I'm holding later this month. You know I don't partake in the dating scene."

"Well, it's reassuring to me that you haven't started believing in romance," I laugh a bit, relieved that she isn't dating Blaise. It'd be unfortunate if I lost my most logical friend to the foolish notion that is "true love."

She chuckles and places her coffee on the table. "The best we can ask for in life is a partner we are completely compatible with, and that definitely isn't Blaise," she states coolly.

"That is what I'm always trying to tell people! The serotonin levels in our brain rising is the explanation for the 'love' people feel. Lust can make people go insane, but what happens when that fades?"

The corners of her mouth turn upward. "That isn't to say that attraction isn't fun while it lasts, correct?"

"Of course not," I wink at her and she gives me a flirtatious smile before returning to highlight sentences in her book.

By the time we say our goodbyes after studying hours, I feel exhausted and can't wait to eat in the comfort of my own home before sleep. The thought of a nice hot bath also keeps my mind preoccupied the whole car ride, because before I know it I'm back in front of the large doors to my home.

"Welcome home, Mr. Kang. I've prepared your dinner, and I am at your disposal for the evening." This maid has a different voice from the one I heard this morning.

"Will my parents be joining me for dinner?" I ask, already knowing the answer.

"No sir, they are currently attending a banquet downtown."

I sigh in relief before heading to the dining room, while the heels of the maid click loudly against the marble floor behind me as she tries to keep up with my long strides.

"Turn the screen on to my usual channel then and draw a hot bath after thirty minutes have passed."

"Yes, sir."

Sitting down, I let the butler place the steak in front of me. After examining my food carefully, I eat it slowly while watching the news on the large screen set before me. "An informed mind is an optimal mind," as Ember likes to say, and there is so much I must have missed in the last few hours.

Just as I'm chewing on a delectable bite of sautéed spinach, the face of a Crossed girl flashes on the screen. She's wanted in New York for escaping the Teorrain that the government placed her in. She looks young. I wave my hand and the screen shuts off at my command. I don't like to see their faces; it hurts me deeply for reasons I can't understand.

I wasn't alive when the laws were made all those years ago, but my father was. He was born back when there were no laws against the mixing of races. It seems crazy to think that he saw a time when it wasn't a crime to be Crossed. There was only a short period in history when interracial couples could exist in America, and their children could freely walk any place they pleased.

Once 2043 rolled around, the government revoked their earlier passing of the law that once allowed persons of any race to procreate with another. The American government decided that to preserve different cultures, they must not let them mix.

There was a fear among those of many different cultural backgrounds that the number of multiracial children was becoming too great. They each feared a day would come when their blood would become so tainted with that of societies other than their own, that their traditions and customs would cease to exist.

Now the year is 2084, and not much has changed since that time except for the names of some states and major cities. We still haven't been able to cure the common cold, we fight over our differing beliefs constantly, and the same mindless sitcoms are available across thousands of streaming platforms.

The only real modifications are that technology has advanced yet again, it's commonly accepted that the FBI watches our every move with technology and being with someone of another race is tremendously unlawful.

Friendship is encouraged between cultures, and polite exchanges are supported. As long as you don't step over the invisible boundary between friendship and romance with someone of another kind, you should have no reason to worry.

The last of the mixed-race people, or "the Crossed," as they prefer to be called, are forced to live out their days in special towns built only for them. There are fifteen circular fortifications with steel walls on the outskirts of numerous cities across the country. Each one has enough people inside to be considered a small town.

Even though the Crossed are separated from us by a barrier, they occasionally find ways to escape. This stirs up problems for our political party. My father has dealt with backlash firsthand and avoids discussing anything about the Teorrains in Geal. I've begun to believe it's because he doesn't even know what life is like inside the walls. Our city, Briste, is the capital of Geal and happens to possess a rather large Teorrain.

Thinking about the Crossed haunts the inner workings of my mind. It isn't their fault they were born into this life, and the system often reminds me of the untouchables in India. I read about how they were treated poorly for so many years. Maybe the Crossed really do live a decent life behind the barriers, as my father claims they do. After all, the government did promise that they would be treated equal to us.

It's still difficult for me to understand the reason why they are not part of our society. My father has told me it's best to not think about it, but that's impossible. That's why I've majored in journalism—it's the best subject to study for someone like myself whose mind has a voracious appetite.

The days go by like this, with my thoughts scattered like paint on a blank canvas. Little by little the hours pass me by, and I have no surprises left in my life that I haven't thought up. I've pondered each scenario that could happen to me, so I have no fear of the future.

For now, I will enjoy the comfort of the steaming water in my bath, before spending my remaining waking moments trying to forget about the astonishingly human face on the news tonight.

CHAPTER
2

Violetta

"*G*uess who!" My hands can barely reach high enough to cover my friend's eyes.

"Considering there's only one other employee who works with me, I'll have to guess it's Violetta?" I can hear the amusement in his voice, along with his pronounced English accent.

I let my hands fall from around his eyes, which flutter open to reveal his warm golden irises. "You got it this time! I'm impressed, Santiago."

He rolls his eyes in a playful way. "Sign in and get to work."

"Back to playing the role of the big, bad boss so quickly?" I sigh at him, walking into his office.

He mumbles something inaudible from outside while I write my name down in the log and check the time on the government-sanctioned clock above me. Tightening the ponytail atop my head, I briskly walk to my boss's side.

"How are you this lovely morning?" I smile up at him sweetly.

"Just fine," Santiago says, without looking up from the aging book he's carefully writing in. "We're getting a new shipment of fiction novels from a generous donor, so I need assistance carrying all the boxes in from the truck. Would you mind helping?"

"What else am I here for? It's not like anyone actually comes and visits our library," I say coyly, and immediately his vexed gaze falls on me.

He hates it when I say things like this. He actively tries to ignore the fact that many people inside the borders don't seem to care about reading. They're too busy with their jobs and trying to survive to sit down and take up literature as a hobby. Santiago ignores suffocating realities. He's hopeful in a way that others may call slightly delusional, but I find his sentiments endearing.

"You never know, someone could come in here just dying to read Shakespeare one day," he retorts back in his usual playful manner, trying to mask the frustration in his tone which desperately seeks an escape.

"The average Shakespeare aficionado that lives in the Teorrain? Can't wait for the day I see them waltz into the library questioning my knowledge of *Romeo and Juliet*." Sarcasm fills my voice.

He peeks up at me through his glasses. "Violetta, I will never quite understand your optimistic yet quietly cynical outlook on the world," he huffs at me. "May I remind you that not everyone who lives within this boundary is unintellectual?"

Noticing his irritation slip out, I begin to retract my earlier statements. "I'll lay off the skeptical attitude for now and keep my expectations high for the multitudes to make their appearance sooner or later at our fine establishment."

He looks at me briefly as he gets up from the chair and cleans his glasses with his faded sweater. Delicate strands of ebony hair fall in his face while he wipes away the smudges. I'm only 18, and even though Santiago is no more than two years my senior, he acts much older.

His parents raised him in England, a country unencumbered by the Crossed laws. To his great misfortune, both his parents died in a car accident when he was thirteen. The only living relative who was able to care for him was in the US, but he didn't even make it past customs before being arrested.

He was thrown in the nearest Teorrain with the other Crossed people. There was no way to contact the British embassy or his family. He waited for his Aunt to get him out for years, but she never came to his rescue. He is convinced they've lied to her about what happened to him. Eventually, he accepted his fate here, and has tried to make the most of it.

He was placed here at the library since his mother had been a literature professor at a university in London. Even at the age of thirteen, his knowledge of the subject was quite extensive. The library building was run down when he arrived, but he has made it much better. It is dusty and it lacks color, but it has this unmistakable soul that he awoke in it. He doesn't seem to be aware of how lively he's made the place. Santiago's cheerfulness rings through the halls like a melody that stays in your head hours after you've heard it.

He talks of his parents often with me. It's almost as if he's trying to keep their memory alive by letting his description of them fall on my ears. His father hailed from India, and his mother was from Spain. They shared a love of upbeat music and old books.

Santiago's hair is as dark as the night and stops below his chin in a wavy shag cut that makes him seem more relaxed than he really is. He towers over me, and always looks like he hasn't had much sleep. Curious eyes live behind the pair of wireframe glasses which sit on his nose, although they are too bright for the lenses to hide them away—like the sunset on a Fall evening. He's handsome, but that doesn't matter here anyway.

Looks get you nowhere in the Teorrain. Especially since the Crossed aren't allowed to date or marry. The government has a strong fear of even more children of mixed blood being born. They hope that by putting us in the Teorrain, we will all just die off eventually and the Crossed will become extinct in America.

So far, it's been working. Our numbers have been decreasing quickly over the course of time. Their main issue is that people outside of the Teorrain, who we call Pravis, keep breaking the law. They continue to produce more Crossed children who are sent to die here when they are caught. Men can make as many laws as they want, but there will always be those who were born to defy the rules, like my own parents.

I never got to know my father or mother well. My dad was injured badly when I was a child, after Pravi civilians found him trying to hide my mother and me. They had to turn themselves in because of the actions of their fellow Pravis— landing themselves in prison willingly to protect me. The government placed me here in a Teorrain before these "vigilantes" could take my life.

Pravis argue and bicker about things, but it appears they can agree on the fact that their individual races should never be "corrupted" with the blood of another. They will all rally together when a Crossed person is created and threatens their way of life. That's why the only Pravis I trust are my parents, who ruined their own lives to save mine.

I have some photos of my mother, and she was stunning in the classic kind of way. I still faintly remember the soothing hymns she would sing to me as I fell asleep. There's only one photograph of my parents together, and my mother's crystal blue eyes held all the adoration in the world as she looked at my father. Sometimes, I even wonder if she knew he was black, or if she was so color-blinded by love that all she saw was his bare soul.

I was placed in the orphanage where all Teorrain children end up and was raised by the Crossed women employed there. I haven't the slightest idea where my parents are now, but I pray for them every day. They must be out there praying for me, too. Hopefully, they'd be proud of the girl I've become, even in this desolate land.

I've stuck to my beliefs and have managed to educate myself to the best of my ability with the books that surround me at work. I'm thankful that the government lets us work for our basic needs. We may be poor, but we aren't starving. That simple truth keeps me happy, especially since eating is one of the most enjoyable experiences of my days.

Santiago hums softly as his fingers flip through the pages of a book, the sound bringing me out of my hunger-induced daydream. I begin to examine his subtle features again and remember my original thought process, before my ponderings took my mind somewhere else.

All this is to say, it is an outright shame that a man as handsome as Santiago will go his whole life being unloved and unnoticed. If the laws weren't in place, I'm sure he would undoubtedly make some girl happy. There have been times I've caught him watching me while I read, and it's made me wonder if he could have feelings for me. But, he's a strict rule follower, and I'm just a co-worker to him.

Even if Santiago doesn't feel that way about me, it's especially sad that he can't experience love, since he is such a secret romantic. The way he talks about the admiration his parents had for one another could warm even a heart made of ice.

A wonderfully crooked smile stretches across his face when he illustrates how his mother would smile contentedly with a cup of tea in her hand, watching his father cook dinner. It makes me believe in some crazy kind of earthly love. It's unfortunate he will never be allowed to experience it, but at least he has the knowledge of these tender tales of affection.

"I think this is the last box. You can look through it to see if you want to read any of these before they go to their designated shelves," Santiago says, panting as he places the heavy box on the ground next to the wooden bookshelves.

"I looked them over briefly and I didn't find anything too interesting," I shrug my shoulders.

"Well, we somehow managed to obtain a copy of *To Kill A Mockingbird* that looks like it was printed in the 2020's before the Crossed laws. You should give it a read; there's even an inscription." He teases me because books that have inscriptions are of great interest to me. Every inscription is so carefully written and tells a story of its own outside of the book. Reading those small notes, each addressed to someone in particular, makes me feel as if I've lived a hundred lives.

"I've never read *To Kill A Mockingbird* or really heard of it for that matter, but you got me with the inscription," I admit.

"Be sure to take good care of it; this is my absolute favorite book." He passes the faded book to me.

"This is your favorite book? You talk so often of Shakespeare, Lewis, and Austen, but I've never heard you mention this author."

"It's by Harper Lee," he says matter-of-factly, like I should've already known. "My parents gave me my middle name, Atticus, after a character in it. The message is close to my heart." There is something almost sad in his voice.

I take the book from his hands and hold it carefully in mine. The cover has faded quite a bit, but the artwork is visible enough for me to imagine what it would've looked like when it was printed many years ago. Santiago doesn't strike me as the kind of man who would ever go hunting for birds, or even read a guide on it. I get the feeling that this book must be about something that really matters to him, especially if he shares a name with a character.

"I'll make sure to put it deep in my bag and read it at home."

"Please let me know what you think of it," he pushes his glasses up higher onto the narrow bridge of his nose. "I quite enjoy having the company of another avid young reader."

With those kind words and a soft look in his eye, we go back to arranging the books we had previously received until we close. After locking up, I give Santiago a quick hug before beginning the trek back to the apartment I share with my closest friend. I can never help but walk home from work with an extra skip in my step, because nowhere feels more like happiness than my cozy old room. Not to mention, it's relaxing to watch the beautiful evening sky for a while before entering the worn-down apartment building where we reside.

"Violetta, is that you?" Nova calls out as soon as the door closes behind me. I can already smell the strong scent of whatever she is making us for dinner, and I'm once again grateful that she gets off work an hour earlier than me.

"Nope, it's a Grey Guard. You're under arrest!" I yell back at her while taking my scuffed shoes off and placing them neatly beside her pristine white ballet flats.

I trot down the hallway to see my petite roommate stirring something in a pot on the small, rusty gas stove that sits next to our cots. Her eyes are locked intently on the pot, and her hair is tied up in the same ponytail she always wears to keep the wild locks out of her face.

"That's fine with me!" she says, chuckling into the pot that is steaming below her. "I'm making us my famous soup for dinner, because it's a very special occasion."

"Special occasion?" My heart stops and I'm afraid I let something important slip from my mind again. "Did I forget something?"

"We received a large amount of food at the Donation Center today, and they let me have extra portions since I've been putting in so many hours." She gestures towards the soup in front of her, and a large smile spreads across her face. "So, let's celebrate."

"I didn't think we would be able to eat any extra portions until Friday!" I say, observing Nova closely as she giggles; she looks almost too excited to be cooking. Typically, she treats cooking like a chore—it's only when she's eating that she seems this jovial.

"This soup reminds you of home, doesn't it?" I ask.

"Yes, it reminds me of life in the country. My grandmother's recipe for Sopa de Lima comes in handy on days like these," she says, smiling happily to herself.

Her family used to live in a secret Crossed base in the countryside. There are apparently a few of these scattered around the country, where mixed families hide together from the Grey administration. Nova describes it as a place where Crossed people and their families could live in harmony, completely off the grid.

Her whole family, including her younger brother, were able to live there until she was eight years old, when they was found by the authorities. Now her parents are in jail, and she was sent here to Teorrain #14. Her brother, Graham, was placed in Teorrain #8. She's been stuck here for almost eleven years now, with many memories of her family, and no hope of seeing them again. It's because of people like Nova that I'm sure it must be a good thing to not remember what life before the Teorrain was like.

"I wish I knew more about my heritage like you. All I have left of my parents is my mother's bracelet." I sigh a little, disappointed to think that my knowledge about my cultures isn't much compared to my friends here. Both of my parents were raised in America, but that didn't mean their roots were meaningless to them. I'm sure they would've loved to tell me all about their backgrounds.

"There's no one who can understand you better than me." She chokes out a pitiful laugh to hide the hurt she feels, and I reach out to give her arm a reassuring squeeze. It's important to be reminded that someone is there for you, even if you don't know what to say. Santiago told me that once and it just stuck.

We eat our dinner on the floor next to our beds, and it's just what I needed after lugging around all those heavy boxes at work today. We chat about anything and everything on our minds. That's one thing I'm glad the government never took from us: our right to talk about anything we want—so long as it doesn't encourage a revolt or anything crazy like that. These small chats with Nova over dinner are the best part of my day. I'd like to think she enjoys them a good bit as well.

As I'm brushing my teeth after dinner, I pull from my bag the book Santiago lent me: *To Kill A Mockingbird.* I look down at it, curious as to whether it's really something more than a book about murdering some poor birds. I try not to think about it as I look at my reflection in the cracked mirror one last time.

Suddenly, an unfamiliar pair of dark eyes seem to stare back at me just for a flash, forcing a yelp of surprise from my throat. They are gone from my sight just as swiftly as they appeared, and my shaking hand rises from my side, reaching out to touch the mirror. As if hypnotized, my fingers trace the spot where those eyes appeared, looking both uncertain and hurt all at once.

A few moments pass and I suck in deep breaths, hoping maybe if more oxygen can get to my brain this strange sensation will pass. While my hand still rests on the mirror, my silver bracelet gleams slightly, reminding me of my mother, and easing my fear.

I must be working hard with too little sleep and now I'm imagining things. I'm left feeling breathless and confused, but there's no use in analyzing my odd hallucination right now. Perhaps the sight of my mother's bracelet shining in the light after that frightening vision was her way of calming me. My eyelids have become heavy; I must need more sleep.

Nova is already on her cot waiting for me, and I bury myself under the thin crochet blanket of the cot beside her. She's trying to dig the grime out from under her fingernails before she falls asleep so that they look somewhat presentable for her shift, which starts hours earlier than mine. Another reason I'm always thankful for my job at the library is because it feels like an escape, unlike Nova's, where she sorts through donations all day at a food bank and decides how many rations the people without jobs will get. I look over at her and she smiles warmly at me before turning off the light.

Nova turns over and falls asleep after only a few short breaths, and I envy her. Praying in my head always pushes the scary thoughts away, but not tonight. Even in the dark of the night, underneath my blanket, I can see the shadow of those daunting irises.

CHAPTER
3

Hart

"You know your proposal is ridiculous, right?" Ember laughs so loudly that the whole campus cafeteria must hear her.

We set our trays down at a glass table in the Student Union. "Haven't you ever wondered what one of them looks like up close?"

"I also wonder what a tiger looks like up close, but I'm not trying to find one to pet!" I compartmentalize her terrible analogy, as she needs to be lectured on her comparison choices later.

"These people aren't like tigers. We are being told they're dangerous, but in what way?" She looks at me with a curious expression as she waits for me to continue. "What if they aren't so different from us?"

She thinks for a moment before swallowing a bite of food. "Father told me that their blood makes them diseased. Your reputation could be ruined if one of them infected you!"

"There's no evidence to suggest they're *diseased*. Calling them all lepers is a bit Old Testament, wouldn't you say?" I slowly lift a cup to my lips and take a sip of piping hot tea.

"Nice Bible reference Hart; I forgot you were the expert on all things spiritual. Although who knows? You could be morphing into someone else with all this talk of getting close to the Teorrain."

"You don't have to come with me if you don't want to, but I'm going either way, in the name of journalism."

She sits in clear indecisiveness for several moments. Her hand loosely grips her fork as she moves the food around aimlessly. After she's done with this, it isn't long before her eyes meet mine and she lets out an exasperated huff.

"I'll come with you, but this is going down on my terms." She finally takes a bite of her food, covering her mouth as she chews. "Also, I am only doing this because you are intolerable and would probably get killed if I left you alone."

I beam at her. "Be at my place tonight at 7 pm sharp, and we will plan this out."

"Whatever you say."

We go back to our usual discussions of all things philosophical, and the occasional ordinary topic such as our plans for the week. Lunch continues like this for about an hour before Ember leaves for her third class of the day. She takes as many classes as the university will allow, yet she never lets on that she's stressed at all. I take only the required number of classes, as my schedule is already packed with political events and parties.

In the small amount of free time I have, you certainly would never find me packing on classes. I'd rather be playing instruments or creating art, and that is exactly what I do when Ember departs for class—spend time in the empty practice rooms on campus until I head home for the day.

My driver is careful not to hum along to the classical music flowing from the speakers on the way home. I'm appreciative, since I'm in no mood to reprimand him again. Staring out the car window at the scenery of light blue waves washing over the fine sand that coats the beach would normally be peaceful, but not today. Maybe it'll never feel serene again, since my mind won't stop torturing me.

Once the car stops, I stroll into the estate while ignoring whichever maid is trying to give me "vital" information about my father's schedule. Pushing past her, I climb the staircase completely out of breath and close the door of my bathroom behind me. My hands grip the sink before I sneak a look at the man in the mirror—someone I almost don't recognize.

Yes, I want to go to the Teorrain. Does that desire make me a fool? Quite possibly. There's exactly fifteen minutes till Ember arrives and I'm here trying to talk myself out of this like a lunatic in a bad film. A feeling of insanity has sunk in. It's been over a week since I last felt like myself. The night all of this started I had eaten my usual meal before nightfall, watched the news until one of *them* came on the screen, and went to sleep.

That's when I saw *her*, or at least her eyes. In my dreams, I saw a girl's eyes, colored violet, with panic filling them as if she needed my help. I called out to her and received no response, but the knowledge that she was stuck behind the boundaries was present in the dream. My hair was rumpled as I woke from my nightmare, and my heart was racing faster than ever before. It seems like it hasn't ceased since then.

This could very well be my guilty subconscious trying to make me reconsider my hesitant support of my father's stance on the Crossed laws, but I need to be sure of that. I want to find out what's beyond that wall—at least to figure out why she's stuck in my head.

Aware of how my mental state is quite clearly deteriorating, I willingly think back to those eyes. I don't know who she is, where she is, or even what she looks like. Even though I know almost nothing about what I'm getting myself into, finding her now is important because she has shaken me—and that's something no one has ever been able to do to me before. She's the only person who can help get me back on track to my normal life.

My choice to be a journalism major is the only thing that is saving me from looking like a complete madman. Even then, it took me a whole week to come up with an excuse to give Ember. You'd think that at my age, it'd be easy to invent a lie a little quicker than that. My mind has been uprooted from its mundane routine and taken through a chaotic battle-field of unanswered questions. The worst part is that all the answers are hiding from me behind walls where a governor's son has no business being.

I enlisted Ember because it's unknown what kind of horrors await me in that circular town. Ember is quick-witted and manipulative; she could get us out of a difficult situation efficiently. I will keep my ulterior motives a secret. She already thinks I'm foolish enough as it is.

"Sir? You have a visitor waiting downstairs," a maid calls from outside my bedroom door.

"Please escort her to the recreational room on the lower level." The tone of my voice is harsher than I intended.

There's no sound of her walking away. "Would you like me to prepare refreshments for you both?"

"No, in fact, please take the rest of the night off. Same goes for the others—have a good evening." Not even the staff can catch wind of my plans; that could be catastrophic.

There's no response for a moment and then a small, shaky voice says, "Are you sure, sir?"

"Absolutely positive, please go to your quarters and rest," I say in a firm way that reminds me of my father.

"Thank you, sir! If you need anything at all, please summon us."

Once her footsteps become barely audible, I loosen the tie around my waist and let my white robe fall to the floor before changing into more suitable clothes. A simple white t-shirt and floral jacket with grey pants are laid out for me, and once they're on, I head to the recreational room.

After placing my hand on the scanner, the door slides open for me. The room is too dimly lit for my taste, but it is filled with lavish furniture. Ember is sitting in a brown leather chair with her legs crossed. She is wearing all black with dark makeup and is clutching her E-pad, the latest 3D drawing device.

I snort at her, "Why are you dressed like we are going to go rob a bank in the 1920s?"

"To look as inconspicuous as possible!" She stands up and twirls around for me, clearly trying to show off the fact that her tight clothes are designer. "What do you think?"

"As much as I *love* discussing your attire, I think we should focus on making a plan," I say, and she nods while laying the rectangular glass on the marble tile below us.

The E-pad lights up and projects a 3-dimensional outline of our city. The glowing blue lines are so pleasing to gaze at that I almost forget what I'm doing for a moment. Ember coughs to get my attention and I shake my head and gesture for her to explain.

"This is our city, Briste, as I'm sure you can plainly tell," she says, before swiping the image away. The outline of the city changes to a red one, with a whole new portion attached.

"And this is what our government doesn't like us acknowledging: The Teorrain."

"Everyone knows where the Teorrain is, Ember. While I appreciate the spy movie getup and theatricals, why did we need this?" I quip at her, slightly annoyed that she hasn't gotten to the point.

"I just wanted a dramatic introduction before you saw this." She smiles devilishly, swiping away the old map to reveal another, new one that is lit up with an emerald color.

"What is this? It just looks like a bunch of random tunnels."

"It *is* just a bunch of random tunnels, and one of them leads straight under the Teorrain and into the basement of their old donation center. The good news is, it seems to have been abandoned since they built the new one several years ago." She looks at me triumphantly, and I stare back at her, dumbfounded.

"Wait. How did you get these blueprints?" I pace across the floor of my home, confused as to how she's gotten her hands on something so private and so very illegal.

She shrugs. "My dad is the Chief of Staff, Hart. It wasn't that difficult."

I stop pacing for a moment to eye her suspiciously. "Your dad just handed over these blueprints?"

"No, I snuck into his office while he was in the bathroom and hacked his home system," she states casually, as if this is a completely normal occurrence in her life.

"You hacked a government official's home system?!" My voice lowers into a harsh whisper. "How have we not already been arrested?"

"Keep it down, Hart! I'm a technology engineering major; I think I can hack someone's stupid home system without getting caught." She continues cautiously and puts her hand on my shoulder, trying to calm me down. "After we talked this afternoon, I asked Vara about what life is like in the Teorrain and it caused a glitch in her system. I even tried running an old-fashioned Internet search, which led me to find tons of articles that were censored by the government. You aren't the only one to have curiosity curse them."

I pause and just stare at her for a few moments. My plan was just to walk by the boundaries casually and pretend we were lost if we got caught. I could possibly see if there was another entrance and go back alone. Now I'm standing here intently, looking at my friend who has always been so collected. I never thought she'd be practically begging to go along with a dangerous plan like this.

"You are aware we could get caught no matter how careful we are, correct?" I stare at her, looking for any signs of hesitation.

"I'm aware, but I want to see what's behind that boundary now." She looks up at me, confident, with no hesitation on her face whatsoever. She is completely sure of herself.

"Then tell me, what's our plan?"

She walks across the room to the E-pad and looks back at me as the corners of her mouth turn up into that same diabolical grin. She snaps her fingers and the lights go out, while the shimmering outline of the tunnels are illuminated once again before us. The jade-colored light bounces off her face, and her eyes glance at me with a mischievous glint swimming behind them.

"Well, how comfortable are you with getting your hands a little dirty?"

CHAPTER
4

Violetta

"I've always related to the Boo Radley character. Locked away somewhere, and wrongly seen as a menace to society. The racial tension back in the day is also quite interesting to read about. It's humorous how history proves that society never let go of prejudice; it's simply the direction of the target that changes," Santiago explains as he blows the dust off a novel and delicately sets it on the cart next to him.

"It's nothing shy of brilliantly written. My only issue is that its kind of made me feel angry." I sweep the basement floor, trying to find the right words for the state I'm in.

The book Santiago gave me made me think a lot about the conditions I'm faced with every day. I've never really known anything but life behind these walls, so I don't think about the injustice here. Reading about similar issues that took place so long ago makes me wonder if the future isn't so different. The Crossed aren't given fair trials either, but there aren't any kind-hearted lawyers like Atticus Finch who would defend us.

"That's the power of the written word, Violetta. It's powerful and can make you feel raw emotion at times."

"When I read *Pride and Prejudice,* I felt frustration at Mr. Darcy's arrogance. I even felt like I was soaring when he professed his love for Elizabeth the second time and she accepted him..." Santiago coughs to snap me out of my reverie as I start imagining the scene before my eyes. "I'm just saying I felt all those emotions, and it's why I loved that novel so much. But this book you've given me is unlike that; no book has ever made me so fearful and angry."

"Literature is meant to make you feel every emotion. This is the first time this book has entered the inner walls of the

Teorrain to my knowledge; I'm sure the government doesn't know it's here either. If it got into the hands of a gang like the Vermillion, it'd only fuel their want for a rebellion. They've been careful to not give us books like this. These words can move and shake people, enough to cause them to take action." He says this solemnly while he continues to set books on the cart.

"I can see why this book shouldn't get in the hands of any Vermillion, if it even made *me* upset." I pause my sweeping, placing the broom against the wall, and come to join him in stacking the books.

"Which is why it must stay here in the basement, so no one checks it out."

"You're probably just being cautious, but you know no one comes in here, right?" I look up at him questioningly.

"The lack of crowds in our library doesn't matter." He places the novel into a drawer, where we keep all the books that Santiago at one point felt could get us in trouble. "It's better to be too cautious than to be deemed a conspirator."

"You have a point," I say, crossing over to his side of the room to take one last look at the book.

He watches as I examine it, before closing the drawer solemnly. "I'm sorry."

"You're more mature than me anyway; I trust your decisions." My shoulders slump at my own words.

His face softens. "You're much more mature than you give yourself credit for. We may have only known each other for a couple of years, but you've become one of my greatest friends."

"You really mean that?" I move closer to him in the dim glint of the basement light.

"Have I ever lied to you?" He reaches out to touch my arm reassuringly.

"Not that I know of."

"Then there's no reason to dismiss my proclamations of friendship." He hesitates before saying friendship, as if he was going to say something else. This small pause twists the aura of the room almost entirely.

His sparkling gold eyes and long eyelashes attempt to hide behind the round glasses that sit just below his high cheek-bones. My eyes move down his face from his cheekbones to his strong jaw and rest there for a moment. Finally peeking at his eyes again, I notice that they seem to be examining me as well.

With his hand now slowly moving up my arm, I step even closer to him. He inhales sharply, in shock at my sudden movement, and his trembling hand cautiously touches the ends of my curls ever so slightly, before he looks down to meet my eyes. My mind is racing as I try to guess what will come from Santiago's mouth next. His lips have begun to part in anticipation.

"Violetta, I'm—"

Just then the lamp begins to flicker and he freezes im-mediately, almost as if the words got stuck in his throat. We both step away as the confusing strain from words left unsaid dissolves into thin air like an illusion. He stares at me for a moment, seemingly surprised at himself. I grab a piece of my lengthy hair and twirl it nervously while Santiago smooths his jacket down, avoiding eye contact with me.

He awkwardly clears his throat. "If you could finish sweeping up in here before you clock out tonight, that would be splendid. I'm not feeling well so I'll be headed out a bit early if that's alright."

"I don't mind that at all," I choke out in an equally rushed manner. "I'm sorry you don't feel well."

"I'll see you on Monday then. For work," he yells out behind him, already stumbling up the stairs, reaching for the handle to the door.

"Yeah, for work," I say, annoyance in my voice.

He briefly glances back at me. "Goodbye then, Violetta."

"Have a good night, Mr. Singh."

He flinches at my formality. My sudden coldness doesn't stop him from closing the door and leaving me alone in the silent basement. The quiet only enables my panicked thoughts. I can't seem to wrap my head around what just occurred only minutes ago. Did I imagine it? Was there some sort of invisible force at work pulling Santiago and I towards each other? Do I now just have to ignore it forever?

My feet feel stuck to the ground where he left me, and my head begins to ache from the stress brought upon my mind. He just left without saying anything about what just happened between us. Nothing irritates me more than when people run from their problems. I can't stop all the upsetting scenarios playing in my mind of what could happen the next time I see him. He's my boss, and he's one of my only friends. I refuse to lose him or this job because of this situation. Nothing technically happened. I *will* pull myself together, before my sanity loses the battle against the voices floating in my head.

Reaching up, I take the rubber bands from my hair. Long, cinnamon-colored strands fall around my face, and I push the thick locks behind my shoulders. As I'm playing with my hair, I feel my lungs burning and realize I've forgotten to breathe once again. A bad habit of mine is depriving myself of oxygen anytime I feel discomfort in my heart, but I didn't feel that way in that moment with Santiago. Breath filled my lungs as usual. Does that mean what happened didn't affect me as much as I think?

There is no way to defeat these questions, which are insistent on ravaging my brain. I must find something else to preoccupy it. He wanted me to sweep up, so that's what I'm going to do. He's my boss and I follow his orders. Although it's dimly lit, and I've already done a bit of sweeping, it's obvious the room does need to be cleaned, or else Santiago's perfectionist rants will kick in. I turn around and begin walking back to the other side of the room to pick up the broom.

As I reach out to grab it, I trip on the edge of a bookshelf and begin to fall. It feels like I'm falling in slow motion as I cover my face with my arms so they take the brunt of my inevitable collapse, but the impact somehow doesn't come. A pair of strong arms has wrapped around me, saving me from facing the certain harm of landing on my face. Santiago. There is no frustration in me towards him anymore; all is forgiven as soon as I realize he's come back to talk, refusing to leave things as they were.

I breathe out a sigh of relief. "Phew! Santiago, you came back just in time." I push away his arms and look down at my unscratched body.

"Santiago?" echoes a distinctly American voice, that surely does not belong to my English boss.

The face that meets mine is unknown—it's a stranger standing in front of me. I instinctively look to his neck. There is an absence of the white tattoo all Crossed are given. I begin to back up in fear when I realize the man standing before me isn't just any common stranger. He's a Pravi with horrifyingly familiar eyes. The same ones flashing in my head constantly.

My lips part to scream, but I'm swiftly silenced by another pair of hands reaching around me from behind to cover my mouth and pin my arms to my sides. I struggle against them with all that I have in me, which isn't much right now. Unfortunately, I've had a rough night, and the fear in the pit of my stomach grows tenfold when my efforts to be released aren't working in my favor.

"Let her go!" The Pravi, still in my sight, whispers harshly at whoever is holding me.

"Are you kidding me? She was going to scream and get us arrested!" A high, feminine voice speaks loudly near my ear, and I wish I could cover my ears with my hands.

"You can't just manhandle the Crossed like this. We need to reason with her," he says, and I laugh audibly into the hand on my mouth. *Does he really believe that he can "reason" with me?*

"She just laughed! She's not even scared of us, and you think that we should just let her waltz back onto the street, Kang?"

The male stranger, apparently named "Kang," stares at me for a moment with an intrigued look sketched onto his hazy face, before approaching me cautiously. I'm befuddled as to why a man who has the upper hand would act like I'm the one to be feared. He stalks the last few steps towards me as if I'm a reckless animal, before coming to a halt in front of my face. His facial features are sharp, and unlike anything I've ever seen on a person in the Teorrain, which makes him appear to be fierce. He has fair skin, golden hair, and deep-set eyes like the ones that have been flashing in my mind throughout the past week. If I weren't so terrified of him, I might even go so far as to call him flawless. I might even question if he knows why I've been seeing his stare everywhere I go.

"Take your hand off her mouth. Now." He speaks roughly to the woman behind me, and I feel a sense of slight relief wash over me.

She exhales in defeat at the command, and reluctantly gives in to his wishes. Removing her hand from my lips, she's sure to keep a tight grip on my arms.

"I hope you know what you're doing right now," she says to the man still standing in front of me.

He glares at her for a moment before saying, "I do." He then looks back to me and examines my whole face now before he speaks, softly this time. "Do you have a name, angel?"

"I do have a name, and it's not 'angel.'" I begin with a confident tone because I refuse to show weakness right now, even if fear is consuming me. "Lose the polite act, and just finish me off already. I know what your kind thinks of people like me."

He steps back and holds his hands up in surprise, as if my words are abrasive to him. "I didn't come here to harm anyone, let alone kill a random girl. I only asked for your name."

"Why should I give you my name when I don't know yours?" I spit back at him sassily.

"She isn't going to talk with us cordially, and she has no reason to. Let's get out of here before we get arrested or wind up dead," the woman holding my arms says to the young man.

That's when I realize that these are just two idiots who probably wanted to see the inside of the walls out of some twisted curiosity. Even though I'm being held back, they don't have the upper hand because they're in my territory. I can scare them into going back to where they came from.

"The best-case scenario is that you two are arrested for whatever insane reason you're here. Just consider yourself lucky if a member of the Vermillion doesn't spot you the moment you walk out of this library," I say boldly, though this is information which any Crossed would know is a lie.

The man furrows his onyx eyebrows at me and asks, "What on earth is a Vermillion?"

"If I didn't tell you my name, why would I tell you anything else?"

"Now do you believe me?" The woman breathes out in anger. "We need to get out of here." She lets go of me brashly as she turns off the lights, so that I'm clueless as to where they are headed.

"I'm going to call the authorities, and they will find you!" I yell into the darkness and run towards the dying footsteps.

"My name is Hart by the way, for future reference!" I hear the man's breathy voice call out from what seems to be behind the concrete wall to my left.

Even though I'm more flustered than I've ever been, I somehow manage to find the light and switch it on. I look around the room, and there is no trace of the Pravis that tried to attack me here tonight. Well I guess they didn't technically attack me... but they may as well have. One of them even touched me! The worst part is that I still don't know how they got in and out of here, or why they were even in the library to begin with.

The basement suddenly feels like an unsafe and frightening place, and I never want to be in here again. This place where I've felt happy organizing books has turned into a daunting room where I both possibly ruined my relationship with Santiago and realized that the eyes from my dreams belong to a treacherous Pravi man. I don't know how to forget everything that just occurred, but I need to, because I hate the prospect of dealing with the Grey Guards. Plus, they'd probably take the side of those Pravi maniacs.

I leave the basement without cleaning up and sign out before I find my feet running all the way home. While I'm sprinting towards my apartment building, I decide it's best not to tell Nova about the encounter just yet. She may think that my absolutely deranged mind imagined it all; I would think that too. Maybe I just dreamed the whole thing up. There's no convincing way to explain how they appeared and disappeared so quickly. It must be scientifically impossible.

We don't have access to the latest technology in the Teorrain, so there could be a transporting device that's been invented, one that they could've used to get into the library. As I reach my front door, I become certain that mentioning this to anyone would result in my doom. I'm just going to lay in bed and pray to God that the past few hours were another deception from my overworked brain. Turning the key in my apartment lock, I suddenly recall a horrific thing the male Pravi said to me. Fear strikes my heart and goosebumps run down my arms, because I can almost hear the tiny detail that my consciousness chose to dismiss earlier.

For future reference.

CHAPTER
5

Hart

he door to my room has barely closed before Ember starts ranting at me, a reaction she'd been holding off until we reached my home. The silence between us on the way here said more than any words could—uncomfortable quiet is not something I'm used to experiencing around my best friend. I didn't enjoy it. She may be furious with me for my earlier actions, but at least now she's talking to me.

"Are you kidding me, Hart?!" Ember flails her arms at me in an unattractive manner. "Do you have any idea what kind of danger you just put us in?"

I throw my entry card onto my nightstand and take the wallet out of my back pocket. "The girl was about to fall flat on her face! I had to grab her."

"Oh, you just *had* to grab her. Forgive me for ever thinking you were sane."

I snort and roll my eyes in her direction. "She's clearly harmless. Even if she told someone, who would listen to her? The son of the governor waltzing into a library in the Teorrain sounds far-fetched to say the least."

Arguing with Ember on this matter is futile. My words are falling on ears that aren't willing to listen. She has a right to be frustrated, since I did something exceptionally risky and honestly, I do fear that a knock on the door from the authorities will come any moment now. I won't give Ember the satisfaction of knowing that she's right, though; I need to act coolheaded, even in the face of a catastrophic situation.

"It doesn't matter who she is! You let her see your face and told her your name, too!" She continues in a rage that I've never seen, and her face becomes the color of a ripe poison apple. "What was the point of using our last names as code names if you were just going to tell her your first name any-way?"

She probably already knew who I was, I think, before in-stead saying, "We got out and are safe now. We even got to see a Crossed person up close and talk to her, isn't that worth it?"

Her mouth twists into a scowl as she shakes her head at me. "Who are you? I want my level-headed friend back."

"I'm just growing," I move near to her, mustering up sin-cerity in my expression. "If I'm going to replace the great Luke Kang, I want to be sure of my position on certain controver-sial policies, such as the Crossed laws."

She hesitates for another moment—she must be trying to discern the motivation behind my actions. Thankfully, my mother taught me not to show hesitation to anyone. Ember feels that she can tell me anything, and expects the same in return, but she doesn't know of my aversion to being in the political field. She assumes that being the president is my life goal, and I let her believe that just like everyone else. I'm hoping that she lets this go and believes the utter lies fleeing my mouth, since I have better things to do than continue this discussion. I would prefer it if Ember would leave so I can focus on my analysis of the Crossed girl, and how I'm going to handle the police if I'm caught.

"Fine." She relaxes and moves away from me as she un-locks the door. "I need to go home, but you're buying lunch tomorrow after class; we should talk about this more."

"Goodnight, Ember," I say politely, trying to hide the an-noyance creeping into my tone.

She says nothing as she closes the door behind her. I pull up the estate's security cameras on the screen to my right. As soon as the live feed shows that she's gone at least a few feet from my house, I dash to my closet and pick up my art supplies. I am possessed by the need to paint the Crossed girl so that I don't ever forget what she looked like. She must be the same one who has taken up residence in my dreams.

I begin by tracing a strong outline, and then etch in even the smallest characteristics I can remember: light, violet eyes like I've never seen, and long, tight curls cascading down her back. The unique structure of her face was complemented by her glowing skin, and the splash of freckles scattered about her nose and cheeks. My sturdy pencil glides along the canvas. My fingers tremble as the outline of her face comes together fully.

I spend hours trying to recall every detail, from her heart-shaped lips to the uneven holes in her black jeans. An unwilling chuckle escapes me when I remember how she sized me up. She dared to throw threats in my face, even though I evidently had the upper hand with Ember holding her back. She was fearless. I've never tried to capture someone so unparalleled in a painting before.

Art can be such a wonderful resource, but the girl's grit can't wholly be captured on a canvas. While I've drawn many things in my life, I feel as if this will be my greatest painting yet. This could help me understand myself more, too.

My clothes are getting splattered with oil paint, while I mix colors together until I get the exact shade of espresso of her hair. Slowly, her voluminous locks come to life. All the dark colors that I use to illustrate her clothing contrast the bright tones of her eyes. It's fascinating, since these different colors would normally clash, yet they blend together so seamlessly on her.

Even by the time the light starts peeking through my curtains, I haven't quite finished the piece. I've been awake all night, painstakingly working on this portrait of her. Standing up and pulling back the drapes, I look at the sun rise over the trees. Up until a few hours ago, I was positive that there was nothing more stunning than this sight. Now, I'm sure I was mistaken.

My father always said that my curiosity would be the death of me. I've been more inquisitive than most others since my youth, believing that knowledge is the most valuable asset a human can possess. This has been a good thing so far, especially in school. I never trusted my father's warning, but perhaps it's a topic to revisit. It could be unhealthy that my mind feels as though it won't rest until I know everything about her. She clearly wasn't intrigued by me, but I didn't make the best impression.

There's no such thing as destiny. Yet, I think there must be a reason we met. What are the odds that she was in the basement that that old, grimy tunnel led to? Finding her wasn't even a treacherous task. Besides taking the train to the far reaches of the city, clearing away debris in front of the tunnel opening, and finding the concrete wall panel that led into the basement, it wasn't too difficult. She was right there, just like in my dreams, even like the ones that occur while I'm awake. It must be her; she's absolutely unmistakable. No one has eyes like that.

I have to wonder why someone like her was in that basement by herself at night. President Grey has always been insistent that the cities inside the Teorrains are no different than ours, but the concrete walls of that room tell an entirely different story. Judging by the fact that she was sweeping up at the end of the day, I'm assuming it was her workplace, but it would be considered unsatisfactory for any establishment in the state of Geal. The quiet, grey room was filled with dusty books and unopened brown boxes everywhere. Saying that that room with its bad air quality made me feel claustrophobic would be a generous description.

There must be a deeper truth the government is hiding from us. Protests of the Crossed laws have increased over the years, but there is little information about them online. If Luke Kang wasn't my father, would I know about the riots? Do I only know so little because he hides the truth from me?

Time has been escaping me, even when I'm typically very good about managing it. The slow decline of my brain since last night is becoming more apparent, as hours have gone by and obsessing over this girl is all I've done. She must not have turned me in yet, because there's been no word from the authorities. If she didn't turn me in, I want to know why. There are so many questions only she can answer for me.

Ember shouldn't know of my plans to go back to the basement since she will just try to stop me. I'd try to stop her, too, if she was trying to do something foolish. The consequences that could occur if the Crossed girl decides to report me are great, but I just don't think she will. I don't even know her, and yet I feel as though something is telling me to trust her.

Chapter 5

I'll be damned if I let that be the last time I speak to her. No one can stop me now, not even myself. I will go back to the Teorrain to see her. My subconscious is already regretting this decision, but perhaps enduring the emotional turmoil is worth it when regret wears the face of an angel.

CHAPTER
6

Violetta

" *T*was starting to get worried that that boss man of yours was overworking you when you didn't show up!" Nova runs to hug me and the brown messenger bag slips off my shoulder, hitting the ground loudly.

I hug her back for only a moment. "I've been putting in late nights fixing up the basement for a new office."

"It's about time you got your own! You've been slaving away at that rundown place for years." Nova releases me and smiles, with her hazel eyes shining.

"My boss just finally realized that he couldn't be around me all day," I laugh nervously while following Nova to her makeshift vanity made out of cardboard boxes and string lights. She brushes her smooth hair carefully and I avoid eye contact with her in the mirror. Ideally, she won't notice the strange inflection in my voice—keeping this from her is already proving to be challenging, and it's only been two minutes.

"Oh please, he adores you," she says, and I feel a pang of relief realizing this conversation is headed elsewhere. I don't want to discuss Santiago at the moment, but I'd rather talk about him than the Pravis.

"No, he tolerates me," I tell her this lie mostly to ease my own concerns. "I'm his subordinate."

"He has a funny way of acting around his *subordinates*, then, from what I hear." Nova eyes me in the cracked mirror, and her nose scrunches up as if she can tell I'm hiding something.

My cheeks are getting hotter by the minute. "What is that supposed to mean?"

"I've never met him, but from all the stories I've heard, it seems he thinks you hung the moon."

"He does not."

"Although I'm not sure why he does when he can't make a move on you." She hums while raising an eyebrow at me.

"He barely even likes me as a person!" I retort in a high-pitched tone that sounds nothing like my regular voice.

"I'm just saying that your boss acts very fond of you." She turns around and casually strolls toward her mattress. "It's not just the cute work stories either. He wants you to read his favorite books, and consistently asks you to join him for afternoon tea. My boss never does anything like that."

She slips under her blanket and I take the hair pin out of the left side of my head. Crossing over to our room, I blow out the candle and lie back on my bed uncomfortably. Her questioning about Santiago is flustering, I'll admit that. I had almost completely forgotten about what happened with him, though it was only hours ago—which is surprising considering how much it had startled me in the moment. I suppose meeting that Pravi boy shocked all other thoughts out of my head. Our interaction was short, and he made me angrier than I've ever been in my life, but there was something about his eyes that left me questioning myself.

"I'm sorry if I upset you, V." Nova speaks up again, scattering my thoughts as her voice continues to float in the dark silence. "I shouldn't be talking about these things when there's no good that could come from it."

I smile into the darkness, because I remember that as much as Nova likes to fantasize, she is also a strict rule-follower, like myself. She never questions authority, and never gets herself into trouble. She wouldn't encourage anything between Santiago and I.

"Don't hide anything from me, okay? That's not how the two of us work." She hesitates before continuing, as if she's going to tell me something reassuring, but instead says, "Goodnight, V."

"Night, Nova."

I begin counting backwards in my head as a way of putting off my thoughts. I want to fall into a pleasing state of unconsciousness, instead of dwelling in the dreadful awake plaguing me. I don't get far before Nova's soft snoring fills my ears. It doesn't bother me, but nothing about her ever has.

I'll never forget when they placed her in the orphanage on the cot next to mine. She took to me immediately, telling me stories every night before we fell asleep. She would talk about the world outside of here, a fantasy place where we could be free and live with our families. She told me that even if we don't see them again, we shouldn't let the Teorrain take those dreams from us. She's been such a good influence on me; even if I tried, my mind couldn't possibly fathom a life without her here to encourage me.

We know everything about each other. There isn't anything I've held back from her, at least until now. I've never felt so fraudulent in my life. Not only am I omitting a questionable moment between me and Santiago, but I'm also staying quiet about the other monstrosity of an event that just occurred. I will tell Nova eventually, but first, figuring out the best course of action is vital.

I'll fix my friendship with Santiago somehow, while staying on my guard in case the Pravi intruders come back for me... but then, all I can think about is *him*.

Hart.

A lovely name with a lovely face to match. I could barely find the will to fight back when I looked into his fierce eyes. The charismatic way he spoke showed his confidence, which bordered on arrogance, and forced me to roll my eyes—especially when he called me "angel." I must admit I was shaken when he actually asked for my name. I wouldn't have expected a Pravi to be curious about me.

I don't trust a man so well-spoken. If literature has taught me anything, it's that charming men are rarely genuine. Especially the ones with pristine skin, shining hair, and a smile that could make even the most determined girl question herself.

My inquisitive nature dares to get the better of me. Vivid pictures of him continue to poke around in my mind. I can't grasp his behavior. He told the woman to let go of me, gave me his name, and didn't actually try to harm me. He also implied that it wouldn't be the last time I saw him. That terrifies me in a delightful way, almost like a pleasant nightmare.

His striking brown eyes... they are the same ones that have been following me all throughout my days recently. I'm sure of it. It was upsetting me so much that I even visited the doctor that lives below us to see if she had some insight into my adamant imagination. She gave me ginger tea and prescribed more sleep. Needless to say, it wasn't helping, and now I have some insight as to why. His eyes weren't just a hallucination, since he was really there in front of me. Some part of me must want him to come back to solve my daydream mystery, but another is telling me it's unethical to wish for such things. The Crossed laws certainly wouldn't approve of it.

Could it be possible that not all these people are the villains we've made them out to be? Before I can answer this, sleep creeps in. Tomorrow a new day will begin, one in which I am going to have to face my newfound fears.

Santiago looks at me perplexed and frowns. "I don't understand what you're saying."

"I just don't think I want the office space anymore," I attempt to say casually, after having spent hours organizing stacks of books outside his office quietly.

He tightens his grip on the pen in his hand. "You were so excited about having your own space a couple of days ago."

"I changed my mind."

"But, why?" He averts his eyes away from me and coughs slightly. "Did I do something to cause this?"

"Absolutely not," I continue, stepping around his desk. "I just decided it's too much of a commitment for me."

"You've been working here for years. I finally give you a personal workspace and it's a commitment?" He stands up to look me in the eyes again, while buttoning the cream-colored vest over his grey t-shirt.

I raise a hand in protest. "It's not that—"

"—I know what this is about." He cuts me off quickly.

"You do?"

He can't know.

"You feel that if you commit to this job, it means you're committing to me."

My mind searches for a response. I can't tell if he's alluding to what happened yesterday or if he thinks I have a better job waiting for me somehow. He sighs after I don't answer him. Moving towards me, he looks into my eyes with an intense gaze, and then we are standing too close for my comfort again. He bends down so we are on the same level and raises his eyebrows before he speaks with candor.

"What happened yesterday was a moment of weakness on my part; it won't happen again. I'd be remorseful if you didn't stay here because of me. I'm sorry for crossing the line." I freeze before he continues with this last pleading statement: "Please forgive me."

He's never looked so vulnerable, with his messy hair and troubled features. I want to tell him about what happened last night after he left, to explain my behavior. My mouth opens to confide in this man whom I trust with my life, but it shuts just as quickly, and I realize that the words refuse to leave my lips. How could I tell him about the Pravis?

He is so petrified of their kind, enough that he might abandon this place and never come back. This library is a sanctuary for him. He's told me that being surrounded by these old books makes him feel like his parents are with him. As much as the basement is a reminder that Hart could come back to see me, I also feel the need to protect this place for

Santiago's sake. I'll never forgive myself if I'm the reason that he leaves the library.

"There's nothing to forgive, Santiago," I say with a half-hearted smile. "But I expect the finest desk the Donation Center has to offer for my new office."

Santiago's face quickly changes as he's overcome with relief. "You shall receive nothing less."

"I'd better get to cleaning up," I chime hurriedly.

"I'll be up here, so if you need anything just let me know." His toothy grin doesn't go unnoticed as he speaks.

Smiling back, I give him a thumbs up before I head for the staircase, where the possible horrors of the basement await me. While walking down the stairs, I decide that my earlier interest in Pravis was simply the trauma of the moment taking root in my brain. It's impossible for my subconscious to *want* Hart to come back. It also may be illegal for me to even think about the possibility; I'll have to look that up in the Crossed laws handbook later.

I look around the basement, searching for possible ways they could've gotten in and out so quickly. There has to be a secret door or something that leads into this place, because I'm pretty sure magical powers don't exist. Even a crack in the wall or floor could give me some hint as to how they entered, yet I see nothing of the sort so far.

It feels like hours go by as I carefully explore the floors and walls of the small basement, searching for clues. No cracks, no secret doorways, nothing to indicate they were ever here. But it's just then that I see it: a short, golden strand of hair on the floor.

So, I didn't imagine him.

I get on my knees to pick up and examine the strand of hair. It's fragile and light, like any other hair that I've seen, but it must belong to Hart because of its unusual color. Now that I think about it, I should probably stop calling him by his name. I could accidentally summon him or something. Stranger things have happened, even in this basement.

I sigh into the empty space and mutter to myself, "At least I have proof."

"Proof of what?" Asks an unwelcome voice that causes me to jump up and yelp. I spin around to see *him* leaning against the wall only a few feet away. Exactly as I remembered him, secretive eyes and a mischievous smirk to match.

I freeze up, expecting someone to pin my arms behind me like last time. If I don't struggle this time, it'll hurt less. But no one touches me, and the blond-haired boy just stares at me, as if to question why I'm standing so still.

"I didn't bring her again, so you can relax. It's just you and I, angel," he says, realizing that I'm waiting to be restrained.

I put up my fists and take on a defensive stance. "Why did you come back?"

"I wanted to see you." He shrugs casually, as if that's a normal thing to say.

"We don't know each other, and that shouldn't change."

He pushes off from the wall. "I find you fascinating."

"The feeling isn't mutual." I lower my arms and step back in response to his movement.

"I don't believe that for a second, angel." He looks at me with a lopsided grin that makes my pulse quicken. "You're curious about me."

"The only thing I'm curious about is how you keep getting in here!" My voice rises as frustration runs hot through my blood.

Suddenly, I hear footsteps making their way down to the basement. Hart's assuredness is melting away and being replaced with a look of panic. Santiago must've heard us.

"Violetta, are you alright down there?" He calls out to me as his loud footsteps continue down the staircase.

Before I can think up something to yell back at him, I see those chocolate-colored eyes in front of me. They're silently begging for help. If I don't do anything, Santiago will find him and have the authorities here within seconds to arrest him. My life will become infinitely less complex and I can leave behind all the anxious feelings about Hart that have been bothering me. There could be a chance his eyes won't intrude upon my daydreams anymore if he's far from here.

I almost audibly groan in exasperation when these rationalizations become overpowered by the quiet plea of this Pravi boy. Grabbing Hart's hand, I run to the boxes of books stacked high in the corner with him in tow. I push him behind them and put a finger to my lips, gesturing for him to stay silent. He makes the same gesture back to signal that he understands.

"I'm fantastic!" I yell back finally and run towards the broom like my life depends on it. Santiago reaches the bottom of the stairs to find me sweeping up the area where my desk will go.

"Oh, I thought I heard you yell down here. Just thought I'd pop in and make sure you didn't get hurt," he says, putting his hands in his pockets.

"I tripped and fell." The excuse flies out of my mouth and an awkward laugh follows it. "You know me, I'm just an unco-ordinated clutz."

His brow furrows in confusion at my unusual sentence. "Are you alright then?"

"Perfect! Not even a scratch." I smile that same deceitful grin that I continue to feel guilty about.

After seeing nothing out of the ordinary, he nods and says, "I'm going to head down to the Donation Center to see if there are any new desks that I can use for your office."

"You're the best!"

"That's debatable." He laughs, and it soothes my nerves slightly to hear it. "Will you be alright here alone for an hour or so?"

"Of course." I beam up at him, trying to pretend that there isn't a male Pravi hiding a few feet away from us.

"Then I'll be on my way. See you soon."

"Be safe, Santiago!" I call out, as he walks back up the stairs and shuts the door to the basement behind him.

Letting out a breath and relaxing a bit, I make my way back behind the boxes to see the Pravi smiling at me.

I lean in towards him and talk low. "Okay, he's gone. Do you know how dangerous—"

"—*Violetta.*" He cuts me off with the sound of my own name.

"What?"

"Your name." He smiles wide like he's won something. "It's Violetta."

I stare at him confused. "That hardly seems important right now."

"It's beautiful."

"What is?"

"Your name. *Violetta.*" He says it in a tone that causes heat to creep onto my cheeks.

"Stop saying it like that," I hiss.

He bats his eyelashes innocently. "Like what?"

"Like you're talking about a fine wine from the 1900's."

He looks at me with that same sly look in his eyes. "I just like your name, that's all."

"My mother's parents were from France." I hesitate before continuing my explanation. "Since I was born with these unusual eyes, she named me Violetta, because it means 'little violet' in French."

"It fits you well. Do you know any French, then?" He eagerly questions, as conversation between us starts to flow.

"A small bit. I had to teach myself since I've been here for a while, but it was worth it."

"Tell me something in French then," he says.

"How about you tell me why you're here instead?" I cock my head and wait for his answer, but he simply freezes up.

For the first time since we've met, he doesn't seem too sure of himself. His suave demeanor is at a standstill as he wars with himself on what to tell me, I'm sure. This excuse better be good.

CHAPTER 7

Hart

S he's asking a question that lacks a logical answer. I'm risking my future to harass a girl for no reason other than the horrible truth that I can't stop thinking about her and she's haunting my dreams. If I told her this, she would call her coworker to come back. That guy would most definitely rat me out. If there's ever a time for quick thinking, it's now. I'm reminded of our prior conversation, there has to be something to use as an excuse—anything to get her to not report me.

"I want to know what a Vermillion is," I blurt out.

She rolls her eyes before turning around and starts to walk back towards her broom. "You can just be on your way now. It was less than pleasant interacting with you, Pravi."

"You call people like me 'Pravis'? There's clearly so much I have to learn."

She snorts. "Like I'd teach you anything."

"I don't see why not." I shrug.

"You're a Pravi."

"Weren't your parents Pravis?"

She stops sweeping and looks up at me with an icy stare and clenched jaw.

"They were," she says through gritted teeth. I've certainly made her angry now.

I cock my head to the right. "And besides their crimes, weren't they good people?"

"They were good people *because* of the 'crimes' they committed." She sneers at me with her teeth bared.

I try to hold back laughter at her delusions that going against the rules made her parents upstanding citizens. "Well, if they were good people *and* Pravis, then what makes you think I can't be one too?"

"I think it was 30 seconds ago when you called my parents falling in love and their creation of me 'crimes'." She continues with the same piercing tone, "As if they were hurting anyone."

Dropping her broom and stepping over it until she's directly in front of me, she glares with unapologetic frustration. Several hairs have escaped the ponytail that sits low on her neck, and I notice her clothes are completely faded of whatever color they originally were. Still, she's more bewitching than any girl I've beheld. Her spirit alone is so powerful that it forces me to notice how inadequate I am in comparison, and our close proximity distracts me from her irate statements.

"Who are you of all people to think that you know what's best for humanity? You are obviously nothing more than an entitled and arrogant fool." Her voice drops to a harsh whisper as she lingers on the last word.

With that piercing assertion and a flip of her hair, she turns around as if she couldn't care less about me. I stand there in shock at her words; no one has ever spoken to me like that in my life—they've always known their place. She doesn't know who I am in society, but something tells me her behavior wouldn't change even if she did.

There's an inherent fury inside of me, but also a need to understand why she sees me like this. My brain absolutely refuses to register the cruel things she's said to me. She saunters up the stairs and her hips sway from side to side as she turns around, just to call out to me sternly.

"You better be gone before Santiago gets back."

Defeated, I trudge towards the concrete wall and start to tap my fingertips in the particular order that causes the wall to slide open. As I'm about to leave, I feel stuck in place and lose the will to continue my shameful exit. I can't let it end like this.

"What are you doing?!" She turns when she hears me running up the stairs towards her.

"Teach me," I say.

She eyes me suspiciously. "What?"

"Teach me about your life so I'm not ignorant anymore."

"I shouldn't have to *teach* you to care about my people." She stares at me with no indication of remorse.

"I already care a great deal." I must sound so desperate at this point, and I can tell she's intrigued. "But our government has made it impossible to find accurate information about the Crossed. I'm simply asking for you to educate me about all the things the media is desperate to hide."

There are riots all over the country that happen each year to protest the Crossed laws, but she doesn't seem to know about this. She clearly isn't aware of how many people are already on her side. Omitting this information can be used to my advantage. I'm not proud of this, but it's what has to be done to convince her.

She ponders the thought for a second before shaking her head and staring at me with more indecision than anger now.

My shoulders square back and I regain my composure, seeing her loosening up.

"This isn't the beginning of an unlikely friendship, blond boy." Her voice becomes unsteady, like she doesn't trust what she's saying. "My life isn't pretty, and nothing I could say to you would change the fate of the Crossed."

I capture her hand in mine, forcing her to look me in the eye. "Don't you see? You've already begun to! Even one Pravi who knows the truth could change everything."

Her brows knit together and her light pink lips open to say something, but then she just stares down at her hand in mine with an inquisitive look. My gaze follows hers, and I notice the stark contrast of color between our skin tones. How oddly pleasing and entrancing it is to look at. My thoughts are clouded by the sight of her small hand in mine. A warm feeling rises to my face like an unyielding fever. She drops her hand too soon and grips her left forearm instead, and with that the temporary spell is broken.

She clears her throat. "Fine. I'll teach you on a trial basis."

"You will?" I ask, as she stands on the step above me like an angel in a painting.

"Only if you treat me like an actual human being and never patronize me."

"That's the least I'll do," I say in a suave tone, smirking.

Her eyes narrow at me with annoyance. "And you must follow my number-one rule above all else."

"Anything," I breathe out.

"This relationship is nothing more than a professional and educational agreement, so don't cross the line. Ever." She folds her arms together in front of her.

I raise my left eyebrow at her. "So, we can't even be friends?"

"It's unlikely." She scoffs at me.

"What if we became more than friends?" I'm pushing the boundary, and her mouth drops open slightly. She looks flustered and unsure of how to respond, so I decide to cut her a break by taking it back. "I'm kidding. Don't worry, I'll comply with your rule."

"For your information, flirting is included in crossing the line," she says once she regains her composure.

"Then it's out of the question," I flagrantly lie to her with a wave of my hand.

She starts back up the stairs. "Whatever you say, Pravi. Be here tomorrow night at 8 pm."

"My name is Hart by the way, in case you didn't hear me last time!" I yell after her.

She turns around at the top of the staircase. "Goodbye, Pravi."

"See you tomorrow, Violetta," I say with a ridiculous smile that I can't seem to control.

She tries to hide it, but it seems like she's holding back a smile of her own. That repressed grin must be the most coveted prize I've ever received. When I hear the door click, I walk back toward the wall. My fingertips lightly tap the translucent keypad and the concrete panel quickly slides back for me to enter the tunnel. There's a sense of gratification welling up in me as I applaud myself for not being so distracted by her that I was unable to speak. As much as I stared at her like a complete idiot this time, it was nothing compared to my demeanor yesterday. Though I *was* left terribly baffled when I saw her silky hand in mine tonight.

You'd think as someone who draws and paints in his spare time that I'd be used to the contrast of two colors, but this was inexplicable. I can't explain with words the true warmth that came over me. How am I supposed to admit that I may be wrong about certain aspects of the world I've been raised to believe are true?

My stable mind once told me that we are all simply souls inhabiting a body and seeking approval in life until our eventual death. "Love is a myth"—that fact is one I've constantly reminded myself of, and constantly heard ring true in my mind. Humans confuse animalistic attraction for a "spark," but the best thing to hope for is a like-minded creature who thinks as you do. Logic is the way I've always chosen to live my life. Now it seems that every time I see her, logic gets thrown far from where I stand.

The train on the way home creaks to a stop to let in passengers of all kinds. Two men of different backgrounds watch a video on their mini E-pad together and laugh. Four women from varying ethnicities are adorned with heavy jewelry and short, tight dresses as they sit and discuss their plans on their way to a club. A red-headed teenage girl shares her grape soda with a boy who looks similar to me.

Scanning the room, taking in the contrast of hues interweaving through the train, I'm only now noticing how odd it is that we can all interact socially but not romantically. The diverse conversations, lives, and souls all intertwine in fantastic ways. But the one solid bond most of these people have is their strong intent to keep their bloodline 'uncontaminated' with that of another ethnicity; this is why they get along so well. Still, America is the only country to implement these laws thus far. Have I been brainwashed, just like Violetta said?

Violetta looks like she's about my age, yet she possesses moxie and wisdom unlike any of my friends. I could feel her ferocity as she challenged me. She questioned my moral integrity, and this in turn is making me uncertain about not only my society, but my own methodical way of rationalizing everything around us.

How is it that a person with such charisma, wit, and allure has been locked away in a town separate from society? Geal could use a bright mind like hers to better the future. We must be missing out by not letting Crossed people join us.

This particularly unsettling question that continues floating in my mind is briefly brought down to earth as the train stops near my home. I pull my black baseball cap down further to hide my face while walking the two short blocks to my home. Just as the large silver gates outside my home come into view, I do something I've never done before; I look up at the stars and admire them. I ponder the great questions of the universe, and what my place in all of this is. I ask myself the hard questions—the ones there aren't any particular answers to.

How am I ever supposed to feel like myself again now that I've met her?

I slip into my home through a door that leads to the servants' quarters. There's no reason to do this, since my parents are at a fundraiser, but I'm overly paranoid that the security guards will start asking about my whereabouts. Quietly closing and locking the door behind me, a smile and a slight laugh slip out as I think of my exchange with Violetta tonight. A lot of it was damning and made me feel like the fool she claims I am, but her attitude is something that I've been missing in my life.

I'm looking forward to these lessons about her life, even though I don't know that she will be able to fully change my mind about anything. It's easy to get distracted by her beauty to the point of not listening to her, which isn't good for me. I can't tell if she's going to teach me or ruin me at this point.

Though the hallway is dark, it's easy to imagine the pathway to the main corridors. The idea of striding towards my room to finish up my painting has never sounded so heavenly. In the hypothetical event that the tunnel to Teorrain #14 is ever sealed up, the painting will always remind me of what she looked like.

The remnants of her voice fill my ears when I put the painting of her on my easel directly under a pale light in the corner of my room. My hands tie the smock securely around me and I pick up a fine paint brush. All her features pair together softly to make her seem innocent, which is not at all like the kind of person she truly is—the type of girl who would risk her life just to get the last word in.

The night wears on until every inch of her is filled with ornate colors, and her name is written in cursive on the back. Dropping the paint brush into a tall cup of water and commanding the rest of the lights to turn on, I brace myself for the reveal of this finished product. The portrait staring back at me is complete with her luminescent eyes and electric smile, bringing goosebumps to my arms. It's perfect.

I pick up the canvas and place it neatly in the vault hidden in my closet. Unfortunately, it must stay here so no one discovers that I've been spending my free time in such a frivolous manner. Before closing the vault, I sneak one last look at the high-spirited girl in the painting and a feeling of dread hits my senses. The painting may be sublime, but I'm afraid nothing compares to the real girl. If that tunnel is ever sealed up like I fear, what will become of me?

CHAPTER
8

Violetta

"You're late." My eyes stay fixed on the analog clock that states it's 8:06 pm.

Hart reaches up and grabs the back of his neck, avoiding eye contact with me. "The train wasn't on time."

"You take a train to get here?" I ask, genuinely curious about transportation beyond the walls.

He hesitates before answering. "Technically, yes I do."

"What are trains like?" I look at him expectantly, even though he ought to be the one asking the questions.

"They're crammed and terrible, but sometimes they can be pleasant." He shrugs and takes the black baseball cap off his head.

"I've only read about them." I try not to stare at his hands running through his blond locks. "How do you get into this basement?"

"I thought you were supposed to be the one teaching me?" He asks with a hand still in his hair, obviously amused by my questions.

"If I'm going to trust you, I'd like to understand how you can just enter and leave a concrete basement in the middle of the Teorrain as you please."

This isn't a large request, considering the situation at hand. Had the book in my hands not been so engrossing, I could have caught him sneaking in. While chewing on my lip in anticipation of the next line, I'd heard a noise and realized he was standing in front of my desk, in dark clothing similar to what he was wearing yesterday. Five minutes later, and he's thinking about whether he should expose this secret he's keeping from me. He lets go of his hair before placing both hands on my desk and leaning closer to my face.

"Teach me a lesson or two. Once I feel like we know each other a good bit, I'll tell you," he states plainly. "Mutual trust."

"It's a deal." I cave to his request.

He takes his hands off the creaky old desk and straightens his posture, before clapping them together. "So, what's the first thing I should know?"

That's a good question. No one has ever been curious about my way of living, mainly because I don't meet people outside of the boundaries. After searching the vast landscape of my brain for several moments, I recall advice that Santiago once gave me. He told me the best way to teach is to demonstrate. This gives me a brilliant and semi-dangerous idea that I'm going to act on before talking myself out of it.

"The look on your face is freaking me out, Violetta," Hart remarks.

My teeth clamp down on the inside of my cheek to keep a smile from forming at hearing him say my name. "Keep your head down and stay as silent as possible."

He opens his mouth to say something but closes it when I take hold of his strong arm, pulling him up the stairs with me. We pass by Santiago's empty office on the way up the second staircase, which causes a twinge of guilt to form in my gut. I let go of him suddenly, embarrassed. Still, he willingly stays in tow up the staircases after me, not mentioning my awkwardness. Finally, my hand turns the knob of the faded green door that leads to the rooftop.

We are both out of breath as we step out atop the tallest building left standing in the Teorrain. The sun is already down, and although it's dark, there is a lot that can still be seen from the streetlights. Motioning for him to sit down carefully near the edge with me, we let our feet hang off the side.

"This is the Teorrain." My arms spread out like a hug to the small, grey city—halfway-finished buildings, roadside markets near the Donation Center, and the children's home that is always over capacity. I point each out to Hart, making sure to include the lake and fields near my apartment. The orange glow of the streetlights makes it easier to see everything. There are few people walking home at this hour, and they don't notice us watching them. The soft scent of grief for a life lost is constantly lurking, yet I possess only the deepest sort of love in my heart for the city. Even though it's far from idyllic, there's a certain charm to the town that I adore, especially from way up here.

He breathes out. "Wow."

"It's not much, but it's home." I laugh quietly.

He looks to me curiously. "So, you like it here?"

"I've known nothing else; it's my home. I have the same routine every day, just trying to keep my head down and out of the clouds where my thoughts tend to get stuck." I chuckle again, trying to make this less awkward.

He turns his body towards me now. "They get stuck in the clouds?"

"I read many books that are donated here. Sometimes they fill my head with dreams of another world."

"Like Neverland?"

"Exactly but waiting around for Peter Pan is pointless here." I try to keep my focus on the city below and not the perplexing boy next to me.

"I never truly grasped how hopeless the town would look." He frowns at me with a look of pity on his face.

"It may be hopeless, but it's not loveless," I say, in a deadly serious tone. "That's all that matters."

"What do you mean?" He raises an eyebrow at me.

Scanning the town, I find a notable example near the barber shop and point my fingers in that direction. An old woman is teaching a young girl how to properly tie her new second-hand shoes on the dusty street corner. The woman is bent down, with both hands tying the laces into bows and crossing them over each other, while the girl nods at her as if she's trying to memorize the movements of her hands.

"Look at how that woman helps the young girl. She has no obligation to worry for her, but she does."

"So, this old woman is why you think love exists here?" He asks slowly, like he's trying to figure me out.

"It's well and alive. The Teorrain is filled with strangers who've lost their loved ones, but instead of closing themselves off, they care for each other. We make our own family." I mean every word; it really is extraordinary that we can band together like this.

He pauses for a moment before his lips part. "You're not allowed to marry though, isn't that right?"

"We aren't." I nod before adding on to that statement. "But romantic love isn't the only love that exists, Hart."

"So, you do know my name," he says triumphantly.

"I suppose," I respond nonchalantly to him, while silently reprimanding myself for slipping up.

"Have you never wanted to fall in love?"

"I haven't thought much about it." The falsehood comes out of my mouth quickly, because I don't like talking about this with him. "Focusing on that stuff only leads to disappointment."

"Well, I wish you were free to be with someone you care about."

"I'm not too upset about it." I tuck a lock of hair behind my ear. "Many people face different trials; this is simply mine."

He doesn't appear to be satisfied with this statement and looks away from me to the town below us. His diverted gaze presents the opportunity for me to admire him. From his strong jaw to his pointed nose and pillowy skin, his face is unlike any I've come across. He must know how charming his features are, otherwise he wouldn't be so full of himself. Maybe if he didn't dress like a burglar, he would be more approachable.

"Well anyways, there has to be *someone* who is bitter about the whole situation," he finally speaks.

"We are all upset about our circumstances, but there's nothing we can do. Although some people have been known to take it too far. We just don't talk about them."

"Are they the Vermillion?" He guesses correctly.

I tilt my head at him. "Yes, and they are the kind of unforgiving people who wouldn't be happy if they found you here."

"Who are they?"

He turns to face me again, but I'm considering not telling him anything about them. The lesson should probably end here for the night. My mind is boggled with the lack of a reason for sharing any of this information in the first place. It made so much sense when he explained it not long ago, but we barely know each other.

This is quite unlike me. I'm not open with strangers, and he's one of *them*. There may not be an explanation for why I continue to inform him about my people and our ways. The way his eyes plead with mine is a chilling temptation that I find myself giving into every time.

"The Vermillion is our resident rebellion gang. They haven't done much except threaten to revolt, but we think they don't have enough of a following."

"We?" He asks.

"My boss, Santiago and I—we talk about them from time to time."

Looking down at the ground far below me, I think about my conversations with Santiago. He truly is a terrific boss, and I'm glad we are back to normal.

Hart huffs with suspicion. "You two seem to have an interesting relationship."

"He's none of your concern," I snap at him and he's speechless for once.

Hart is worse than I had earlier perceived him—having the audacity to imply with that self-righteous tone of his that something other than a friendship is going on between Santiago and me. Nothing is happening. Technically, nothing ever did. That's the end of the story, and I'm choosing to believe that. If he tries to insinuate one more thing about my relationship with my boss, I will get up and leave him on this roof to fend for himself.

Hart's intense stare would normally be enough to make me shrink up inside. I don't let my emotions show through in my expression; my disposition remains fierce and unchanging. My eyes dare him to say something else, but he steers the conversation away from the subject he wants to ask about.

"Does he know anything special about the Vermillion?"

"No, he tries to stay as far from trouble as he can. He doesn't even know what Othello looks like."

A perplexed look forms on his face. "Othello?"

"I've said too much." I avert my eyes and hesitate before saying more. "Let's just look at the view for now."

"I'd rather look at you."

I snap my head up, the temperature in my cheeks rising again. "Hart! What was my only rule?"

"I'm not being flirtatious!" He scoots closer to me and examines my face. "I just genuinely don't think you comprehend how breathtaking you are as a person."

My voice struggles to stay composed. "That's a high compliment coming from someone so vain."

"You perceive me to be vain?" He shrinks visibly at my words.

"Look at you." I gesture to him now while rolling my eyes. "You're attractive, tall, and your hair is meticulously styled. You must care about what others think of you."

"You think I'm attractive?" He asks in a teasing tone. "I never thought you'd be the one to break your own rule."

His selective hearing is irritating. "That's seriously what you got out of that?"

He looks me up and down briefly before winking. "Listen angel, you're the one who thinks I'm wildly alluring."

"I never said that! I was just pointing out your narcissistic behavior, which is even more apparent now that you're only focusing on my comments towards your looks." I feel my face flushing as he sits unbothered.

Hart leans in, smelling like the delicious vanilla cookies that Santiago makes at Christmas. His black eyelashes are long, and something wild creeps behind his inky irises. My emotions are mixing together to form a hindering shade of anxiety.

"How can I focus on anything else when you've admitted that you find me attractive?" His voice comes out deep.

"I warned you, this isn't about to become some timeless love story." As I stand up to leave and march towards the door that leads downstairs, it takes everything in me not to glance behind me. This lesson has to end here for the night—he's becoming too bold. "I need to head home."

He chuckles and pushes himself up from the side of the roof. "Don't worry angel, I'm only teasing. I don't believe in love," he says as he hurries to catch up with me, but I recognize the dubious nature of his words. I've also become good at deceiving myself lately.

I look over my shoulder sorrowfully at him. "Oh Hart, I don't think you know what you believe anymore."

CHAPTER
9

Hart

*I*t's my birthday today.

That's right, I'm finally 19. Only one year away from being 20, which means I'm on a downward slope towards retirement. Making a big deal about my birthday is not on my to-do list. What is the excitement in getting older? Every year is just another dreadful stride towards following in my father's political footsteps. Unfortunately, I'm somewhat of a celebrity around here because of that, which means that my birthday is always celebrated in the most lavish ways.

This day is an excuse for my father to host an elaborate ball and show his elite son off to the city. Today my birthday has fallen on a Friday: lesson day. It's been about a month since our first lesson on the rooftop, but it's felt like I've been meeting Violetta for much longer. At our last session, I conveyed to her that I might not make it tonight, but she casually responded that she would wait up for me anyway. As surprising as her answer was, I wasn't going to question it. I've been thinking maybe she's starting to like my company.

These past four weeks have altered my reality in ways that I didn't think were possible. Violetta's stories about living in the Teorrain have opened my eyes. Each time I sneak back to my mansion after visiting her small town, it's hard to not notice the imbalance in our country. Everything has been handed to me, and each day here is another reminder that it isn't enough. Violetta has so little, but she is thankful for even the smallest of things. She's enthralled by something as simple as paper and ink bound together. It's like her consciousness is stuck ages in the past.

Recently, it seems she's not been too disgusted by me. She's a mystery to me most of the time, but her actions tell me she is starting to see me as a good acquaintance at least. I've learned to leave my flirtatious comments out of our lessons, and she's begun to inquire about existence outside the walls more. Still, I know she wouldn't speak to me again if she knew who my father was. I appreciate that she's let her guard down a bit, but I must keep my personal life ambiguous. My entire temperament has been built on charming the public, so it has been difficult to shed my act. Violetta seems to appreciate the genuine version of me.

If this party was actually about me, I'd be attending it with her. Instead, my plus one will be the persona I invented for myself so long ago. It's dreadful, but it's my reality. When I'm with Violetta, however, I feel like someone else. I have a persistent desire to keep meeting her, even though she defies me ruthlessly. She's something fearsome… and I'm absolutely entranced by her.

"Happy Birthday, son!" My father interrupts my peaceful dinner, and I pretend not to be annoyed.

"Thank you, Dad."

"Are you excited for the ball? Ember's father told me that she has a surprise for you." He winks and it takes everything in me not to gag.

"She's been telling me this as well; I don't have the slightest clue what it is," I respond while reaching up and patting a linen napkin against the side of my mouth.

He sits down at the head of the table beside me. "I'm sure anything coming from a beautiful girl must be wonderful."

That comment causes me to choke on my water and I begin coughing as my father looks at me quizzically. I eventually catch myself before clearing my throat, swallowing my shock at his gross implications, and begin to clear things up.

"Ember and I are only friends, Dad."

"For now," he quips back.

I use the napkin to pat my mouth. "Excuse me?"

"I'm just saying, I had a best friend like that at your age and fell in love with her," he says, and my jaw goes slack. I've never heard him describe my mother as his best friend, let alone tell me he's in love with her.

"Well, Ember and I aren't like you and Mom. We are just friends," I say again sternly.

He's the one to cough now. "Son, I'm talking of another woman that I loved very much, before your mother."

I am staring at him not only with my mouth open, but my eyes wide. He's never shared this much information with me while sober before. I'm starting to think he's either very ill or near death to be telling me any of this. I lean in closely and catch a whiff of the strong scent of whisky almost immediately. I suppose if he's going to get tipsy and tell me all his secrets, I'm glad it's a little past dinner time.

"Who was this girl?" I pry while I still can.

"She was my absolute best friend growing up. She was stunning. Had blonde hair, just like you, only hers was natural. We did everything together. The three of us were inseparable."

Three? That doesn't add up.

"Don't you mean the two of you?"

Chapter 9

He shakes his head sloppily. "No, the three of us. Clara, Kit, and I. Clara was the daughter of my father's right-hand man, and Kit was my closest friend. Clara knew that I loved her, but she wasn't Korean. She convinced me that going against the law would only ruin both our lives. It seems ironic now." Shrugging, he takes a sip of my water.

"Why is it ironic?" This story is too good now for him to end it there; I finally find him interesting for once.

"She ended up eloping and running away with Kit. I should've alerted the authorities right after reading the letter she left on my desk, but my love for her stopped me. I even pretended to not know where they could've gone when her father questioned me, so they could get a head start." He sighs with his head hanging down now and there's a crack in his voice. "I was heartbroken and foolish. I should have let them get arrested for what they did."

"Why would they be arrested for running away together? I could understand if they were disowned but being arrested seems unfair."

Before he can answer me, I hear my mother's loud voice coming down the hallway. The click of her heels is horrid, and I already dread the nagging that is coming for me.

"Hart! Why aren't you dressed yet? I laid out the suit that Lorenzo made special for you; it's not going to put itself on." She sneers at me and I stand up to rush past her.

"I'm going. Fix up your husband while you're here, will you?" The feel of her eyes glaring at the back of my head follows me up the staircase.

When will being defiant become less amusing? Perhaps when I'm at the ripe old age of 20.

"Just when I think you've reached the epitome of handsome you outdo yourself again." Ember's voice floats over from behind me, and I turn to greet her.

"Ah, look who decided to show up! The party has been in full swing for a couple of hours." Her elaborate yellow dress is puddling on the floor around her.

"You know I have to show up fashionably late." She flips her shoulder-length blue hair with a coy laugh.

"I thought maybe you'd make an exception for a dear friend's birthday," I pout at her teasingly.

"Every news outlet and young girl in the city has been lovingly wishing you a happy birthday. You can't expect me to be one of them—I am going to treat you as any other friend."

This is refreshing to hear from her. "So then, what's this talk of a surprise? Even my father seems to know about it."

She raises her eyebrows and her pale lips open to speak. "Follow me."

I nod and do as she requests. We maneuver through the crowds of elegantly dressed people. One might think this is an award ceremony with how lavish these outfits are; earlier I saw a reporter wearing a blue velvet dress with a ten-foot train. I dawdle a bit, being distracted by all the glitz, until Ember grabs me by the hand. She leads me, while weaving in and out of various hallways, until it's just the two of us in our old wine cellar. It's well-lit in here, and the hundreds of bottles are all neatly arranged behind their glass panels.

"I hope you like it." She pushes a large box towards me that's wrapped with paper the exact color of her dress.

"Nice touch," I say chuckling.

"Open it!"

The wrapping is so intricate that I'm almost sad to re-move the large bow that sits atop it, but it must be done. The paper is easy to rip away, the tear revealing what seems to be an authentic painting by one of my favorite artists from long ago, Mikaela Merid. It's a piece that is instantly recognizable by the subject of the portrait, the artist's late husband. The brushstrokes are clearly visible on the canvas; it's an original.

Words seem to be caught in my throat for a moment. "How did you get this?"

"I have my ways." She shrugs, before my outstretched arms embrace hers in thanks.

Our hug lasts for only a few seconds before I begin to let go, but she holds me tighter. She smells like aerosol and foreign incense. What if there is a future in which I'm content with Ember for the rest of my life? The whole world thinks we are practically bound for each other; maybe it wouldn't be so bad.

Then I remember Violetta, whose mind is like no other. Her lilac eyes which follow me, and her voice, more graceful than a hummingbird's singing in the sky at dawn. My arms force Ember away at this thought. The idea of being content doesn't seem to be enough anymore. It's time for me to exe-cute my plan.

"Thank you, Ember. It means the world—" Bending down to the ground, I clutch my stomach dramatically mid-sentence.

"Hart!" She exclaims, looking at me with panic. "Are you okay?"

My head shakes so violently that my hair almost moves out of place. "No, I think I'm feeling ill. Medicine and rest should fix it."

"But your party is down there!" She's reaching for my arm and I can't help but notice how different this feels from Violetta's touch.

I let out a slight cough. "Can you stand in my place?"

At this she lights up; never has she looked more radiant. Of course, she would love nothing more than to host a party for me and give everyone the impression that she's my future wife. I'm sure that this is a mistake, but it's a problem to deal with another day.

"You can count on me." She's already fixing her dress slightly as she holds her chin higher.

"Thank you, Ember. Please let the maids know not to disturb me for the evening."

I start my race down the hall dramatically, still with a hand on my waist, as she calls after me that she will take care of everything. She also notes that she will have the rare painting sent to my room at the end of the night. The painting which had already almost completely left my mind.

I'd hidden sunglasses and a large coat next to the dumpster bin earlier, outside the staff exit—a disguise is necessary for this procedure. Paparazzi finding me sneaking out of my own ball? That would end quite poorly. My hand sneaks into my pocket to check that my chip is there; it holds enough money for several round-trip train rides to the outskirts of town. Walking briskly towards the nearest train station while also trying to hide my face is no small feat, but when I'm safely on board, it seems easy.

If anyone knew about this, they would be utterly baffled. The governor's polished son is on a train headed for the Teorrain, while he's supposed to be getting intoxicated with attention at his birthday party.

Thinking of this paradox makes it difficult not to laugh, but while stepping on the damp dirt down the tunnel that leads to the library, I almost feel guilty. Am I so enticed by Violetta that I'll abandon everyone else to spend a couple of hours with her? This was probably a mistake, but it's too late now, since the entryway is already in front of me.

Violetta finally learned how to enter and leave the basement. It's a lot safer than before, since we came up with a secret knock for when I arrive. After knocking on the wall, the same sounds are delivered back to me in no time.

The wall slides open and the lighting is dimmer than usual. There are small candles scattered around the floor, too. They encircle a blanket with peculiar-looking food sitting atop it, complete with a small, unfrosted cake in the middle. Something shifts above the blanket, and my eyes catch sight of Violetta, standing there with a humble smile. She's wearing an old, white-colored dress that falls past her knees, with lace sleeves billowing around her arms. The large bun atop her head is filled with pins to secure it. Judging by the state of her dress, it's clear that it's been handed down. Her feet are covered with white ballet flats that must be at least a size too tight, and her full, round lips are painted a deep red.

Looking at her now, there is no doubt in my mind that I made the right decision by abandoning my party.

Although she is waiting for me to say something, there's no clever comment coming to me, because I'm certain this is not real. Surely, she's expecting someone else.

"I wasn't sure you'd actually show up." She speaks up since I'm standing frozen in place.

I take my sunglasses off. "Violetta… Is this for me?"

"The last time you were here, I noticed your watch lit up to remind you that your birthday was coming up. I assumed you would cancel on me, but you said you'd try to find a way to make it. You should at least celebrate your birthday a little, Hart." She gestures to the food spread out below. "Even if it's with a Crossed girl who finds your company less than ideal."

She laughs like a melody, and those vibrations of her voice are contagious; I find myself laughing right along with her.

"I can't believe you did this for me." I'm completely awe-struck by this gesture.

"Treating your friends well is important."

"Are we only friends, though?" I wink at her.

"Hart, remember my rule. If you do that again, we won't even be acquaintances." She rolls her eyes and crosses her arms. "Sit down and eat."

Her words intended to have a bite in them, but a glimpse of friendliness is there. Her nose scrunches in concentration while she cuts into the small loaf and places it gently onto a plate. She lets out a satisfied breath before elegantly holding it out to me with both hands. I take it gratefully, and she goes to cut herself a piece of bread with an elated disposition.

It's funny that a little over an hour ago, I believed Ember's gift to be unrivaled. Now, biting into this bland bread, I'm certain that no treasure on earth, not even an authentic Merid painting, could compare to the piece of heaven that is this impromptu picnic.

CHAPTER
10

Violetta

This Pravi boy does not like my food, that much is obvious. He's trying to pretend that it's delicious, but I can read him like a book. Sitting on the floor in a giant black coat and chewing cornbread with a bewildered look, even the low lighting can't hide his downturned lips.

"You don't have to eat it." An airy laugh leaves me.

His eyes go wide as if he's been caught. "I like it! I just haven't had food like this."

"What do you usually eat?"

"Um… well, usually food that's prepared fresh for me, tailored to a diet based on my body type."

I touch my hair to make sure it's still in place. "So, your mom cooks for you then?"

"Something like that." He chuckles awkwardly, not caring to elaborate.

"I'm sorry if this isn't what you expected for your birthday; I thought if you were spending it with me then you must've not had big plans." I bring a paper cup of water to my lips, diverting my eyes from him.

"Let's just say I've never had a birthday quite like this, and I fear the future ones won't measure up," he says, much to my disbelief.

Turning my face away, I hide the blush that must be forming across my cheeks. "Your birthdays must be pretty dull then."

He looks at me earnestly. "They just aren't as special, and I enjoy my present company much more."

"Probably the most unlikely company you've ever had." I shove a large piece of cornbread into my own mouth.

He glances at me with a lopsided grin. "Tell me about the best birthday you've had."

The question causes me to think back on my life, and memories begin to flood into the forefront of my mind. My friends, mostly Nova, have never let me forget my birthday, and it's always great. That being said though, there is one such day that stood out among the others.

"Last July, when I turned eighteen." The crumbs on my fingertips are begging to be wiped off.

"Wait, so are you younger than me?" He places a hand over his chest in feigned shock.

"Yes, by a few months, and it's truly astounding when comparing your lack of intelligence to my brilliant young mind."

"Very funny." He playfully shakes his head at me and hands me a napkin. "Why was last year your favorite birthday?"

Gently, I clean my hands with the cloth. "Santiago let me have the day off work, so I got to spend time reading at the lake."

"I must be misunderstanding this." He grimaces before continuing, "Last year was your favorite birthday because you were able to read *alone* beside a body of water surrounded by bugs?"

"Reading is something adventurous to me, and the lake is serene. Watching the ripples calms me; they move in a pattern as if they're speaking to me."

He looks at me now with that same Hart stare. "You are—"

"—Odd?" I interrupt and begin to laugh.

"Remarkable." My jaw drops slightly at this, but he picks up his cornbread again as if he was simply commenting on the weather.

Instead of responding, I find myself unexpectedly mesmerized by how he looks in this light. His hair is accentuated by the soft flicker of light being emitted from the candle flames. He's gone back to concentrating on the food in front of him, and the hard features of his face are glowing. Over the past month of meeting with him, I've begun to notice how pleasant his company can be when he isn't putting on an act. There have even been times I've looked forward to seeing him and felt that we could be good friends one day. But the subject of his life seems to be one he wants to hide from me for now. I examine his expressions and wonder if he looks like his parents. They probably live happily in a cozy house with a red door like the families in books.

"Enjoying the view?" His face becomes smug while he plays with his food.

Straightening myself up, I regain my composure, in fear that he will start flirting again. There's nothing I detest more than when he does that. At least that's what I tell myself.

"I just noticed that you're wearing a huge coat indoors." *Nice save, Violetta.*

"Oh, I forgot to take this off." He wipes his hands on the gruff cloth before standing.

Unbuttoning the long black coat, he carefully takes his time sliding out of the sleeves. Finally shrugging it off himself, he lays it on my desk and turns around. When he walks back over to me, his figure becomes clear, and what he's been wearing under his coat this whole time causes me to go numb.

It's the most striking clothing I've ever laid eyes upon, a deep blue suit made of a material that glitters like the lake on a bright day. It resembles fine silk, and almost looks like it was made just for him. He loosens the berry-colored tie around his neck, and his muscular arms come to rest on his hips as he quirks an eyebrow at me. I curse myself silently under my breath for how obviously I've been admiring him. Is this how everyone beyond the walls of the Teorrain dresses for their birthday?

"I've never seen a suit like that."

Self-consciously, I glance down to the long sleeves of my ratty lace dress. It's kept only for special occasions, and it's the nicest thing I own. I borrowed Nova's flats since they're prettier than my boots, but they've been pinching my toes. He must have passed judgment on my clothing the second he walked in. This is by far the most embarrassing situation of my life.

"I've never seen a dress so divine," he says without hesitation.

The temperature of the room must be rising. "You tell me such beautiful lies, Hart."

"I mean it; don't take my compliments lightly." He unbuttons the top button of his blazer.

"Did you dress up to see me tonight?" Ignoring him is the best tactic.

"My mother forced me to wear this for a small dinner we had." His voice freezes over at the mention of his mother.

"Why aren't you still with them?"

"I'd much rather be here, so I snuck out."

"Aren't your parents going to be worried about you?" The image of worried family members abandoned at a birthday dinner is an upsetting one.

"They didn't even notice I left." He breaks eye contact with me before slipping his shiny, navy-colored shoes off.

I don't expect this response from him, and there's so much I want to ask, but it could cross a proverbial boundary. Perhaps his parents are poor compared to others outside the Teorrain. Although, if the less fortunate of the world dress like Hart, what do the rich clothe themselves in? Perhaps he is wealthy, and his parents work too hard, leaving him to be neglected. From what I've learned about him over the past month, there's one thing I do know: Hart does not like the world outside of here. The same one I'd be ecstatic to explore.

"My life is not what you'd think." He walks over to me and reaches a hand out, helping me stand. "It's lonely. I didn't know until I met you, but I'm not someone who has deep relationships with anyone."

"Why is that?" He reluctantly lets me pull my hand away.

"No one cares about me, and honestly I never cared about them." I eye him suspiciously as he says this, but then he sighs and elaborates. "It's almost like a utopia. My life is a seamless counterfeit of what others think to be the perfect existence."

It's at this exact moment I see Hart for who he really is, a boy who is wounded and has been suffering without even knowing it. One who has a distinct absence of love in his life, and in turn has learned to trust everything except emotion. This could be why I saw his eyes before we ever met, maybe God was telling me to help him grow. Lately there's something different about him that's more sincere, more human.

I speak up. "Don't you have friends?"

"There's no real care in my friendships. Sometimes, I think they just like me for the ways I could help them."

"You'll never know if you don't give them a chance to prove themselves." I try to convince him, because surely not everyone can be looking for favors.

He looks doubtful. "What if it only confirms my suspicions? Caring for someone who doesn't care for you is a worthless cause. There's no logic in the matter."

"Life is unpredictable, and you never know what could happen. One day you may wake up alone to realize you're the only one who's been living a life based on calculations. Then where will you be?"

"At least I won't have been hurt by others." He turns his nose up at me.

"It seems like you're already hurt by the crimes that you're convinced they'll commit."

He winces when I say this, as if my words held power. He must have not recognized his own emotions. I can tell by the wide eyes he's giving me that he is shaken by the truth of my statement, but the Crossed laws will be abolished before Hart ever admits he is wrong. Instead of continuing this line of conversation, he loosens the collar on his dress shirt hastily like it was suffocating him.

"How about that lesson?" Walking over to the blanket again, he looks at me expectantly.

"Sure!" I'll go along with the change of topic; it was getting too serious anyway. "The history of Crossed people and the good they've done."

He sits back down, ready for the lesson, but I notice the uneaten cake beside him.

"Before we start, I have to do something!" I race to my desk, grabbing the birthday candles.

Hart will never know, but I had that cake mix saved for my own birthday in a few months. I'm not sure what compelled me to abandon that plan and make it for him. Some part of me must care about being a good teacher. I sit down and put the thin, white candles in the cake before lighting them with my last match. I hold it up in front of Hart and smile at him warmly, since the story he told me made me feel the slightest inclination of sadness for him.

"Make a wish, Hart."

He beams back at me with dimples forming in his cheeks and closes his eyes as if this wish is his last hope. Then he leans in and blows out the candles, one by one. The smoke swirls up into the air between us and when his eyes flutter open, his stare has intensified.

"What'd you wish for?" I ask.

"If I told you the truth, I'd be breaking your rule."

His voice comes out flat and deadly serious—there's not a trace of flirtation. Tension hangs over our heads like the smoke in the air and the candles reflect fire in his eyes. My heart is racing, and this novel, new feeling in my gut is perplexing. He isn't breaking eye contact with me and I'm suddenly aware that the last thing I'll ever do is be friends with this Pravi. That would be crossing the line and will only lead to disaster. He needs to learn his place. Caring for him just isn't an option, and in my soul I am positive of what he wished for.

Caution must be heeded when it comes to Hart, because somewhere deep inside... I wished for the same thing.

CHAPTER
11

Santiago

Voices have always been of a particular interest to me. I find that a person's voice can be the best way to determine their intelligence, personality, overall character, etc. Inflections in one's tone can reveal the intent of their words, which is something quite unique to humans. Words can often get in the way of what people are truly trying to say. This is why it's imperative to pay attention to the implications behind the words. The tone in one's voice is what can help us to be sure of what they truly mean.

People have often laughed at my voice, which is a distasteful act in my opinion. At first glance, I fit in well with the people of the Teorrain. I'm tan and ethnically ambiguous as many here are, and yet my accent makes me stand out. Some of the people here find it odd, but it reminds me of my youth back in Britain, when life was filled with opportunity instead of restraint. My voice is deep, quiet, and sturdy. It affirms my thoughtful and inquisitive nature.

Being just a boy when I was thrown behind the boundaries of Briste's Teorrain, I have always been told what to do. People tried to be helpful, sharing with me their lists of places to avoid, people to stay away from, and ways to survive. These fellow broken humans whispered careful instructions on how to live caged in this city. They often spoke of the loneliness that would swallow me if I didn't learn to rely on other people. It was made clear to me that there was no chance to live a marvelous life. Dreaming is for those who are weak, and they often end up dying a slow death.

The main reason that the Crossed laws were able to be passed here in America is because of the motto that they advertised, "Separate but equal."

Throughout time, this key phrase has been used to trick the upper class into thinking they aren't doing injustice to anyone. We are separate, but far from equal. Most Crossed haven't the faintest clue of this because they haven't lived outside of the Teorrain, but the knowledge of an existence outside of here follows me like a ghost. I lived a posh life once, but only a few months after my parents died, I was arrested at the airport and thrown onto the streets behind the boundaries to fend for myself. After trying to plead my case to the Grey Guards multiple times, I eventually gave up, as one does when they've lost everything that ever mattered to them. There was no choice other than to take the advice of the locals and try to live an ordinary life here.

Getting the orders that I was to become the head of the new library was a surprise. Only 17 then, I was fearful when the Grey Guards delivered the papers. Numerous sheets of documents explained that due to my affluent knowledge of literature, they felt I was the most qualified person for the job in Teorrain #14.

The government here may be evil, but they need to have a few different buildings functioning to make it seem like we live an equal life to the people outside. People in the boundaries aren't even aware that they do this, but I know all too well since my parents often discussed news reports on the Crossed laws in America. The press could ask how we are being treated, and President Grey can always respond with something like, "Each Teorrain now has a functioning library where the Crossed can read any time they want, just like we do."

It's horrifyingly brilliant.

This well-thought-out tactic makes it easy for Pravis to feel at ease with what's happened to us. Many sleep peacefully at night knowing that we are going to die out humanely in a nice place that's simply isolated from them. Society won't ever have the threat of being contaminated with such "lowly" creatures as us. I wonder if they would care if they knew how bad it is behind these walls—how abused we truly are in the Teorrain.

There are bodies constantly being dragged out of Galgen Lake as more people take their own lives, but no one seems to notice these tragic acts anymore. It's heartbreaking to say the very least. People only donate to us because they feel the need to cleanse their souls by at least letting us have their old clothes, food, and other miscellaneous objects.

The cautionary tales from locals about the trials to come were helpful in my journey here. They taught me to heed caution and keep my head down and away from places it doesn't belong. What I wasn't warned about was Violetta.

My voice cracks often when she is around, weakening my usually sanguine tone. I see a flash of her abundant, walnut-colored hair and suddenly I sound like a boy going through puberty, with no way of controlling how I feel.

I have one of the most atrocious memories when it comes to people. Reciting *Hamlet*'s "to be or not to be" monologue is no issue, yet recalling someone's name is near impossible. Part of me believes that I simply have a bad memory, but the other part knows the truth: I don't want to get attached to anyone for fear of losing them. When it comes to memory and Violetta though, I can't forget a thing.

I can recall the way she scans my face while talking to me, as if she's trying to compartmentalize every one of my features, and the day she was supposed to be organizing the new donations but instead was reading a children's fairytale book with a look of awe. Memorizing her different kinds of laughs and favorite literary characters is easy. The feel of her long curls when I reached out to touch them not too long ago is burned into my memory, too. Most of all, I remember the day I met her.

The government had given me an order to hire a subordinate to help me with all the people who would be coming in to check out books. A year had passed by, and people rarely stopped in to even look at them, which disappointed me greatly. On one fateful day though, the door chimed and I snuck downstairs. I ran my hands through my hair to look presentable before strolling into the main hall of books to offer my help to whoever had walked in.

That's when I saw her. My spotty memory could do its worst, but that feeling of seeing her there for the first time will never be expelled from my mind.

She was holding a copy of *Peter Pan*, sitting on the floor by a bookshelf like this place was her home. Biting her lip with a look of concentration, she had already found herself engrossed in the novel. Though she was flipping through the pages anxiously, she held the small, beaten-up novel in her hands with reverence. I couldn't do anything but watch her; my feet refused to move. An invisible force was keeping me from stepping towards her and breaking the trance.

She turned a page before tucking a strand of her hair behind her ear—which was riddled with piercings. She looked rough around the edges like everyone else here does, but fragile at the same time, like a daisy that blows with the wind. I could tell by the way her eyes danced and gleamed as she read that she was special.

I must've let out a breath that was too loud and caught her attention, because she suddenly gasped and turned towards me with a look of pure fear. We watched each other for a moment before her eyes darted to my nametag. While she relaxed her stance, I forced myself to wave at her.

"Hello." I moved cautiously, trying not to frighten her again. "I'm called Santiago, is there anything I can help you find?"

She hesitated before speaking. "No, I wouldn't want to bother you."

"It's alright! Although I must apologize for startling you. You seemed so surprised I thought you might drop your book," I rambled on, in hopes that she wouldn't leave.

"No one could ever scare me enough to let go of a good book." She extended her hand towards me as a greeting. "I'm Violetta Akan."

That was it. That was all it took to come to the revelation that I was absolutely and remarkably under the spell of the girl that stood before me.

We spent the rest of that day discussing our favorite authors, eras, and poems. She had been taught to read and write well at the children's home—one of the workers that cared for her even left their book collection to her. She was so intelligent that I offered her a job right on the spot. She responded with tear-filled eyes and a resounding yes. She even jumped up and down before hugging me, a gesture which had become foreign to me. Her warm-hearted nature made it hard for me to let go, and even more difficult to continue to be her boss for the next couple of years.

On nights like this, I sit at my desk in the empty library, attempting to write about anything but her. It isn't easy to be infatuated with someone, interact with them every day, and refrain from conveying your emotions. That's the main reason I decided to give her the basement as an office, because we need space from one another. This decision was necessary, especially after what happened that night.

How foolish I was to almost tell her that I love her as though I was completely ignorant of our situation. After over two years of working with her, I'd learned to control myself in any circumstance. I pushed down my feelings when she laughed at my jokes, hugged me at the end of each day, wore her hair in that exquisitely complex braid... but then I completely messed it up.

She's been uncomfortable around me as of late, and this is for good reason. Being not much older than her doesn't change the fact that I'm her boss. Even if that factor wasn't present, it's strictly forbidden in the Teorrain to have a romantic relationship. The government doesn't want more Crossed people born within the boundary; it would derail their plans. I could get caught for even admitting my feelings and we would be sentenced to death immediately. No one would fight on our behalf, because we broke a clearly-stated law. There is no such thing as a fair trial in the Teorrain.

This is assuming that she would even return my feelings of affection, which is quite presumptuous based on the lack of evidence. She could even see me as a brother for all I know.

I can't help but shudder at that thought.

A crashing sound interrupts my thoughts, causing me to stand abruptly. It sounds like it came from the basement— which alarms me, because Violetta signed out hours ago. Taking my knife out from under my chair, I walk slowly down the hall and open the door that leads to the top of the basement stairs.

"Violetta? Are you still here?" I call out and am met with no response.

This is simply delightful. I always *love* the opportunity to face a potentially dangerous situation.

My legs shake as I slowly make my way downstairs, only to see an empty basement. All the books are intact, and Violetta's desk seems to have been left untouched since earlier this evening when I said goodbye to her. I search around the room a bit more before essentially giving up, reaching the conclusion that I've gone undeniably mad. Home sounds like a good place to go. Although I didn't see anything out of the ordinary, something has unsettled me here this evening. No longer will I spend another night here to write. I march back up the stairs, mindlessly grabbing my coat, locking up, and letting the cold air greet me.

The walk home only reminds me of my solitude and the lack of adventure in my life. As a child, my parents would read me stories and tell me that I could do anything. What a grim lie to tell a child. Especially one who had to greet adulthood at an early age and meet a fantastic girl, only to be told he could never be with her.

Arriving at my flat and brushing my teeth never felt so needed. Cleaning my teeth isn't engaging enough to take my mind away from the upsetting ideas in my head, though. Would she notice me if we didn't live confined to these walls? What a frivolous thought this is, since we probably wouldn't have ever met if it weren't for these laws. That's the one favorable thing about being here: seeing her 5 days a week.

Sitting down on my favorite wooden chair with a fantasy novel, I let the story take me away. No longer do I exist, and neither do my issues. I'm in a place where Violetta isn't.

I do have a bad memory, yet every time my eyes close, I can still feel her around me, and that is a tragedy of Shakespearean proportions.

The words on the page begin to fade and blur as I feel a sweet slumber circling me. Before I let it find me, a daunting realization hits me so fast I'm snapped out of my daze. I sit up straighter in the dimly lit room out of fear. I'm only now processing that there *was* something unusual in the basement, something that wasn't present when I said goodnight to Violetta earlier.

A large, muddy shoe print next to her tidy desk.

CHAPTER
12

Hart

Chapter 12

The plan for tonight is dangerous, but as usual, the prospect of danger isn't enough to stop me. I stumble over the uneven path of the tunnel, while carrying a peculiar-shaped piece of luggage that weighs down my arms. Adrenaline runs through my veins as I continue on my way to meet Violetta.

Since my birthday a few weeks ago, Violetta has been acting quite guarded. She gave me the best gift I'd ever received, accompanied with a terribly glorious cake, and a deep conversation that has since bettered me. Then, at some point during the night, she put on the guise of someone unrecognizable—a guise which has yet to go away. I've been determined to rekindle that friendship between us, and tonight is the night.

After our talk last month, I've genuinely started to care about people in ways I never did before. I've started picking out my own clothes, inquiring as to how my driver is, and even being polite to my mother on occasion. Violetta made me realize that maybe not everything in life needs to be so calculated and contrived after all. And if I can become a more amiable person, I'm sure Violetta can go back to being one.

The dirt beneath me becomes increasingly wet, causing me to grip the luggage higher against my chest. I suck in a breath of relief at the sight of the tunnel door to the library in front of me. This will never get less daunting, but I trust that Violetta will knock back every time. Not the authorities, or worse, that aggravating boss of hers.

My heart skips a beat when I hear her light taps against the wall in response to mine. The entryway slides open and she's there, waiting only a few feet away. She's like a vision of pure grace with her arms folded, leaning against her desk. I avert my gaze before speaking to her, proceeding tentatively in her direction.

"So." My throat didn't feel this dry before.

She stares at me, eyeing my luggage with suspicion. "So?"

"I wanted to show you something tonight from my world for a change."

She raises her sculpted brow at me as if to question my motives.

I speak before she can raise concerns. "If you don't like it, it'll never happen again. I swear on my mother."

"Alright, but if you're going to swear, I'd prefer it be on your own life."

I suppress a laugh while leaning down to unzip my bag, slowly revealing the instrument inside. The quizzical look on Violetta's face tells me she isn't completely sure what it is. This is unexpected, although it makes sense that she wouldn't recognize it. Music doesn't seem to be aplenty in the Teorrain.

"I'm aware you like to chastise me, but this is special. Please hold your laughter until the end." She rolls her eyes while motioning for me to begin.

Placing the back of the violin on my shoulder, my jaw gently settles on the chinrest. I take one last peek at Violetta for inspiration and close my eyes to find the right tune. The music slowly and softly enters the room as the notes begin coming to mind. This calming rhythm causes me to sway, and I play effortlessly, as if no one is watching me. The melody I'm composing encompasses my body. It dictates the movements of my fingers as they glide up and down the finely-crafted strings so familiar to my hands.

After several minutes of moving with the sound, I let the piece finish with a long note that lingers in the room long after my bow has left the strings. My eyes flutter open to witness her standing there, gawking at me with an expression of fascination and wonder. She's never looked at me with such fervor in her eyes before. I could be mistaken, but I think that she enjoyed it.

She clears her throat. "That was incredible, Hart."

"You mean that?" The sound of my brittle voice startles me.

"I do." She nods at me with a small smile. "I've never seen a violin in person; I guess there are some things to learn from you."

"There are some things I wouldn't mind sharing my expertise on." I smirk, taking a step forward with my confidence regained.

She becomes guarded as she moves back, darting her eyes to the floor beneath us and finding a way to change the subject.

"You tracked mud into my office?" She glares up at me.

"I'm sorry, I usually remember to clean my shoes off before coming inside." I give her my best apologetic look, the kind that usually turns girls to puddles. She stares back at me with unwavering frustration and walks behind her desk to pull out a small towel. She bends down to the floor, wiping up my footprints, which lead all the way up to her desk.

"At least let me help you with that." I half expect her to politely decline my offer, but she stands, handing me the towel without hesitation.

"Okay, you do it."

Alright, this is not the response I was expecting. The assumption that Violetta is going to act like the other girls in my life is wrong. She's nothing like any one of them, and I need to keep reminding myself of that. She's unpredictable, wild, intelligent, and… making me clean her office floor while she sits on her desk and reads a book.

Of course.

"You could help me," I mutter under my breath, immediately regretting it when a clear scoff reaches my ears.

"Help clean up the mess that *you* made? No, thanks."

I pick up the small cloth again and sit back on my heels, staring at her. She peeks up from her book when she feels me leering at her and makes eye contact with me.

"Please?" I pout my lips at her.

She looks as if she's about to make another sarcastic remark, but then she blinks at me for a bit in surprise. Placing a bookmark in her book before setting it on her desk, she opens a drawer to grab another rag.

"Only because you asked nicely." The desk drawer slams shut as she walks over to the mess on the floor.

Her knees gently meet the ground as she kneels, and she cleans quietly in front of me. The mud is being carefully wiped away, and she begins humming while she works. I don't take much notice at first, but as she continues, it's obvious that it's the same tune I just played for her. I sit up again, and her humming comes to a stop.

"What?" The circular motion of the cloth in her hand is halted.

"I noticed you're humming the song I played." The smug look on my face is impossible to repress.

She opens her mouth and closes it again before returning to scrubbing the floor. Her hair is falling on her face as she cleans. I think she's actually embarrassed and it's a rare sight. "It's a nice song, but don't go getting an even bigger head." She's pretending to be concentrated on the floor, but her expression is transparent.

"It's an original song," I say. "I made it up on the spot."

She doesn't even know it's about her.

"You did not."

She looks surprised to see that I'm glaring at her now, still sitting on my legs. She stands up aggressively, a move to size me up. Her attitude is frustrating. I wish she would morph back into the girl who made me that birthday cake a few weeks ago.

"Why are you so sure that I didn't?" I move to stand.

"I've been getting to know you for over two months now, and you've basically proved to me that you're a robot." She takes a challenging step forward, expecting me to back away. I hold my stance and look at her with unwavering calmness, although my brain is anything but calm.

"I'm no such thing." I emphasize each word with a step towards her.

"You could've fooled me." She holds her ground, though my patience is wearing thin. "You don't have faith in anything, you don't believe in love, and you run your life according to numbers! Do you even have feelings under all that pretense?"

As she spits out the last word, I'm certain she must be aware she went too far. I wait for an apology. Instead she continues glaring up at me, maintaining tenacious eye contact for what feels like an eternity. I'm not one to have my feelings hurt, but what she said sliced through my innermost being. In any other situation, I would turn and leave, slam the door, and never speak to her again. But while her words leave me to bleed, they also leave me to wonder why I ever let people tell me that my blood was worth more than hers.

I'm at a loss for what to say now; there are too many conflicting thoughts fighting within me. She's slightly nervous, though she doesn't want to show it—I can tell from the way she's chewing on her bottom lip. I close my eyes, picturing different scenarios of how this might turn out and thinking about the best way to react, before opening my eyes and looking at her again. I'm done with the calculating. She wanted to see the real Hart, and now she will.

"You're right."

Her eyes widen at my confirmation. "Excuse me?"

"I've never trusted in anything or anyone, but you don't care what I think, do you?" I stride forward as she steps back, edging closer to her desk with each step. "You'd rather see me as the villain in your little story of misfortune."

"Wait, Hart. What are you doing?" The anger in her eyes is replaced with panic.

"You've made me delirious. Everything that I thought was fact has been taken from me and ripped apart. An entire nineteen years were spent building a perfect worldview, and it only took two months for that to completely unravel. That's all your fault," I say with bated breath, and her gaze lingers on the stairs as if she'd like to make a run for it.

Violetta bumps into the desk and reaches behind her to grip it. I lean in close to her, brushing her hair away from the side of her face. I move my lips near her ear to be certain she hears me loud and clear this time.

"Violetta, the only thing I'm certain of is that you've lit a fire inside my soul that I can't put out," I whisper in a low voice. "You ignite me."

Her breath hitches and I move away from her ear slowly. As her hair falls back into place, she gazes at me, dumbfounded. The atmosphere between us is heavy and I'm completely consumed by thoughts of how she's going to respond.

Before she can say anything, her arm slips slightly, knocking several hefty books off the desk. She looks at me with wide eyes as if to warn me, but I can already hear her boss's footsteps. After hurriedly restacking the books, she grabs my hand, running to the other side of the room and gesturing towards the tunnel opening. I grab my violin before running through the entrance with lightning speed.

I enter the code on the keypad and the entryway is sealed shut, leaving us in the unlit tunnel together. The last thing we hear clearly is the door to the basement opening. I switch my watch on flashlight mode to see Violetta putting a finger to her lips. Pressing my ear against the wall, I listen to a man's voice, which I find myself irritated at, calling out for Violetta. She's trembling next to me as we wait for Santiago's retreat up the stairs. A sense of relief trails over me when the faint creak of the door closing once again makes its way to my ears.

Violetta is still shaking. Her nervousness makes me want to reach out and hold her in comfort. I decide against that though, for obvious reasons—the most important being that doing this would most definitely break her rule.

"I didn't even know he had come back. How could I have been so absolutely careless?" She fixes her gaze onto the ground.

"It's okay, you couldn't have known."

"Just stop!" She says harshly, her voice carrying through the tunnel.

"Violetta, what's wrong?" I approach her, but she draws away with a look of disgust.

"What's wrong is that you know my name, my story, and my life. We are breaking so many laws and neither of us has actually stopped to consider the consequences." Glistening tears appear in the corners of her eyes. "If we ever got caught, you would live out the rest of your days in *jail,* and they would kill me!"

I advance towards her, in one last attempt to stop her from pushing me away. I need her in my life; I can't fathom an existence without her. She challenges me and makes me feel secure at the same time. How did I survive so long in the shadows without the light to pull me through?

"Whether you want to admit it or not, you like being around me." She peers at me like I've just condemned her. "You don't know why, but you want to keep seeing me. Something is pulling us together and it can't be stopped by any mere human law."

Violetta snorts through her tears. "Stop flattering yourself."

I place my hand over hers and she flinches at my touch. She looks down at our joined hands and sees it too. The light coming from my watch exaggerates the untamed allure of our hands. The feel of my hand in hers grips me and delays my next words. An anxious feeling enters my veins again, yet it won't stop me from confronting her.

"Say it. Tell me you despise me, and I'll be gone in an instant." My voice echoes down the tunnel. "I dare you."

She looks at me through the tears in her eyes, not saying a word. *I'm getting to her.*

"Is there anywhere in this world you can go to forget me? Any place where you'll be able to escape the memories we share?" I cover the top of her hand with my other palm. "Tell me these two months haven't felt like a euphoric eternity."

A gasp escapes her, and she hesitantly looks back at our hands. There is no doubt that she wants to give in to me; I pray she won't let the rules win and force me away.

She inhales deeply and raises her head. "Even if I can't forget you, I will still be alive. Living is worth more than knowing you."

She snatches her hand away and wipes the single tear that has fallen down her cheek. Creeping towards the wall again, she enters the code and the opening reappears. The dim light of her office shines into the tunnel. Her frigid demeanor leaves me wounded as she prepares to abandon me there.

"I warned you not to break my rule. Go home, Hart." Violetta steps into the office, taps the keypad, and lets the opening drift shut while she says her last words to me. "Don't come back if you know what's good for you."

I slam my hand against the wall and rest my forehead there, soaking in my misery until I gain the energy to walk to the train station. Meeting the frosty night air after being rejected is not as pleasant as one might assume. The worst part is that all I want is to run back to her. There isn't a word she said that came across as believable. She wants me in her life—that much is without question. I'm not in agreement with the logical side of myself. It'd be absurd to go back, but what can I do?

I've never known what's good for me, after all.

CHAPTER
13

Violetta

I allow the wall to shut behind me and sink to the uncomfortable flooring. My arms wrap around my knees, pulling them close to my chest, and tears stream down my face. Nova once told me that there is no shame in crying, although she never does. She said tears aren't weakness and being vulnerable is what makes us strong. She must be mistaken. This is the weakest I've felt in a long time.

You ignite me.

Those words will follow me for the rest of my life. Thoughts of what he said lurk above me while I struggle for breath. I'll just hope to forget him, though there's a voice deep inside begging him to stay. This doesn't matter anymore, because he'll never come here again. I made sure of it. The second those cutting words left my mouth, his features turned from determined to devastated. My face continues to dampen with sorrow. I may never cease my wallowing over the golden-haired boy who ruined my life with his violin.

Hart's song has been ringing in my ears since he played that final note. The persistent rhythm repeats in my head, not even pausing when I cover my ears with my hands. I've heard many say that a composer plays their instrument well. They've even used the word "passionate" at times, but these simple words cannot hope to express the magic that flowed when he played his violin. He played almost as if he were drowning in open water, and the strings beneath his fingertips were his only saving grace—like the music breathed air into his lungs, and he didn't need to try so hard anymore.

The right thing isn't easy to do, but foolishly sacrificing our lives for this friendship must be wrong. If this was a different world where I was born a Pravi girl, I'd say the things on my mind. With his hand holding mine, I'd tell him how much I've grown to enjoy his company. He would know that his beautiful tune left me feeling faint in a delightful way, and that he doesn't have to leave. Most of all, I would confess the fact that's been evident to my subconscious all along:

That he ignites me, too.

"V, are you seriously going to spend your day off like this?" Nova's voice seeps through the comfort of the blanket wrapped around me.

"I don't feel good today, Nova." I wish she'd leave me alone.

Feeling a dip in the old cot, I get frustrated with my annoyingly persistent roommate. She's just trying to help, but that's the last thing I want. Nothing can fix this except time, which supposedly heals all wounds. She gently tugs the blanket off my face and looks at me with unease.

She places her palm to my forehead. "You feel slightly warm. Dr. Meisburg is just downstairs and owes me a favor; let me ask her to examine you."

"Nova, I'm just going through some stuff." I move her clammy palm away from my head.

She looks at me perplexed when I get up, walking past her into the kitchen. This should ensure she won't question me.

"What kind of stuff?"

Ah, no such luck with that tactic.

"I've just been thinking about life lately." My eyes are trained on the water as I pour it into my cup.

She looks at me in a way to suggest she wants me to go in depth with my explanation. I'm going to have to keep the truth from her, yet again. This is the last thing I want to do, but I'm in too deep to turn back. This web of lies has begun to suffocate me. As hard as this is, telling her the truth would be worse for both of us.

"Work has been stressful."

"What?" Nova looks stunned because I've never expressed this before. "You love that job."

"I do, but it's just rough occasionally." She clicks her tongue at me in skepticism, rightfully so. "It's nothing, forget it." I place the cup down, having little will to drink.

"This wouldn't happen to be about your cute intellectual of a boss, would it?" She eyes me skeptically.

"Nova!" My protest is anything but genuine. "We've been over this, that's *illegal*."

She shrugs with her mouth turned downward thoughtfully. "It's not illegal to look."

"I can't believe you thought it was about a man. Like I'd *ever*," I scorn her, trying to act offended.

I turn to hide my face, because this defensive performance is a little dubious. She should know it's not Santiago, but I also can't have her figure out there's another boy. It's only been a short while since Hart and I started meeting secretly; how long can I keep this hidden?

She walks up behind me and gently puts her hand on my shoulder so that I turn to face her.

"You don't have to tell me, but I'm here if you ever want to talk about it."

I admire her uneven hazel eyes, which hold a mix of colors like a meadow, and her lively attitude that usually makes me feel like everything is alright. If only she knew how horrid she's making me feel just by being herself. I need to find friends that are far more cynical.

"Do you ever wonder what it's like outside of here?" I ask instead.

"Right now? It's sunny and bright! I went out earlier for a walk," she responds in an upbeat fashion.

"I mean outside of the Teorrain."

She looks slightly startled by the question. "No."

"Really?"

"I've lived outside of the boundaries; I already know." She attempts to fix the bow on the side of her head.

"What was it like in the country?" I must've asked her this a thousand times, but I find myself wanting to hear her answer again.

"We were all friends, the air was crisp, the food was fresh, and it was incredibly carefree." Her starry gaze falters.

"I'm sorry you ended up here." I adjust the bow for her so it's symmetrical.

"Everything happens for a reason," she says. "I'll see my family again someday."

No matter how much she tells me she's okay, she'll always be homesick. I was always glad to have forgotten most everything besides life in the Teorrain because I didn't have to learn what I'm missing. But ever since I met Hart, it almost feels like I have.

"Do you think there are Pravis who want us to be free?" I ask.

Nova's appearance becomes sullen. "If they wanted us to be free, they wouldn't have put us here in the first place."

"But what if some of them are different?" I poke the beast cautiously.

"There's no such thing as a Pravi who would fight for us, and there probably never will be. Simple as that." She slips on her ballet flats and walks to the door. "I need some fresh air; I'll be back soon."

I sit there somewhat shocked for a bit, before moving to my bed to wallow with a good book again. No matter how hard I try to focus on the pages, my mind reverts to Nova and her sudden disappearance. She rarely gets so upset; I haven't seen a reaction like that from her in years. Her eyes were unyielding as she made her last remark, almost like she was another person. This must be the one subject that upsets her thoroughly. At least I didn't give in and tell her about Hart— that could've had catastrophic consequences.

The day passes me by while I do nothing but think about all the stressful things that are going on in my life right now. A few months ago, everything was divine. Now, it seems like I'm watching my life happen from the outside, not knowing if I chose the correct path.

Nova comes home at the end of the day and I'm still lying on my bed. I don't bother asking her where she's been, since that could make her more frustrated. Nova's agitation becomes even more apparent when she remains quiet as she brushes her hair and teeth in the bathroom, preparing for bed. When she reaches her cot, I notice her look of affliction matches my own.

"I'm sorry for letting my temper get the best of me earlier." She twists her hair around red curlers while she speaks.

"You don't possess the capacity to have a temper, Nova." She laughs as I reassure her and move to sit up. "I'm glad you came home."

"I'll always come home, V." She gives me a knowing look. "You can't get rid of me that easily."

"I'm glad to hear it." I turn off the lamp beside me as she lies down. Once we say goodnight, she drifts off to sleep soundly.

I don't fall asleep. The hours go by as I lay awake all night, dreading my return to work when the weekend ends. I shudder at the thought of being in the office filled with memories that Hart knew I couldn't escape.

My mission this morning is to shake off the thick grey fog that encompasses my mind. This way, I will be amiable when greeting Santiago. I pick fuzz off my sweater a bit and make an effort to smoothen my hair—which is more unkempt than usual. Bracing myself, I put on an imitation smile that could fool even myself.

"Good morning, Santiago!" I chirp, walking into my boss's office cheerily. "How was your weekend?"

He's sitting in his chair, quickly filling out what seems to be some government paperwork. His clothes look wrinkled, and the circles under his eyes have deepened in color. The metallic frames are slipping off the bridge of his nose again as he writes, but he's too focused to even push them up. At least I can be sure that some things will never change.

"Fairly bland as usual. You?" He doesn't glance up from his work as he speaks to me.

I shuffle around his desk and stand next to him. "Just hung out with Nova."

He barely nods, not paying much attention to what I'm saying. I snicker to myself, because his glasses are seconds away from falling off his face and he hasn't even noticed. He's so transfixed on the pages. I stretch my hand out and properly adjust his glasses, and he stares at me in surprise.

"They were about to fall off," I try to say coolly.

He blinks rapidly before glancing over my face. When he doesn't say anything, I just clap my hands together uncomfortably and head for the door to avoid acknowledging the strangeness of my gesture. I thought we were close enough for me to simply fix his glasses, but I should've kept in mind that he's my boss. That must've been so inappropriate. I'll just blame my lack of shuteye.

My hand is just about to reach the handle when I feel Santiago lightly grasp my wrist, and suddenly I'm being pulled close to him. He's still staring down at me; his hand releases my wrist, but he draws closer to me still. My mouth hangs open at this sudden abrasiveness, to which I've never been a victim before.

"Violetta," he says, looking deeply into my eyes.

"Yes?" I manage to get out somehow.

"I'll continue to get the wrong idea if you keep making these types of gestures towards me, please don't do that anymore," he says sternly, with a clenched jaw.

With that, he turns around and sits back in his chair. He returns to his writing as if nothing happened, and it takes me a beat to register the events that unfolded. I'm so disoriented that I can't even tell if my mouth is still hanging open. Time slows down as I attempt to process everything he's said, and what it could've meant.

Without looking up from his desk he adds, "It'd be best if you went back to your office now."

This is a good opportunity to get out of here as fast as I can. Running all the way down the stairs to the basement, I fall into the chair at my desk and let out a loud whine, knowing that no one is in earshot. My brain feels as though it's sinking into this overload of emotion, and I cover my ears again to try and make it stop. Nothing works, so I'm forced to simply take deep breaths.

Once my initial panic dies down, thoughts rush into my head all at once like a monsoon that can't be stopped. If I wasn't absolutely miserable before, I assuredly am now. Even if it were suddenly okay for me to marry, would I want to be with Santiago? Would I just be using him as a distraction?

He is genuinely good-looking, he loves books, and he's encouraging like Nova. We have so much in common and if all were perfect, I guess he would be a wonderful man to end up with.

Unlike Hart.

Hart is the complete opposite of me. He's rude, arrogant, and narcissistic. Not to mention, he never stops trying to flirt with me, even though he detests the idea of love. It forces me to wonder what he meant when he said the things that he did. It was shocking that he could care about me so much after living his proper Pravi life in a world I'll never know. He was an absolute jerk when I met him. He's changed since then, but that's not enough. Hart was willing to risk going to jail just to continue making my life arduous, and I don't even know his middle name.

I'll win against whatever is pulling me to him. I will learn to never think of Hart again. There's a determination inside me today that refuses to back down and be ruined by any man. I'll remedy this unspoken tension with my boss, while doing whatever it takes to make Hart return to being a nameless Pravi boy.

I'm taking control for once, even if it means unrepentantly running from Hart and addressing Santiago with full force.

CHAPTER
14

Santiago

*O*nce as a small child, I drank an entire bottle of cough medicine. My parents were quite lenient with me as I was never devious, but one of the few things they commanded me not to do was drink medicine without their permission. Concern plagued them because of the way I would constantly stare at it. The behavior I exhibited compelled them to place the medicine atop the icebox where it would be safe from my stubby hands—but the thought of tasting that cherry red, candy flavor kept me up every night, until I devised a plan to drink it while they were asleep.

I took a chair from the kitchen and climbed it. Capturing the forbidden fruit medicine, I speedily drank all that I could before falling off the chair. The crash woke up my father, who rushed me to the hospital after he realized what I'd done. The doctors told him if he had arrived there any later, the amount I consumed would've killed me. As they pumped my stomach and my mother cried, I noticed something about myself that I've tried to keep in mind:

There is an undying desire in my heart for what I can't have, and I will put my life at risk to get it. That glistening bottle of delightful poison still exists in my life, and now it's Violetta.

The yearly paperwork on my desk that begs to be finished has become blurry. Even though my mind tells me that I sound idiotic, I'm not one to focus on the rational. I am a creature of extreme emotion, though I may not seem like it from my exterior. I have always said that actions speak louder than words, and while writing may be my forte, speaking is not.

Chapter 14

It's become evident to me that I can't ignore my feelings for this girl, not for lack of trying, though. My heart will never comprehend the negative impact that surely only falling in love causes. If the Grey Guards found out about this, they would kill me quicker than any overdose would. Can I willingly poison myself again?

I won't lie, every fiber of my being can't help but be horrified with my actions earlier.

What was I thinking? She will most likely quit after that if she has any sense. The way she ran out of here proved this to me. I don't even know what's come over me or why I did that; it's almost like I was possessed. Every time she's near me, I try to keep my composure, but it looks like my self-control has become a mere thing of the past.

I shuffle the papers together and stack them neatly. Opening the drawer next to me, I take my mother's rosary out, and pray on each bead that I'll be released from this torture. As I finish praying on the last bead, I remember something that breaks this trance.

If I act on my reckless emotions and she reciprocates these feelings for me, I'm not the only one who would die. They would kill her too, I've seen this kind of thing happen before, and the Grey Guards have never hesitated to murder the couple.

This fact is like a bucket of cold water washing over me. I clear all thoughts of betraying the law for no other reason than that I fancy this girl. I thank God for the sudden clarity, put the wooden rosary away, and repeat to myself that it's not just about me; it's about her safety as well.

Loving someone is putting their needs above your own. I've read enough literature to be aware of this. I must let her go fully, for the circumstances are too dangerous. I refuse to put her in danger, and perhaps it's in my best interest that she quits, since my heart can't stand this torture any longer.

I glance at the clock. I've been thinking about this upsetting matter for over an hour and it's already teatime. I adjust the wire frames on my nose as I begin to heat some water. The fresh turmeric will soon be distilled to create a soothing drink. The scent of it calms me down. For now, I will be at peace.

Slam!

I fearfully turn as I hear the door to my office slam shut and see Violetta staring at me with a sense of determination. I'm assuming she has finally become outraged by my outlandish behavior from earlier and is here to tell me off before she resigns. I remind myself that this is a good thing; tensing up will do no good.

"Violetta, would you like some turmeric tea?"

She doesn't respond and walks across the room until she is standing only mere feet from me, with her arms crossed tightly.

"What did you mean earlier when you said that you might get the wrong idea?"

Well, this is quite an unpleasant turn of events. I attempt a proper answer but continue to simply stand here looking like a complete buffoon. My bloody brain has a million and ten things to say, but I can't get one word out.

"Do you have feelings for me?" She's standing her ground.

It's now or never. Time to be brutally honest.

I adjust a button on my cardigan. "Yes."

"How long have you felt this way, Santiago?" Her words are clipped.

"A while."

"Be more specific."

"I would say it's been two years now." I shove my hands in my pockets nervously.

"Were you ever going to tell me?" Her voice grows loud with frustration.

"What good would come from telling you, Violetta?" I start to raise my voice back at her.

"I don't know!" She shouts at me in exasperation. "You still should've said something."

"Well that's my judgment, not yours."

"Your *judgment* was irrational; you weren't even considering my feelings," she says, and unforeseen vexation builds up inside me.

"How is this irrational? We could both get killed!" I say intensely, and it feels peculiar to hear my voice ring out so loud.

A look of understanding crosses her stern face and her arms fall to her sides in defeat. This is not at all like any of the scenarios I'd dreamt up about finally confessing my feelings.

"I'm sorry." She looks down and twirls the ends of her hair. "Sometimes I forget how unsafe it is to even be having a conversation like this. You did the noble thing by protecting us both, even though it must've been hard for you."

"No, I'm sorry for letting my emotions get the best of me and having to be found out in such a deceitful manner." I feel a pang of guilt in my stomach for speaking to her like I have and place my hand on her shoulder. "I hope we can move past this."

Smiling back at me with a tender nod, she says, "It's already in the past, my dear friend."

Friend.

That word has never sounded so dreadful to my ears, and my heart feels as if it's dropped to the floor in despair. She takes one last long look at me with sympathy and pain as she removes my hand from her shoulder with hesitation. She turns to open the door and though I should just let her go, I can't without knowing her thoughts.

"Violetta?"

She stops without turning around. "Yes?"

"If we lived in a world where I could love you without a looming threat of death surrounding the both of us, would you hypothetically have feelings for me too?"

She rotates ever so faintly, so only her profile is visible. "If you had asked me that question a couple of months ago, the answer would be yes. But lately, I've changed, and I can't be sure of anything. A piece of my heart will always wonder how our relationship would be if things were different." The sorrow in her voice hurts me deeply. "Maybe our questions will diminish in due time."

With that she closes the door quietly and leaves me reeling. I reach for my chair to sit down, feeling lightheaded to the point of seeing stars form around me. I warily look at the hand that her own lingered on as she carefully eased it off her shoulder and feel like a blooming fool for not telling her sooner.

From what she said, I can gather that this exchange would've had a much different outcome had I confessed months ago, and it leaves me to ponder what could've changed in her life recently to make her feel as she does now.

CHAPTER
15

Hart

*I*t's my 20th birthday today.

I look in the mirror at my black tux and smile slightly at my appearance. Happiness glosses over my entire being when I find my way into the ballroom, which glitters of gold like the thread woven into my jacket. The sight is so pleasing that I'm in awe of it. Family, friends, and strangers are gathered around the dance floor. The music stops as my feet reach the bottom of the twinkling staircase. Nervously, I twitch in anticipation and, despite my best efforts, my jaw drops at the sight of her atop the stairs.

Violetta Akan.

The most incredible girl stands there looking at me with a knowing smirk, and the white lights illuminate her perfectly crafted features. Tight coils of hair fall on either side of her face and spill down to her sides, hanging there like an ornate decoration. She's embellished with diamond teardrop earrings and a locket necklace with my initials on it—taking my breath away. She descends the long staircase as the train of her purple-colored dress follows and her eyes, similarly colored, never leave mine. As she takes each slow step down the marble stairs, I know she is all I ever needed; she is all mine.

There's madness and then there's Violetta: an incandescent exemplification of the raw insanity which sparks adoration in a man. She's light and darkness. She's absolutely and wonderfully herself.

The sound of her silver heels comes to a halt as she reaches the glistening tile of the ballroom floor. The flowing music starts up again and she stretches her gloved hand out to me, which I gladly accept. Vivaldi continues to play as I spin her around, waltzing across the lavish dance floor. Although there are many watching us, all I can see is her small face staring up at mine. She throws her head back in laughter when I dip her, and I've never felt more alive. This moment is like a dream; I can't believe this is really happening.

Wait, this *is* a dream.

I wake up immediately and stare at the clock with disappointment. I've woken up three minutes before my alarm is going to go off. Typically, this would be a great accomplishment for me. It'd be a wonderful sign that my body has adapted to the correct sleep schedule it's intended for. But after that dream, my sleep schedule is the last thing I'm thinking about.

Am I so obsessed with Violetta that even when I try to let her go, she's in my dreams? *Be more logical, Hart. Think of logic.*

Technically speaking, this feeling of elation is just a sudden rise in the level of dopamine in my brain caused by the chemical attraction to another being. I've spent my whole life judging others for their foolish reactions to their animalistic desires. It shouldn't be so hard for me to convince myself that I've simply fallen prey to this archaic human rule.

If I remember that this is essentially my body betraying me, it should be easier to move on. She doesn't want me to be around her anymore, and she's absolutely right for wanting to never see me again. Every reason she gave me was correct. Briefly, after she left me in the tunnel, I was convinced I could give up my future and everything my family has gained because of a girl. But the Kangs worked too hard for me to ruin this legacy. I won't do it.

I feel something wet on my wrist before noticing that I've been pouring milk onto the table. The sad bowl of cereal sits close by, dry and dreary. As I reach for a towel to clean myself off, the sound of a utensil clanging against the ground rings out.

One of the maids is standing there looking at me with shock. The staff still isn't used to seeing me do things for myself. I pick up the spoon casually before handing it back to its rightful owner. She takes it from me tentatively, noticeably shaken by my simple courtesy.

"Good morning, Kate. How is your son?" I did some research on the house staff and learned about their lives to know them better.

She coughs slightly. "He's doing well. He just won his chess tournament."

"I'm always looking for a worthy challenger in chess. Have him come over sometime so we can duel." I pat the excess liquid off my arm with a nearby cloth napkin.

"Of course, sir." She nods excitedly.

"Call me Hart, no need for formalities," I say, and she curtseys with a smile before leaving, with a giddy pep to her walk that wasn't there before.

It does feel good to be kind to people; Violetta knew what she was talking about in that aspect. If only I could tell her how much easier life is now that she's made me into a better person.

More urgently, I must find a way to stop myself from remembering her throughout the day. The more I dwell on it, the more I make it into a bigger deal than it is. I am just going to shove this unappetizing cereal down my throat and focus on the present.

"Have you been eating enough lately?" Ember's comment is so hushed during the lecture that it's almost as if just air is leaving her lips.

"Why do you ask?" I whisper back at her a bit louder, yet low enough so that the professor doesn't hear.

She taps her nails against the desk lightly. "Your face looks slightly thinner and your eyes are sunken in."

"Maybe I've missed some meals here and there." I shrug my shoulders at her.

"You stick to your schedule as if your life depends on it." She shakes her head at me.

This persistent line of questions is tiresome to say the least. "Well maybe schedules aren't always necessary in life."

The moment those words leave my mouth, I instantly regret it. Not the kind of regret that came with visiting Violetta, because I don't really regret that. I squeeze my eyes shut, pinching the bridge of my nose in utter frustration. How could I have said that to Ember of all people? There's no way she won't interrogate me as soon as we are out of this classroom. I hesitantly look at her out of the corner of my eye. My worst suspicions are confirmed, as she is staring at me in disbelief. Her face is distorted as if I just told her I was going to shave my head and become a peaceful monk.

As soon as the professor dismisses us, my drawing device is in my hands as I attempt to make a speedy getaway. If I can outrun her, then I may be able to slow my possible imminent demise.

"Hart Jaehyung Kang." She draws out each name separately through gritted teeth. This must be what it feels like to know you are about to die; I think there's even a vague light in the distance.

"Full name, Ember?" I taunt with dalliance, trying to act like my old self. "Being a little over dramatic here, aren't we?"

Her expression doesn't change. "You're the one who just said that schedules aren't necessary. The Hart that I know would *never* say something like that."

"People are entitled to change their opinions."

"You've never changed." She looks at me with genuine confusion. I want to feel bad for her, but all I feel is extreme irritation at this conversation. "Lately you miss classes, conferences, and parties without a word. Even the press has noticed your absence and it's getting difficult to cover for you, so please explain what happened to cause this sudden radical shift."

"I appreciate the concern, but I've just been busy with personal matters lately," I say in a softer tone than my earlier statements. "Also, the sky doesn't have to be collapsing for me to have different views than earlier."

"So you've changed your mind about things other than the schedule?"

"I don't know." I run one hand through my hair in aggravation. She's asking these questions too fast.

The silence of the now empty classroom suddenly becomes suffocating, and I can't take it anymore. I rush to open the wooden doors and breathe in the evening air. The colors are deeper, and the air is as crisp as freshly cut grass. It almost makes me forget that Ember is intent on driving me to the brink of insanity.

Almost.

"This behavior seems *so* normal, Hart." She raises her voice in sarcasm after following me out of the doors.

"I don't need you butting in like this." I'm clearing my throat, trying to control my temper.

"You clearly need someone to check on you if this is how you're going to act!" She starts to shout at me and a few students begin to look our way.

"You've overstepped, Ember," I whisper in anger, keeping an eye on the people watching us. "Why do you care so much about what I do with my life?"

"Because I love you, idiot!" She blurts out and then immediately covers her mouth as if she had just put a curse on me.

My fixed, enraged glare falters as I study her demeanor, only to realize that I've never seen Ember like this. She's exhibiting the physical signs of being scared. Frightened is something I could've never imagined she'd be, with the extreme poise she exudes. Her hand hasn't left her mouth, as she's still shocked by her own words, leaving only her frantic eyes visible to me.

"Ember." My voice changes from bitterness to empathy, and she lets her hand drop from her face.

"This is not my wisest decision, but it can't change what I feel whenever we are together." Her voice shakes as she shifts her feet nervously and glances to her magenta pumps.

For the past few years, I've always assumed Ember would become my partner in life. Her feelings for me shouldn't be something upsetting, yet it feels like she just told me the worst news I've ever heard. In the back of my mind, I always knew that she probably felt this way about me, but now that it's staring me in the face it hurts, because I don't want to say what I must.

"I'm honored. But, I—"

She cuts me off. "I know you don't feel the same way; I just assumed you'd be with me anyway because you only believe in companionship. But these past couple of months, you've become almost unrecognizable."

"I'm sorry, Em." I use her nickname to ease the fact that I'm rejecting her in the middle of our college campus.

"As long as I'm in your life, I'll be okay waiting on the sidelines," she says lightly, while fixing the gold choker around her neck.

"How can you be okay with loving me and not expecting anything in return?" I ask.

"I'm new to this, but I think that's what love is. It's like lighting a fire inside your heart that keeps you warm. You don't want it to dim, but at the same time it's slowly burning you and forcing you to become something better." She looks at me with bittersweet dejection.

Her surprising answer sets me ablaze. At this moment I should be comforting my friend, but I need to get to the basement of the library as soon as possible. I finally realize why I'm like this, and rectifying this situation is more consequential than tradition or status.

"Ember, I'm sorry but there's an urgent matter I must tend to." I squeeze her forearm in a consoling manner. Without looking back at her only slightly devastated face, I run towards my fire.

There's no stopping me as I drive my car to the nearest train stop. I try not to think about what I'm doing the whole train ride to the outskirts of Briste and the sprint to the opening of the secret tunnel. Each step brings me closer to the inside of the Teorrain.

In the hollow space towards the basement of this library, the sound of my feet hitting the unclean pavement is echoing out. I'm not as perfect as I used to believe myself to be; even I have certain flaws that I must acknowledge. One of them is not breathing when I'm nervous—Violetta noticed it because she also has this unfortunate trait. I must have never noticed, since there have been few times in which I've ever been truly distressed. My life has been fairly planned out. I'd watch films in which the hero has something outlandish happen to him, but that's just never been me. I've never been the protagonist in the story.

My dad has been in the political game since my early childhood. He wasn't always the governor of our state, but he was still the mayor of our city. The public eye has watched me grow, and I've never known what it's like to be authentic. Everyone I met had an agenda in getting to know me.

That's why Violetta makes me feel something completely untamed that my mind hasn't been able to quite comprehend. She hasn't the slightest clue of who I am, my ranking in society, or what sort of power I hold. She doesn't know that my father has no opinions of his own and supports one of the main driving forces keeping the Crossed laws in place. She's the first person who hasn't treated me with the utmost respect that a governor's son deserves, and I am infatuated with her unfiltered thoughts.

Tabloids say I could have any girl, and yet the one person I adore doesn't want me. The only person who is never afraid to tell me how she feels. She helps me become the best version of myself. Violetta has put in the effort to know me, even if she is reluctant. I want to feel enraged from how she treats me sometimes, and yet I don't feel rage. I feel light; I feel fire and warmth previously foreign to me.

Nothing extraordinary had occurred to me and I'd been absolutely content with not being the protagonist until she entered my life. This whole time everything has been a plain canvas, but now it's covered in violet that can't be washed away.

I refuse to stop to think about how this is wrong or what's logical. I've lost myself, but I don't want to find the person that I was. I want to find her. I *need* to find her.

The time on my watch reassures me that Santiago should be gone, and Violetta will be finishing up. I breathe in while tapping out the secret knock. The sound seems to boom throughout the empty tunnel. I hold my breath and within seconds, the knock is returned to my ears. The wall slides open seemingly in slow motion, but it's worth it when she's standing in front of me.

Her expression turns rapidly from concern to frustration as the initial shock of my appearance wears off; I can tell she isn't happy to see me. That gorgeous hair hangs in curls around her face like in my dream, and her pink lips are twisted into a frown. Dark circles surround her eyes, mimicking my own.

"What are you doing here?" She hisses at me. "I told you not to come back."

"I had to."

"You've learned all you can from me and what we were doing wasn't right." Her voice wavers just like last time. "Go home and stay gone this time."

She moves to close the wall on me but I force my way inside the basement. She doesn't anticipate this move, so I take the opportunity to grab her shoulders and stare down at her. I'll never be the same if I tell her, but I'll hate myself if she never knows my feelings.

"Violetta, just let me speak." My hands are still on her shoulders.

"What is it?" She looks away from me.

I lightly tilt her smooth chin upwards, forcing her to look at me. Her eyes widen at this action, but she doesn't resist.

"Until a couple of months ago, my existence was black and white, nothing in between." I pause, thinking of what to say next. "Then I met you and started to question the very fabric of my world. I don't know who I am anymore."

I take a step closer and let my hand gently rest on her cheek as she looks at me, stunned. My face leans in close to hers, and I look into her eyes. "The only thing I'm certain of is that you've mixed the colors of our lives together. You've ignited a fire that I can't let burn out, no matter who threatens me."

"What are you trying to say?" Her voice is so quiet that it's barely audible.

"That this isn't just flirting, or lessons, or friendship. Violetta, I'm in love with all that you are." I keep my voice steady as her mouth drops open. "I love you and I'll never stop."

Violetta stares at me in disbelief and astonishment for several moments, leaving my heart to feel like it's going to burst out of my chest. The hand I have on her cheek slides down her face and hangs beside me in an uncomfortable way.

Panic begins to rise inside of me, and I'm afraid I have made a grave mistake. I don't expect her to say it back to me, but her lack of response is torturous. I must let her know that it's okay if she doesn't feel the same way. Leaving in shame isn't the ideal outcome, but I'm just proud of myself for telling her.

Taking a step back, I begin to apologize. "I know this is crazy, and you don't feel the same way, bu—"

I'm suddenly cut off by her closing the distance between us. She stretches her arm up and places her hand behind my neck as she pulls me down towards her. Standing on her toes, our faces are closer than ever as she gazes into my eyes with a flame behind hers. Without warning, she breathes in quickly and then reaches up as our lips meet. My eyes close after the momentary amazement fades and I'm falling into the sensation of her kiss.

My arms instinctively reach down to wrap around her waist and she tilts towards me further, with her hands clasping together behind my neck. She smells like vast lavender fields and beautiful memories that I've yet to experience. Time has stopped, and I'm here in this moment with the most magnificent girl in my arms.

She draws back from me and sets her heels down on the ground. I'm still lost in the feel of her around me as I watch her keep her eyes closed, before reluctantly opening them. I'm completely speechless at our kiss; it was like a perfect illusion. Was I daydreaming my entire existence until her? Either way, now I'm awake. Never will I daydream again, I don't have a need for that.

"I love you, Hart," she says, wrapping her arms around me and laying her head on my racing heart.

I am now positive of three things in my life: that I'm in love with Violetta, that life is about to get exponentially more difficult, and that logic is vastly overrated.

CHAPTER
16

Violetta

I love you, Hart.

Did I really just say that out loud? The mystification I feel isn't completely about my confession, but my actions as well. Nova has told me she's admired my capacity to be bold and daring. She's often said she wished she could be more outspoken like me, so my brave nature is something that I've admired about myself. Kissing a Pravi, though, is another level of audacity—even for someone like me.

This aura of exhilarating endearment kindles a flame in me, and it's almost like the stars were waiting to align for this. The fire around them must've been burning in the night sky all this time just for the two of us.

It's difficult to focus on anything other than the way he's looking at me. In the split second that he told me his true feelings, every single apprehension about this went away. His words broke the spell over me. The prospect of imminent peril is trying to work its way back into my consciousness, but it's being overpowered by the strong desire to stay in his arms forever.

He holds me close against him now, and I gladly snuggle into his warm vanilla scent. "Well, this wasn't the response I was expecting. You broke your own rule, Angel."

"How was I supposed to stand my ground when you melted my heart with your confession?" I question while he chuckles, resting his head onto mine.

"This must be a dream," he whispers into my hair while his arms stay securely around me. "Real life has never been so good to me. There's no way someone like you could love me."

"There's no way someone like me could love another." I speak into his chest, not ready to let go. "I tried to deny my feelings for so many reasons, but it's been you the whole time. You're my protagonist."

"What do you mean by that?" He asks, perplexed with my statement.

"In books about love, there's always two protagonists that were meant for one another and they find each other no matter what. I was convinced that didn't exist behind these walls, but you proved me wrong tonight. You've been the other lead in my story, and you found me against all odds," I say, and he takes a deep breath as if he's contemplating something.

"Do these stories usually end happily?" He asks with bated breath.

"Sometimes…" I'm aware of what he's getting at. He's frightened that we are being all too careless.

His sigh is lined with melancholy. "What are we going to do?"

My previously weak arms squeeze him tighter. "Do we have to know right now? I feel like nothing else matters."

"I want to keep holding you like this in the future and the only way that's possible is if we have a concrete plan." He loosens his grip on me and draws back enough to see my face. I look up at him and he leans in to kiss my forehead, which gives me the best kind of goosebumps.

"Let's talk then."

He smiles before hesitantly moving from me to the opposite side of the room. He leans up against my desk and cocks his head while motioning for me to come over to him. There's nothing that can hold me back from looking him up and down while walking over. It's almost as if I'm seeing him in a new light, and it suits him. My eyes follow his black leather pants, up to the silky green dress shirt hanging loosely around him. His attire only accentuates his fierce demeanor and immaculate complexion. By the time we make eye contact, I'm positive he's noticed me admiring him.

He chuckles at me knowingly. "Like what you see?"

"Always have." I shrug at him, and instead of saying something witty back to me, he just stares in astonishment.

"I don't know when I'll get used to this." He shakes his head gingerly.

"Used to what?" I ask.

"Your change of heart towards me," he says with another laugh. "I like it."

"I like you."

That came out of my mouth without hesitation, or any prior thought for that matter. He looks at me stunned again, before shaking his head again to presumably snap out of the daze he's in. Though he appears flustered, his features remain as striking as moonlight itself. When did I become so weak for this flirtatious contradiction of a boy?

"You're going to make me lose focus," he groans at me.

"I'll stop for now," I sigh in a defeated tone, and gesture for him to begin. "Let's talk business."

"My idea is that we just date in secret," he says confidently.

"That's it?" I pace back and forth across the concrete floors. "What if we get caught?"

"It's a risk I'm willing to take. Jail seems like nothing compared to not being able to see you."

"It's like you never listen to what I say." If this is about to become our first argument as a couple, I won't be surprised it happened so quickly. "If we get caught, we could both die."

He straightens up and appears more alert. "They can't kill us."

"They kill Crossed people all the time for much smaller offenses."

"They actually *murder* them?" He walks over to me and his expression turns deadly serious.

"Did you think I was joking about something that serious?"

A look of horror sweeps across his face. "Yes! The government tells us that you live safe, just like we do. I knew it wasn't accurate, but nothing as cruel as this!"

"We are far from equal to you all, I've taught you that." I flip my hair behind my back, letting out a breath.

"We should expose them for who they are. If people knew how you're being treated, they wouldn't stand for it. There's a large population of Pravis who protest the Crossed laws every day, including yours truly," he says excitedly, like he's the first person who's thought of doing this.

"You've forgotten, but there's already a group trying to fight back, and it's useless. The Vermillion has spent years hiding and planning, but there is a reason that they haven't acted on anything."

"Why is that?"

"We are outnumbered and many of the Vermillion aren't actually willing to take a life, but the Grey Guards don't hesitate," I say morbidly.

"You think we'd be taking our lives into our hands if we tried to fight?" He flinches.

"We would die without a doubt."

He huffs with frustration. "Tell me about the Vermillion, can we talk to them about this?"

"The Vermillion despise the Pravis for obvious reasons, so they would not take kindly to you." I look away from him and wrap the ends of my hair around my fingers. "We are already doing one very illegal thing; we shouldn't add another."

"What happened to your confidence?" He says with concern in his tone. "I don't want to be the reason you're unsure of yourself."

"The reason I'm unsure of myself is because I've never done anything significant in my life. What if I'm the reason we get caught in the end?"

He speaks out sternly. "You're the only reason I believe we can be together."

"I'm just a normal girl, Hart. There's nothing particularly special or heroic about me."

He looks at me with sadness crossing his features. I'm putting his life at risk and the knowledge that I can't protect him is terrifying. When I look up at him again, his face seems to have changed like he's scheming something, and he opens his mouth to address me again.

"Do you have a mirror anywhere?" He asks.

"What does that have to do with anything?" *This is weird timing for worrying about appearances, even for Hart.*

"Just trust me. Do you have one?"

I eye him suspiciously before giving up and letting my feet carry me to my desk. Opening the drawers, I pull out my handheld mirror with floral designs down the handle. I bought it with Nova's discount at the Donation Center. It was the first thing I purchased just because I wanted to, not out of necessity. My eyes linger on it while walking over to Hart and placing it into his open palm.

He uses his free hand to grab mine and spin me around so that my back is pressed against his chest now. I let out a gasp at his speedy actions and he snickers slightly at my reaction. Placing one arm around me, he holds the mirror up to our faces with the other.

"What do you see in the mirror?" He asks me.

After glancing at us, I speak candidly. "I see a scared Crossed girl and her Pravi boy."

"Look again." His hand settles on my waist while my heart rate increases. "Ask me what I see."

"What do you see, Hart?"

"I see a brilliant woman with fire in her eyes and ambition in her heart. The true protagonist of our story." He kisses my cheek gingerly and my face heats up. "Behind her is the luckiest man alive. Not a Pravi and a Crossed, but two souls who found one another. Two souls who can shake the world."

I spin around, placing my hands on his shoulders. "I just don't want anyone to take you away from me."

"No force on this earth can ever take me away from you." He tucks a loose curl behind my ear. "You have my word."

I nod my head, trying to have faith in his words. "I trust you."

"For now, let's continue meeting in secret, and pray that we don't get caught." He looks deeply in my eyes.

"Did you just say you're going to pray?" I almost let go of his shoulders.

"What can I say?" He says coyly and scrunches his nose. "You have a certain influence on a guy."

"That may be the strangest thing you've said tonight." I giggle at him.

"I never thought people could change to their very core, but love is so demanding that I couldn't help but bend my logic for it."

"But are you prepared to die for it?" I whisper.

"I'd rather die in your arms than live in anyone else's," he assures me in a hushed voice.

"Well then." I stand on my toes and place a chaste kiss on his lips. "I'll try my best to make sure no harm comes your way."

He hugs me tighter and his heartbeat is keeping time with mine. "Even if it does, I'll still be yours."

We stay in one another's arms for what feels like only minutes but turns out to be all night as we talk about our lives. I could listen to him tell me stories forever. Maybe I will get to, if we are careful.

I'm sad when he tells me he needs to leave, though. I never want him to leave my side again. He looks just as disappointed as I feel after we say goodbye and the tunnel door slides open. He starts to walk through, but I have to stop him.

"Wait!" I call out.

He turns around with a worried look. "What is it?"

I run forward and hug him one last time. "You can go now."

"You make it hard to leave, angel," he says, and my cheeks flush at the same nickname that used to make me wince.

His smile exudes the same radiance as the sun, and my soul lights up as it shines down on me. After taking my hand in his one last time and giving me a reassuring look, he lets go to enter the code for the opening to close. There's no trace that he'd ever been here.

A sigh escapes my lips as I blow out the candle on my desk, and I switch off the lamp in my office. He's gone now, but the thought of him keeps me humming to myself. This is the only time I've felt overwhelmed in a good way. Once I lock the front door on my way out of the library, the chilling air hits me with the harsh reminder that I'm still inside the Teorrain and he's somewhere far from here.

I want to leave, be with Hart, and live anywhere else. Yet, as much as I like the idea of freedom, I'd be more than content just getting to meet Hart in a basement for the rest of my life. If destiny will only allow us to be a secret, then that's alright. Just being with him is such a blessing that I never knew I'd be able to have. I shouldn't wish for too much.

I let out an exasperated breath while walking on the path back to my apartment. Hart is the only one who makes me feel like I don't have to think. Like reason and rules can't defy what we have, because we are stronger than all of that.

Before I open the door to my apartment, I try to fix my hair and straighten my coat. I'll have to tell Nova that Santiago made me work late again. It is not going to be easy to pretend like the last couple of hours didn't happen, but I have to protect Hart. I need to be the girl he believes I can be, and that means fibbing until we figure out a solution to our dilemma.

While nudging open the door, I prepare for a long lecture from Nova. Peeking inside, I notice her blanket nicely folded on her cot, without a trace of her. I sigh out a moment in relief, she must've already left for work to get an early start to the day. The apartment feels empty without her, but at least there's no intense interview about where I've been. The most significant problem that dares to challenge me is that I'm a very bad liar, and something in my gut is whispering that Nova has caught on to my charade.

CHAPTER
17

Santiago

*I*f you're willing to search, you'll find that throughout the history of literature many write about the soothing qualities of putting their thoughts onto paper. They like to believe that writing down these musings grants them power. The written word must be mighty because it's lasting. Authors of all kinds have expressed that once your feelings are written down, a sense of peace will then fill you. The sheer act of putting pen to paper will resolve many of your worries.

This theory is absolute rubbish.

It could be that I'm awake at approximately 0500 hours and furious with myself, but writing is doing nothing for my mind. This dainty pen may break underneath the force my hand is applying to it. Nausea hits my body thinking about the scene I just witnessed.

Should I even write about this? If only Mum and Dad were here to tell me what to do. I'm absolutely lost, and which path I should hurry down is unclear.

His voice whispers in my head. He's soothing her, telling her how perfect she is to him. Her laugh, which usually is music to my ears, felt like alarm bells when it came in response to something he said. Her hands on his broad shoulders while he admired her in a way I always have. His arms draped around her as she beamed at him like she's never looked at me.

I hear a crack and look down to realize my pen has snapped in half. *Simply smashing, Santiago.* The state of unsteadiness I was residing in before tonight was bothersome, but pleasant in some way. But now, the irregular harmony is gone. All that's left is betrayal in its most deceitful form: that of a best friend. One whom I wrongly thought cared for me. A friend who I thought felt the same way about me.

Chapter 17

A large part of my heart will always wonder how our relationship would be if things were different.

Dreadful lies. She doesn't see me like that; I don't know if she ever has.

I've spent all night trying to forget the images of her with him, but I can't erase what has been burned into me. The two of them together will be engraved in my mind for the rest of my solitary days. I was just trying to find a misplaced book. If I hadn't come back to the library to find it, I could've lived in sweet ignorance. Instead, I possess the torturous knowledge that everything she told me was simply a myth to protect my feelings. They were so wrapped up in each other that they didn't even notice my heart shattering at the top of the stairs.

She doesn't care for the rules; she's a rebel. She owns no fear of what the Grey Guards could do to her or that naïve boy. How could she let this happen? How could she mislead me and feel no remorse?

He's a rare one to say the least. I can't recall seeing a Crossed dressed so impeccably; he reminds me of the kids I went to primary school with before I lived in the Teorrain. Not only were his clothes ideal, but his hair was a bright blond color that was so well-combed that it looked manufactured. He's everything I've wished to be. Everything that I'd wanted to be for her.

No.

I need to bring my thoughts to a full stop. I can't live my life based on what she wants. Clearly her desires don't include me, and pondering this will drive me to a madness I won't be able to come back from. The most severe issue is that I don't know what to do about this. Do I turn them in like the law compels me to, or do I stay quiet because of my lingering feelings for her?

She chose another man over me even when it's illegal, being positively aware of the consequences. She used the law to reject me when she was defying the rules this whole time. With all this information staring me in the face, it only makes sense to turn them in immediately to the Grey Guards.

With my mind made up, I pick up the emergency red telephone on my desk. I sit for a moment, awaiting a voice to speak so I can get this over with as swiftly as possible.

"What is it?" I hear an aggressive masculine voice on the line.

"Yes, this is Santiago Singh at the library—"

The Guard cuts me off. "It's almost the 22nd century, Santiago. We have caller ID. What do you want?"

After his abrasive answer, I ask myself if this is truly right. I haven't even given Violetta a chance to explain herself. She isn't even aware that I saw everything, and it's my actions that could grant her death warrant. Even if I'm furious with her, my heart would never repair if her demise was the result of my wounded pride.

"Santiago?" The voice speaks louder in an annoyed tone.

"I do apologize, I thought someone might be trying to break in. Turns out it was just the wind," I blurt out rapidly.

There's immediate laughter in the background from several people and the main voice on the phone joins in with a hearty cackle. I roll my eyes out of habit; the Grey Guards always elicit this sort of response from me, whether I'm conscious of it or not.

"No one would try to break into your sad library, so don't call again unless you want a beating," he snarls out.

The extended tone of the line being cut off reaches my ears and it's a welcome sound. The noise is like a symphony playing to applaud me for refraining from making a huge mistake—it is the sound of relief. With trembling hands, I put the phone down on the hook, letting out a long breath.

I must get back to my flat and sleep away my worries. Lacking in slumber won't help this situation whatsoever. I walk over to my journals, neatly stacking them before heading towards the wooden door at the end of the hallway.

The journey to my flat seems to be taking longer than usual, and my mind is going into overdrive trying to answer questions that are impossibly difficult. Eventually I'll have to stop this lunacy, but for now I allow my mind to wander because stopping it would be too time consuming.

The sun begins to rise while I'm still walking, and not even my horrendous train of thought stops me from appreciating the glow of the morning sky. They can put us behind a wall, but they'll never be able to take away our Geal sunrise. I'm enchanted watching the beauty coming up just above the wall when I'm abruptly knocked to the ground.

"Hey man, watch where you're going!" An angry woman's voice rings out at me.

"I'm dearly sorry, I hadn't—"

The words get caught in my throat whilst I pull myself up from the hard cement. She's pretty in a remarkable way, young, with a look of incomparable ambition in her eyes. Even though she's staring angrily at me, she doesn't come off as threatening. I can tell it's because she doesn't really want to. The clothes that cover her body don't seem to match her face, which makes me curious about her. The mousy brown hair atop her head is pulled back into two tight braids, and her clothes match her coal-colored nails. Her style lacks color, except for the crimson-red laces on her high-heeled boots.

"Are you going to finish your apology, Mr. Englishman?" She looks me up and down with a sneer as she stands.

"Yes, I formally apologize." I look down with shame. "There's no excuse for not noticing you."

She begins to relax. "A man with manners, I didn't think they really existed."

"We are an elusive creature, and only venture outdoors in the winter," I tease her, and she smiles at me.

"Then maybe it was worth getting knocked to the ground, since I got to witness this rare sight."

"Glad I could be of service," I bow to her and she giggles. "Are you harmed at all?"

"I can take it. I was just surprised by the genuine apology." She shrugs.

"It's the least I could do for being so inconsiderate of such a kind young lady."

"Young lady? We look about the same age." She eyes me up and down again while crossing her arms.

I look at her for a moment, contemplating my response. "I've had a very horrible night and I can't think straight." I begin to walk past her. "Sorry again for the inconvenience, please travel safely."

"Wait!" She stops me unexpectedly.

"Yes?"

"Do you want to talk about it?" She looks at the old watch on her wrist. "I've got some time."

It's odd that I ended up in an unfamiliar meadow with a total stranger in the early hours of the morning, but it feels right. Typically, I'm quite reserved, always holding back rather than telling people my feelings. Something about this girl makes me feel that I can be honest for once. I mustn't be completely truthful since she is still a stranger, but so far, she's helped me to take my mind off things more effectively than sleep would.

We've been talking in this field for about an hour. It's almost like I didn't see Violetta wrapped around that bloke in the basement of my workplace last night. I can't tell this girl about the situation, obviously, but being vague couldn't hurt.

"So, your bad day is essentially the result of your feelings for someone?" She asks, as she plays with a piece of wild grass mindlessly.

"Pretty much." I leave some key points out, like the fact that there's another man.

"Tell her how you feel, then."

"What good could come of that?" I look up at the dewy sky with doubt.

She isn't aware that I've already told Violetta, and she rejected me anyway. Maybe I'm just searching for some sort of validation that I did the right thing by confessing my feelings. There's essentially no point in talking to this girl about matters out of my hands, but it feels nice to say them out loud.

"You two could be together, wouldn't that be good?" She asks.

I begin to laugh. "In a perfect world yes, but that's extremely illegal, as you know."

"Well, the law is wrong." She sounds exasperated when she states this, causing me to look at her hard features again. "Go get her!"

"I'm not just going to disobey the law. What kind of thinking is that?" I ask.

She stands up and reaches a strong hand down to me. I grab it before letting her pull me up as well. She's silent for a moment while thinking of what to say, and I look at her in anticipation. I may have an advantage over her in terms of physical height, but her presence is taller than I'll ever be.

"What if I told you that there was a way to break the law and not get caught?" She looks in my eyes, searching them for a reaction.

"What do you mean?" I'm starting to get concerned with this line of conversation.

"What if we didn't have to live in this state like caged animals?" She moves closer to me with perilous dreams in her eyes. "What if you could love who you wanted to openly?"

I start to think about this momentarily before the realization of her words crashes into me. A small gasp escapes me; I don't know why I was so ignorant. The determination in her voice, the black clothes... the crimson laces.

How did I not put this together?

Just as I'm wondering how to make an escape, she pulls out a red cloth from her pocket and ties it around the crown of her head tightly before grabbing my hand.

"We could use someone smart like you, and there's a meeting happening under the church in half an hour." She squeezes my hand eagerly. "Join us."

I pull my hand away from hers and begin to back away cautiously, to which she slowly walks forward in my direction.

My flustered voice cracks out: "I'm just a simple man who doesn't want to cause trouble."

"I was a simple girl when I joined. Aren't you tired of this life?" She pleads with me and her eyes are honest. "More people are going to be ripped away from their families just like you and I were, but we can change this place. Not just for us, but for all the Crossed who are suffering."

My movements come to a halt, and I consider her powerful words. It seems they've sparked a ghostly curiosity within me. Until now, I had mostly been thinking about my story and how the Teorrain has affected me. I never stopped to consider the dreadful truth that this could keep happening to people just like me with no end in sight. These laws may never come to an end. This girl in front of me has the capacity to lead thousands with her overwhelming influence, and she started as a simple girl. She began her journey like me.

A hundred more thoughts like these run through my head before I decide that the impulsive decision I make today won't be to report Violetta… it will be to reconsider my stance on the rebellion.

"I can't promise to join, but I'll go with you to the meeting," I say firmly, not completely believing my own words.

"Really?" She jumps up to hug me and I try not to think of Violetta. "You won't be disappointed."

She grabs my hand again, pulling me out of the meadow towards my fate. For the first time in my life, I'm about to do something daring. I don't know if it'll kill me, but maybe I am willing to fight for others now. The adrenaline in my blood is stopping all reason from flowing to my brain. I should at least hear them out on their plans, shouldn't I?

I follow this stranger with her nice smile out to the same road where we bumped into each other. It could be the lack of sleep, but it feels strangely like this is where I'm supposed to be.

I pull back on her hand to stop her briefly. "I almost forgot to ask, but what's your name?"

She turns around to face me and giggles, recognizing that we have talked for a long while without exchanging pleasantries. She holds her hand out to me with poise and introduces herself formally.

"Nova Alejo, 2nd-in-command to Othello of the Vermillion."

PART II

*"... unkindness may defeat my life,
But never taint my love."*

—William Shakespeare, Othello

CHAPTER
18

Hart

*T*he sound of water sloshing around inside my mono-grammed metal bottle is drowned out by the loud music my driver put on at my request. It's a love song that's topped the charts recently—a song that I would've earlier condemned for being entirely too cliché and upbeat. Instead of criticizing it, the evolved version of myself sits in the passenger seat of this town car, belting out the lyrics along with my driver. The lyrics that epitomize how I feel about visiting Violetta tonight.

This being said, Violetta and I try to incorporate reason into our emotions at times. We know it'd be suspicious to Santiago and Nova if she stayed late every night to work. After deliberating for a while, we decided that every Tuesday and Friday evening I would go to the basement to see her for our version of the typical date.

I had some dismay limiting it to only two nights. Although I'm aware of the suspicion it would cause, I can't help wanting to be around her all the time. Remembering that euphoric feeling I get, just from being beside her, is enough to fill me with lovely thoughts every waking moment. It's also enough to make me into the person who is now harmonizing to love songs with my driver.

The cheerful song comes to its closing notes, and it hits me all at once that I'm on the way to school and seeing Ember is unavoidable. This will be the first time we've spoken since she confessed to me. My absent-minded smile quickly diminishes as I come to this realization.

It's been exactly eighteen days since she told me the truth about her feelings, and inadvertently made me realize mine for Violetta. Class attendance is optional for our shared class. Even if it wasn't, my professor would never say anything because of my status. I've had many political events to attend lately, so I haven't been to class since our conversation on campus.

The intense way I feel about Violetta is the same way Ember feels for me, and I've been completely ignorant of that. Even though the horrible feeling in my stomach is telling me to run far away, it's my duty to confront this and earnestly apologize. That is the only noble solution to this issue. It's what Violetta would want me to do.

The main problem with this strategy is that I'd like to tell her my heart already belongs to another. I'm sure that would be the easiest way to avoid hurting her feelings. But, how would I even go about telling her that I kept going back to the Teorrain after she explicitly told me not to?

The only answer is to be vague, staying somewhere between the truth and a lie. That way it will be believable, and I will be able to turn her down in the nicest possible way. I must don the mask of my former self. I'll convince her that I'm the same robotic Hart Kang she's always known and had the misfortune of loving.

I rehearse what I'm going to say while strolling past the shrubbery outside of Classroom Building A. I can see several groups of girls whispering about me, but I'm in no mood to be my usual charming self for the masses. My heart beats rapidly before I open the large door to my class. I can tell she's surprised to see me here.

Her face is bare, which is a sight I've not seen since we were small children, and her nails have been stripped of any polish. Her face goes slightly pale upon making eye contact with me, and she quickly turns away to face the professor once again.

"Mr. Kang, how are you? We've missed you in class," Professor Arnay says in a tone that is soft and kind, unlike her usual lecturing tone.

"Happy to be back," I say confidently.

"We are just as happy to have you, please have a seat." She smiles before going back to lecturing on cost theory.

I slide into Ember's row and sit directly next to her. She shifts from her left to her right to stay further from me without making a spectacle of herself. I decide to send her a message to say hello. This could let her know that I haven't forgotten about her, and that I'd like to remain friends.

I hit send on my E-pad and she stares at her own quizzically before looking back at me and smiling. A weight feels like it's being lifted off my shoulders, but just then her smile fades and she deletes the message, glaring at me.

This can't be going well.

Ember and I sit uncomfortably in complete silence listening to Professor Arnay explain things that we already know. This adds to the intolerable feeling in the room, because neither of us is taking notes. The lecture passes by at an excruciatingly slow pace, and when it ends I'm more than ready to get my apology over with.

As we are packing up our things, I look at her seriously and whisper in her direction.

"Can we talk outside?" I ask.

"Fine," she says in a curt manner.

Knowing that I'm headed for my doom, I trudge out of the classroom and wait for her outside by the shrubbery. She walks over to me and folds her arms in a defensive stance.

"What do you want, Hart?" She asks aggressively.

"I want to apologize."

"Apologize?" She scoffs. "You think you can ignore me for weeks and then everything is going to be okay because you feel bad?"

"I'm just asking for forgiveness." I really hope she doesn't ask further questions.

"You didn't respond to any of my attempts to contact you. That's much worse than only turning me down." She uncrosses her arms and loosens her stance.

"I needed time to process my emotions but handled it in the worst way. There's no good excuse, and I'm sorry." This isn't totally a lie, but it's certainly not the whole truth.

She huffs out a breath. "You could've had your staff send me a message to reassure me that you weren't dead or anything."

"When I die, I'll call you so you can be the first to know." I chuckle and the corners of her mouth begin to turn upward. "You are the only one who I trust to plan my funeral."

"Only white lilies and Mozart's finest pieces playing." She softly laughs with me.

"See? You know me so well." I look at her intently and step toward her. "You're my best friend, Ember. I just don't want to lose you."

"You won't lose me Hart, I just need some time to get over you," she says in a slightly broken voice, and I notice the distress written onto her features.

"How long?"

"Not too long," she promises me with a hesitant nod.

"Take all the time you need."

She lets out a long sigh. "I wish that gorgeous mind of yours would open up to the possibility of love, but that's just not you."

With that, she walks away and leaves me standing there. I watch her ponytail, which holds her deep blue locks, sway from side to side until she's so far from me that it's no longer visible. A part of me feels remorseful when I start my walk away from the classroom building. I hurt the best friend I've ever had. That may have been difficult, but it was the right thing to do. We are on the road to being friends again, that's all I needed to be reassured of.

There are people who walk around at my school holding books in their hands—not the types of stories that can be read on their E-pads like everyone else does, but genuine paper copies of novels. I heard once that libraries used to be places that citizens would check out books and read each page as if it were something precious. Now, they are simply glorified places with cafes, study corners, and rooms for clubs to hold meetings. Books are still available for checkout, but rarely do those pages feel the fingers of a reader flipping through them.

Even though my major is journalism, I can't remember the last time I held a true physical copy of a novel. I was taught that material books are inefficient. My mother says it wastes time to turn a page and pointed out that the weight of a paperback is heavier than even a single E-pad.

Therefore, it's uncharacteristic of me to be holding the faded copy of a book I've never heard about. Violetta stands above me and explains why it's important for the awakening of my mind. It didn't take long for me to read it. I must admit there was a certain thrill when I got to turn to the next page instead of scrolling down. Not to mention, it was less strain on my eyes to study the words on paper instead of a screen.

"I went to the library at my school to find this book, but the screen said there was an error and no such novel existed." I set the book down beside me on the ground and look up at her, just in time to see her trademarked Violetta eye roll.

"They don't want your head being filled with ideas of justice on behalf of the Crossed," she says pointedly.

"The book has nothing to do with the Crossed, it's simply about racial discrimination in a time when they claimed to be executing freedom for African-Americans."

As the words leave my mouth, she looks at me with an expression that tells me I've already answered my own question. It's true that I've never read anything like this book, *To Kill a Mockingbird*, and I certainly have never been more fascinated by a concept. Pain strikes my chest as I remember that my world is simply a censored version of reality. How many more books are there that the government is hiding from us? How many times has my own father been responsible for this manipulation of the media?

Chapter 18

Violetta moves to sit down parallel to me and crosses her legs in front of her as she exhales heavily. Although this is a serious moment, I can't help but feel nervous when she's this close to me. She moves her long, curly tresses to one side of her head and glances at me grimly.

"Have you ever seen any reading materials on the Crossed laws that weren't biased?" Violetta's stare is one that evokes sympathy in the deepest parts of my soul, and I wish there was some way around the truth again.

"When we learn about the laws in class or read political articles, it's usually spoken of like it was a moral conclusion that everyone came to." The inflection in my voice seeks to convey that I don't agree with this choice.

She nods without hesitation. "I assumed if this book was impossible to find, then unbiased reading materials on the Crossed laws would be even harder to come across. It's almost like they're censoring you the same way they censor us."

"Perhaps that's why there have been so many protests about these laws in recent years. People are getting angrier now; even many politicians have taken a stance against the Crossed laws," I say.

Violetta scoffs at this. "I don't trust politicians; they must be terrible to have put us here in the first place."

I impulsively twitch at the mention of politicians. There isn't a bone in my body that doesn't completely agree with her ideas about this. I would know firsthand just how greed-filled and self-centered they can be. My father cares greatly about fame, power, and nothing good. The one thing that keeps me up at night is knowing that one day I will have to defy him and put my foot down. Now that I know this girl, how could I ever actively be a part of his world?

Governor Hart Kang, who will have a lovely Pravi wife complete with Pravi children whose ideals match his own. The masses will listen to him, put their hope in him, and yet there isn't one word he speaks that he truly puts faith in. He'll have everything he could ever want, but his smile will look dreadfully forged. He'll look as if he could be plucked from the earth right then, and he wouldn't be fearful at all because anything is better than his life. What a frightful nightmare indeed.

"If everyone out there could read this book, they could see that the Crossed laws are just history's newest form of oppression towards the underdog." I shake my head in dissatisfaction with the way my society looks. "Crossed people don't dilute culture at all, they bring it to life in exciting new ways."

"Change and mixing isn't something that people are typically excited about, Hart." She frowns and stops playing with her hair. "Speaking of change, what if we talk about something more fun?"

I perk up at the mention of fun and pick up my bag, ready to pull out the ancient artifact I brought for her to see. She glances at me curiously and I smile before grabbing her hand. She scoots towards me and rests her body against mine.

"You can't break up with me once I show you this, okay?" I say jokingly, and her laugh almost makes me forget that I am unquestionably condemned for feeling this way about her.

CHAPTER
19

Violetta

$\mathcal{M}$y frenzied laughter echoes off the walls while I try to keep from falling over from Hart's story. "So, you actually thought that you were famous just because your birthday is February 14th?"

He nods and lets out a deep laugh. "I went around acting all superior because I thought I was Valentine's Day royalty or something."

"You sound like you were quite the charmer."

I try to muffle my giggles with my hand, and he flashes those faultless snowy teeth just before kissing my forehead. We are sitting on an old blanket I brought from my place to the basement. I never thought I'd be here with him, cuddled up like two peas in a pod. He continues to let me flip through a beautiful leather-bound book filled with screens that display pictures of him from every stage of his life.

The most wonderful thing about the book isn't the pictures, but the story behind each photo. Every story he tells makes me feel closer to him, like he's filling me in on what I missed throughout his life.

"I wasn't a charmer back then, but I must be now to get someone like you to notice me."

"That has less to do with charm and more with you trespassing in my office late at night." I roll my eyes mockingly. "Anyone would notice you in that situation."

"Tell me, then, when did you actually start to have feelings for me?" He asks.

I lay my head back on his shoulder. "There was no moment when I was aware that I was falling for you. I just looked at you one day and knew I already loved you. My feelings went behind my back and surprised me without warning."

"Really?" He asks, with giddiness in his tone.

"Yes." My cheeks heat up with embarrassment. "What about you?"

"When I saw you from behind the bookshelves for the first time."

I sit up abruptly and whip my head around to face him, and his features tell me he's being honest.

"I don't believe you," I blurt out.

"Why do you think I risked my life to stop a stranger from falling?" He asks flatly.

I shake my head at him. "Weren't you the one trying to convince me that love doesn't exist from the beginning?"

"That was my own fear speaking for me. It had to reaffirm my former beliefs out loud, because the second I saw you, those great theories I held dear were proven false in the best way." He leans in close to my face and smiles.

"You're just saying that because you're cheesy." I put my hands on his chest and push him away playfully.

He grabs me again and pulls me into his arms so that he can whisper over my shoulder again. "Saying it out loud feels like a great privilege I didn't think I'd ever have, and I'm never going to stop."

I look at him again. "I love you, Hart."

His face lights up in the most surreal way, and I realize my attraction for Hart isn't the kind that I read about in books. It isn't the kind that led me to an epiphany the first time I saw him, and it definitely isn't the kind that made me believe I'd met my soulmate during a chance encounter. It's the type where, over time, his soul began to reflect on his features. His outward appearance began to morph into a boy who was perfect for someone like me; his inner-self made his outer-self beautiful in the most transparent way.

"I love you, too." He opens his fascinating and futuristic-looking book again and points to a picture of himself with braces. "Just be glad that I grew up and don't look like that anymore."

I chuckle softly at his comment. "I wonder if I'd like you if we met when we were younger."

"I'm not sure how we would've met." His hand falls from the side of the book. "It makes me sad to think that if I hadn't broken the law, I'd never have met the only girl for me."

"That would've been sad for you," I say slyly.

"You're supposed to say it back!" He feigns a hurt look, and I try not to laugh since my poor cheeks hurt from smiling too much.

It's hard to concentrate my thoughts on anything other than what he said, though. If he hadn't committed a crime, I'd probably be trying to figure out my feelings towards Santiago. I wouldn't know the difference between convenient attraction and true love. He's only been in my life for a short while now, but I can't even imagine a horrible alternate universe without him.

I glance back down to the book and flip the page again. There's a photo of him from when he was a young teenager.

He looks almost the same in all these photos, and the back-drop also stays the same. He's standing straight upright in front of a stunning mural that depicts a secret pond hideaway. There's a small white bridge and flowers abundantly placed in the trees surrounding it. He's showcasing his debonair grin at the camera, and I notice something slightly alarming.

"Where did you find that bracelet?" I ask in a disordered haze, not quite sure if what I'm seeing is correct. "I have the same one."

He pulls the book up from my hands and taps at the screen while examining his left arm closely. He lets out a con-fused huff at the silver-tinted band wrapped around his wrist, and the holographic words engraved onto it.

"It was my father's; he said it brought him great happiness once. He wanted me to have it." He puts the book down and shrugs slightly. "He said it was custom made, but maybe you have something similar."

"That's my bracelet, Hart," I say, and then hastily push my sleeve up to reveal an identical silver band. "L'amour est l'amitié; it means 'love is friendship.'"

His eyes widen at my words and he grabs my right wrist, examining the French words on the bracelet. "Who gave you this?"

"It was in the bag of things my parents left for me. They weren't able to leave a note, so I don't know what those words meant to them on a personal level."

He looks down at me in a state of pure wonder and then back at my bracelet. He's quiet for a few moments, before looking at the ceiling and closing his eyes, as if he's trying to remember something that could possibly help us understand why on earth we have the same accessory.

"It must be a coincidence, or perhaps it was a trend," he speaks out finally, but I can tell he doesn't believe that at all.

I pull the sleeve back down, but my gaze lingers on his wrist in the photo. "Must be."

There are a few beats of silence, and I know his mind has already moved on to something else. Hart can't stay thinking about one thing too long. He has this uncontrollable cognizance that is such an enigma to me.

"I wonder if there are Pravis who don't get to end up with the people they are destined for because of these walls too," he says suddenly, breaking this silence in the most solemn tone he's ever used.

"There must be," I reply with a bit of sadness in my voice. "If I hadn't met you, I'd probably still think I had feelings for Santiago."

"Perhaps," he says absentmindedly before visibly tensing up. "Wait, you thought you had feelings for your boss?"

"We had a few odd encounters that confused me," I say while fidgeting nervously.

"Violetta, why didn't you tell me?" His features darken in defeat.

"I just didn't think it was important."

"This is extremely important." He stands and begins to pace across the concrete floor in front of me. "Your boss has feelings for you and doesn't even know about me."

Without even noticing, I let out a small laugh at his worrisome features.

"This is funny to you?" He looks down at me with frustration filling his voice.

"It's just that you're cute when you're jealous." I stand up and wrap my arms around his waist.

"How can I not be when he gets to be around you every day?" He looks concerned.

"I can handle myself, Hart," I say with confidence. "He will never come between us."

"I want to tell the whole world that you're mine and I'm yours."

"I want that, too," I whisper.

He wraps his arms around me and we stay there embracing one another. He strokes the back of my head in a calming manner, staying silent, as he knows there's nothing he can do to change our situation. After a short while, he suggests we go back to looking at the photo album, and we start back up with our normal banter. We laugh into the night, trying to ignore the unspoken dangers that loom above us.

"Nova, you can't tell me you're going to spend your whole evening doing this," I say, after tripping over her long spool of yarn.

"What's so wrong with knitting?" She continues to concentrate on the dull-colored yarn, while smiling like she's the happiest girl on earth.

"Don't you ever want to hang out with me?" I ask her.

"You have no right to ask me that question," she says lifelessly, continuing to knit. My mind tries to think of what I may have done to offend her, but I keep coming up with a blank slate. There's no option but to ask.

"Why do I have no right?" I ask in a tone that hopefully conveys I'm not sure what's happening here.

She huffs out, "You really have no idea?"

"Not one."

She puts the yarn down in her lap before scratching the top of her head and looking up at me. "You have been working late a lot recently, and I never see you anymore."

I stare at her blankly, not believing my complete ignorance and lack of consideration towards her. Does falling in love mean you have to lose your best friend? I guess in the books I've read, the main characters always focus on their deep affection for one another. The other characters get kind of left out. I can't let Nova become the best friend that I stop paying attention to. With this thought in my head, I walk over to where she sits beside her mattress and lower myself to the floor.

"Nova, I'm sorry. Let me make it up to you."

Her big eyes stare at me suspiciously. "How would you do that?"

"Why don't we go on one of those walks you love so much." I stand up quickly and reach my hand out to hers.

"Well that sounds like a fantastic start." She smiles up at me and takes my hand.

Chapter 19

After smoothing the ruffles of her old dress, we walk out of the door and stroll side by side around the backroads. She takes me to a field that's close to Santiago's place, and it's very quiet here. She talks about things that happened to her at work and the stress of having to deal with the Grey Guards as they drop off donations. I try hard to listen to her, but my mind travels nonetheless.

I wonder how fields look outside of the walls. I wonder where Hart lives, and how he lives his life. Our daily routines are probably extremely different. My favorite part of the week is when I get to see him, and I hope that's his too.

I think even if I had everything I ever wanted in life my favorite part of the week would stay the same.

I'm pulled out of my thoughts by the feeling of something soft under my uneven shoe. I've stepped on something that doesn't feel quite like grass and lean down to see a piece of fabric. It must be one of Nova's frilly headwraps that she makes with old scraps of clothes. She's still walking ahead of me, talking about how her boss, Jill, let her take home more yarn than she's supposed to because they are friends. I don't want to interrupt her, but I know she will want it back.

"Hey, you dropped your—"

And that's when I see it. As I hold it out to her, I recognize what I'm holding. It's a headwrap, just not the kind I expected.

After gawking at it for a period of time, I look up to see Nova standing there with something in her eyes I've never seen before. It looks like she has no emotions, and I wish she would just brush it off and resume her story. If she said this wasn't hers, I would believe her. Yet, she remains completely still, and her silence is sending chills down my spine.

This can't be happening.

"Oh Violetta, I really wish you wouldn't have picked that up." She begins to step towards me as I try to come up with a rational explanation for why she would be saying this. She moves slowly, almost like she's stalking me. The kind features I'm familiar with have turned into something unrecognizable.

"You can't be one of them," I say, and she stays silent for a few seconds too long. My instinct reacts to her hesitation and I begin to back away from her, prepared to run to the basement where I can pretend this isn't real.

She anticipates what I'm about to do, she knows me too well. The tiniest bit of pity flares in her eyes, before she lunges forward with lightning reflexes I didn't know she possessed. She touches her fingers to a pressure point in my neck and I fall into the grass.

I see her lean down to pick up the Vermillion bandana, and my world goes black.

CHAPTER
20

Santiago

*T*ve become rather accustomed to the fact that I'm in a rebel group, though I've only been involved for a short while. While certain higher-ups in the Vermillion meet three times a week, I attend the weekly meeting on Sunday nights. The people here are kinder than I expected, and there are only about sixty-four of us, which makes us quite a tight-knit community.

When I followed Nova that night, I didn't know what exactly I was getting myself into. It was purely a rash decision made by my broken heart. I was quite surprised to learn that the second-in-command to Othello was the roommate I'd heard so much about from Violetta. Nova explained that Violetta knows nothing of her involvement with the group, and that she intends to keep it that way. She spoke often of how she and Nova would tell each other everything, but she isn't even remotely aware of her friend's double life.

Not only is Nova a figure of hope to the rebels, but she is also physically strong, and equipped with a black belt in Brazilian Jiu Jitsu. She may technically be second-in-command, but Othello does nothing without her approval. He once said the only reason she isn't the head of the Vermillion herself is because he's been there longer.

She lives a hectic life trying to hide from her best friend. Yet, she has no inkling that she's not the only one keeping things to herself. I'm deep in the Vermillion now, but I won't expose Violetta's secret to them. I'm not sure how Nova would react, and this is about making the future better for the Crossed. It is not a story of revenge for my wounded pride.

As I walk up to the church that holds our meeting place, I admire how the ivory exterior causes it to have a peaceful glow. No one would suspect that the rebellion is brewing below its sacred floorboards. There's a small hole in between two connecting walls which is barely visible, but holds the answer to my liberation. I pull a red string—tied to a key hidden deep inside—out of it. After using the key to open the door, I carefully place it back where it stays. Slipping into the church, I feel a whisper of solace when I see the familiar stained-glass scene of Saint Paul at the Acropolis illuminated by the moonlight.

My footsteps are light until I reach the pew closest to the altar. Sitting down in the chair, my feet harshly tap the ground seven times and I wait. The floorboards in front of me shift and open seamlessly, like a portal to another dimension. I lower myself down into the cavity in the floor until my feet hit the first step of the ladder. Some time ago, I overcame my fear of missing a step on the way down, and the once-unnerving feeling of slipping into darkness has become my friend.

Once on the ground, I speak out into the darkness: "The Crossed will rise."

The heavy tread of feet that follows is a welcome noise, and I see a faint flicker of flame as someone appears. The large, shadowy figure approaches to lead me into the room where we will have our meeting.

"Mr. Singh, how have you been?" David asks me with a kind expression.

I can see his bushy eyebrows above the light he holds with his muscular arms. I must raise my head to see his face, as he is several inches taller than me and has a wide build. The fire illuminates his pale complexion, and his gruff features cause him to seem menacing. If I didn't know him, I would fear him greatly.

"I've been well, and you?" I smile widely at my good friend.

"We have been preparing for something big; I am anxious for Othello to reveal his plans to the family tonight," he says as he pushes on a lever that closes the opening above us, before motioning for me to follow him down the hall. I start behind him, following the light around corners and hollow passageways. We pass by several rooms that house the staff of the church, and there is quiet chatter flowing from them. There is no greater supporter of the Vermillion than that of the church.

"Can you give me a hint of what it is?" I ask out of pestering curiosity.

He lets out a bellowing laugh. "If only I was allowed to."

As we reach the end of a narrow hallway, David opens the door to the meeting room. Light hits my eyes suddenly, causing a stinging sensation, and I allow them to adjust to the room before fully entering. Stepping in, I immediately begin to greet everyone, since there isn't much time before Othello begins speaking. The meeting room is a cut above what I originally assumed it'd be. It's quite spacious and well lit, unlike the hallway that David waits in to greet the members. I search the room for my close friend, Ryan, but fail to see him anywhere.

"Santiago!" Ryan's warm voice brings me out of my thoughts, and I jut my hand out for a handshake. He refuses this gesture and embraces me in his arms instead. "So good to see you."

"Always a pleasure to see you as well. How is your bride?" I ask, looking around for her.

He beams at the mention of his wife. "Elizabeth's fantastic. We got to see each other a couple of times this week, and she should be here any minute."

"That's good to hear, since I've been meaning to get that recipe for the bread pudding she made a while back. It would be splendid with my afternoon tea."

"Her father taught her how to make that, so she may be hesitant in giving you the classified family recipe." He laughs and crinkles form around his eyes. "I haven't had it in a while either, since we don't see each other often, but sometimes that wait makes it taste better," he says in a painfully optimistic way, and it reminds me of just how oppressed we are. It's not necessarily the lack of bread pudding in my life that strikes a chord with me, but that Ryan and Elizabeth never know when they can see each other next. I can't imagine that kind of stress, and yet they seem so happy, even when they aren't sure of their next step.

One thing that gave me quite a bit of culture shock was learning that the Vermillion has a considerable number of couples, some who have been married for years on end. A leader in this church founded the Vermillion, and he continues to marry couples in secret. Violetta did cross my mind when I was informed about this. I mean, if these couples can make it work, then why couldn't we? Then I remember the picture of her in the arms of that man, and I remember this isn't feasible in any capacity.

Over the last couple of weeks, I've yearned to confess to Violetta about my involvement in the Vermillion. I want to show her how she could be a part of something bigger, but Nova has continuously insisted that Violetta is not the type to be swayed into joining the group. There's a possibility she would report me instead of joining me.

As I'm still talking to Ryan about the possible difficulties that arise when baking bread pudding, I notice the room has turned silent. That's when I see David walk to the front and softly tell everyone to sit on the floor. We heed his instructions and patiently wait for our leader to greet us.

His silhouette appears before he does, looking larger than life. Othello strides in complete confidence to David's side, and everyone claps as if he's the King of England. He's about my height with fairly short brown hair. He wears all black, with the signature Vermillion bandana tied around his forehead. There's a scar on his right eyebrow just above his light green eyes, and his tan features are sharp enough to look as though they were carved: giving him the quality of an Adonis. Until I met Othello, I had been positive that the boy I saw holding Violetta was the most intimidating person I'd ever seen.

He nods humbly at the crowd, and I can hear several women sigh audibly around me. He knows his effect on people, and he's used it to recruit almost half the people here. After a few moments he gestures for all of us to settle down, and his powerful voice meets the ears of his eager followers.

"I stand here today as a proud Crossed man. Is it wretched to hear that I take pride in the mixed blood pulsing through my veins?" His way of speaking is beyond convincing, and each meeting reassures me that this is where I'm meant to be. "We are unique, powerful, resilient, and strong. Pravis are fearful of what we can do, so they have confined us. They can trap us here, but they can't stop us from being proud of who we are!" His voice rises, and the entire room cheers in approval.

Once the people quiet down again, he continues talking. "I see a room full of incredible people here tonight, and you know what's special about us?" He leans forward a bit. "We are the rebels who will take down the Crossed laws. Nova and I have devised a plan that we have discussed with the others. It's been years in the making, but we believe that the time has come. We are going to publicly protest next month in the middle of the square for all to see!"

The roars of the room get louder. He seems extremely content with the reaction of the room, but his pleased look quickly turns into a perplexed one as he stares at the door at the back of the room. Most people are so lost in their ideas for the protest that they don't even notice his quizzical expression, but I follow his eyes to see what he's fixated on.

There in the entryway is Nova in a frilly dress, with straight hair falling around her face and a single yellow bow attached to the side of her head. The way she is dressed would be enough to shock me completely, but it's the girl she's dragged in that captures my attention.

It's none other than the only girl I've ever loved, Violetta, hanging like a rag doll in Nova's small but sturdy arms.

I stand quickly, pushing through the crowd of people to the back of the room. Snatching Violetta from Nova's arms, I lay her on the ground, whilst being careful to continue holding her head. I push the large curls away from her face and place my fingers on her wrist to make sure her pulse is beating normally.

After I am positive that she's fine, I look up to Nova, who is standing over me. "What happened?!" I yell out, and the room begins to fall quiet again at the sound of my scream.

"We went for a walk when she saw this fall from my purse." Nova pulls out the standard red bandana we all have. "I panicked, hit her pressure point, and dragged her here since it wasn't far."

"How could you do something like this, Nova?!" I raise my voice at her again and she frowns at me, looking extremely guilty.

"Do not yell at my girlfriend, Santiago." Othello's voice looms over my head, and now he's standing beside Nova with his arm wrapped firmly around her shoulders. "She used her instincts in a trying time, and I'll remind you she is your superior, whom you must treat with respect."

I take a few deep breaths and remind myself that these are the leaders I swore my allegiance to. Being disrespectful to them won't get me anywhere. Othello is right, but my concern for Violetta is hard to get past at the moment.

"I'm sorry for my harsh words, but what do we do when she wakes up?" I look up at them.

"We have to tell her the truth and hope she can see reason," Othello answers, and Nova looks at me apologetically.

"And if she doesn't?" I ask with a trembling voice.

"Then we will figure something out," he says, in a grave tone that doesn't leave me feeling comforted whatsoever.

Just as he says this, Nova begins to shed a few tears—a sight I never thought I'd see. I glance around for the first time, to see the whole room watching the four of us. They're all gawking at Nova crying into Othello's arms, while I cradle an unconscious girl on the ground.

"Everything is going to be okay, my love. We've prepared for this day, and she will side with us," he says calmly to her before kissing the top of her head, then unties the bandana on his own, lending it to her so she can wipe away her tears.

As she takes it from him, she abruptly squeaks out, "She's waking up!"

Sure enough, Violetta's eyelids begin to flutter, and she looks up at me. Her lilac eyes are just as stunning even when they're darting around in a daze. "Santiago?"

I breathe out a sigh of relief and peek at Nova, who moves to sit on the ground beside me. Violetta looks at Nova and her face twists in alarm. Her eyes dart between Nova and I before she gapes up at Othello, who has donned his most charming smile for her. He squats down next to us, while Violetta's eyes go wide as she waits for one of us to say something.

"Violetta, it's so nice to finally meet you. I've heard a lot of wonderful things about you from Nova." He reaches out and grasps Nova's hand, to which she offers him a warm look before turning her gaze back to a panicked Violetta.

Nova squeezes Othello's hand. "V, I think it's high time I tell you a story."

Violetta's eyes are narrowed in on her best friend the whole time she speaks. Her eyebrows furrow together like they do when she's deadly serious about something—a look I've seldom seen in my time working with her. Nova continues her story of how she became the second-in-command to Othello about two years ago, and I'm grateful that we have moved to a more private room, letting David take over the meeting to avoid more of a spectacle was the right thing to do.

"After coming to the Donation Center a few times, he asked me if I'd like to go for a walk with him after my shift. Something was pulling me to him from the beginning, and I fell for him and his dreams of freedom. I've always known how you felt about following the rules of the law, so I didn't think telling you was an option." Nova's soft voice flows through the room, while Othello's hand remains on her shoulder as if to offer support for her genuine vulnerability.

It makes sense to me why Othello fell for Nova and begged her to join him. Not only is she exceptionally beautiful and strong, but her compassion compliments Othello's righteous anger. Dynamic is too simple a word to describe the force that they are together.

"I just can't believe you led a secret life and kept that from me for all these years." Violetta shifts uncomfortably where she sits in a stiff chair. "I don't know what to think or who you are." I can feel the tension in the room grow thick enough to be cut with a sword. Nova's right eye twitches at the last sentence that Violetta lets out and I can't help but want to comfort her. That's what Othello is here for though, I suppose.

"You do know me, and I know that you don't believe that. I just want us to have a life outside of these confines." She moves Othello's hand away from her and stands to be closer to Violetta. "Don't you want that?"

"I need time to think about this, but I feel betrayed. You have a boyfriend, you're in a gang, and you managed to drag my poor boss into it somehow!" She looks over at me with sympathetic eyes, as if I'm being held here against my will.

"Violetta, I am here because Nova told me the truth. The Vermillion isn't out to kill or hurt anyone, we are simply trying to be the movement of liberation. If we don't rise up, then when will this end? Meeting Nova is the best thing that's ever happened to me; she gave me the hope I was praying for."

I look from her to Nova, who eyes me warmly as she mouths, "Thank you," and one corner of my mouth raises at her tenderly. Violetta looks like she may faint again, and I understand how unusual this must be for her. Witnessing that her boss and roommate have become good friends without any of her involvement whatsoever must be bizarre.

"I am still in complete shock that you both have been keeping this from me. Omitting is not too far off from lying," she says in a tone that makes me roll my eyes.

"Did you just have the nerve to roll your eyes at me, Santiago?" She asks angrily.

"I don't know Violetta, maybe I think you're being hypocritical. Is there anything you want to tell us since you're such an *honest* person?" I stare her down, and she seems to melt away from me. I can see the fear in her eyes; she is aware that I know her secret now.

"I don't know what you're talking about," she whispers quietly, and runs her fingernails over her arm.

"You're lying. You only scratch your forearm when you aren't telling the truth." Nova steps forward to look Violetta in the eye.

"Why should I tell you anything? Maybe I'll just keep it a secret forever like you were planning to do," she snaps back, and I give her credit for not being afraid to fight back.

"Violetta, I saw you in the basement. If you don't tell them, I will," I say as she glares in my direction, sending goosebumps up my neck. I don't let her faze me; I'm completely done protecting her. She needs to tell Nova and Othello. They could even help her with her relationship, but she's not seeing reason because she is trying to protect whoever that man is. Violetta stays tense with her fists clenched beside her, and I smile triumphantly—she finally has to admit what I've already known.

"I'm in love with a Pravi," she blurts out, and all of our jaws go slack in horror. Nova and Othello look as if Violetta just tried to attack them, and not a sound comes from their lips. Violetta's hand flies to cover her mouth as if she is trying to put the words back.

As for me, well, it seems I didn't know anything all along.

CHAPTER
21

Hart

E mployee 03199: *Master Kang, you have a visitor waiting for you in the east courtyard.*

A screen on my desk displays the message from the doorman, Derek, downstairs and I stand up from my chair abruptly. I wasn't expecting company, but thankfully I'm always dressed for the occasion. Securing the second button on my lavender suit, I make my way to the marble staircase. The third stop on the elevator leads to the courtyard, but my mother taught me that's not the procedure to make a proper entrance if we have company.

With a wave of my hand, the doors to the courtyard open to reveal blossoming flowers that span every color of the rainbow. Spring has never been so magical. The fresh cut grass sings to me and in the white gazebo I can faintly see the outline of my oldest friend.

I walk with excitement towards the structure and hope that she is here to welcome me back as her friend. As she comes into view, I'm sure that my theory is correct. She is standing to the side next to a number of thorn-covered yellow roses, smiling at me. As I continue to stride towards her, her smile falls, and a flare of worry passes over her features.

"You're here!" I call out cheerfully.

"What have you done to your hair, Hart?" She asks me in a disturbed tone.

I reach up and impulsively touch the black strands at her question. A couple of weeks back, Violetta questioned me about why I dye my hair blond. To avoid revealing that my father insisted upon the hair to make me seem more appealing, I told her that a lot of guys dye their hair various colors, since girls like it. Technically, this isn't a lie, but it's not my reason. Violetta nodded at this, before commenting that she would like me with any color of hair. I dyed my hair back to its natural inky color the next day. Her opinion is the only one that matters to me and I don't have to pretend anymore.

Even the staff was surprised at how frantic the news outlets became upon learning that I'd traded in my signature golden boy look for one much darker. Many fans of mine said it's simply a phase, while others supported the look, calling me "The Raven of Briste." Each headline about my natural hair brought a chuckle to my lips that I wished to share with Violetta. Ember hasn't seen me in a couple of weeks, but I was sure she'd seen the reports about my sudden hair color change.

"You didn't hear?" I ask her. "It's been all over the tabloids."

"I've been preoccupied with my studies lately." She shakes her head at me.

I nod, stepping into the gazebo. "Well, what do you think?"

"The last time I saw your hair like this was in elementary school." She scrutinizes the black locks falling just past my brow. "It doesn't seem like you."

I shrug and decide that this would be a good time to change the subject, since I don't want to chat about my vanity for much longer. There is so much we haven't discussed that is far more important than hair. She may be slightly suspicious of me, but that's nothing a sugary drink couldn't fix.

"Would you care for a strawberry spritzer?" Her ears perk up at the mention of her favorite beverage. "I can have a couple sent to my room where we can catch up."

"That sounds nice, Hart," she says with a faint smile.

We walk together to my room, and she sits in my favorite chair. A housekeeper sends a message that she will have our drinks brought up in a few minutes. Ember relaxes sooner than I anticipated. Within seconds, her navy-colored hair is bouncing as she happily gives me a rundown of the latest college drama I've missed while having to keep up with my father's exhausting political events. There's a rumor that he could be chosen as the next vice president, a rumor I suspect he started, so he's been quite the busy bee.

Apparently while I was out, several of our classmates have been involved in quite the scandal, and Professor Casey has been stealing food from the cafeteria every other day. She doesn't mention the awkward encounters we've had, and I'm beyond grateful for that. Being with her like this feels comfortable and familiar; I'm glad to have my best friend back.

Suddenly, Ember lifts her jewel-covered hand to interrupt herself mid-story. "Wait. Why isn't the painting I gave you hung up anywhere around your room?"

My eyes make their way around the large space and the private corridor to my bathroom, but there is no such painting to be found. "Where did you put it after I left the party?"

"I had the help take it up to your room for you." She rolls her eyes at me like I should've known this information.

"They probably put it in the art vault then," I say, right as a knock on the door sounds out.

"You get the drinks and I'll get the painting so we can hang it up together." She stands giddily, and it's hard for me not to laugh at her enthusiasm.

While she retreats to find the vault in my closet, I open the door to find my favorite housekeeper standing in the doorway with two delicious strawberry spritzers on a silver tray. Kate sets the tray down on the coffee table and we chat a bit about her son and how he defeated me in a game of chess last Thursday. When we hear Ember's footsteps, she politely curtseys and closes the door behind her. I bend down to the coffee table and pick up one of the drinks to offer her, almost as a peace offering of sorts, when I hear her open my door.

"The *Crossed* girl?"

Ember's voice trembles with anger behind me, and I spin around to see her holding a different painting than I expected.

How could I have forgotten?

Her fingers grip the edges of the portrait that I painted all those months ago, the one that is the unmistakable likeness of Violetta. She is shaking, and the rage in her eyes is frightening.

"Is this why you turned me down?" She yells at me with vitriolic acid staining her voice. "Have you been going back to see her?"

I hesitate for far too long, trying to conjure up a response. "It isn't what you think—"

"—You've been willingly going back to that damned place?" Her voice rises even louder than before.

Reaching out, I try to touch her arm and calm her. "Ember, please let me explain. Don't do something you'll regret without first hearing me out."

"How could you do this to me?" Tears fill her eyes and she looks at me as if I were a stranger. "She's one of *them,* Hart. Do you know how dangerous this is?"

I can't find the words that I'm so desperately searching for. There is no correct way to respond. She's asking these questions as if I haven't realized how much I'm risking for Violetta. She's breathing heavily, waiting for a response. All I can focus on is the way her long fingernails are beginning to puncture the canvas of my cherished painting.

"Even if it isn't true, tell me you haven't gone back. I'll stand by you," she begs me with her voice cracking. "We can move on from this, Hart."

She begins to sob, and I am certain that I have two options at this point. I could lie to Ember like she wants me to, or I tell the truth and say a final farewell to my safety. There isn't enough time to imagine what Violetta would tell me to do. I need to go with my gut and have faith that Ember will understand. Even if she doesn't, perhaps she will love me enough to not turn us in.

"I love her," I say firmly.

She looks up at me in alarm and wipes her nose with the back of her hand. "You don't even believe in love!"

"Violetta opened my eyes," I insist, noticing her visible disdain at the use of my girlfriend's name. "I was wrong."

"*Violetta?* Really? You're not the boy I fell for." She stomps to the door of my room with clenched fists.

"What's so wrong with belonging to more than one culture? Doesn't that make them unique?" I'm asking her questions in the hopes that one of them will strike a chord with her and make her mind unravel like mine has.

"If we let them into society, then *no one* will be unique anymore. The Crossed probably wouldn't even know how to function in normal society; I've heard they are all primitive," she says with a sense of certainty that makes me nauseated.

"They're just like us!" The pitch in my voice rises in frustration. "Violetta is kind, intelligent, and everything good in this world. She tells me stories of her friends, and they are just as incredible as her. Their blood doesn't suddenly make them savages, Ember. If you just spoke with one of them, you'd know how wrong you are."

"The only thing I was mistaken about is your integrity and self-discipline. They're not special, Hart. They aren't even normal." I shoot a glare in her direction, and she says her final words, words that she knows she can't take back: "And if the whole species is anything like that out-of-control loudmouth, I hope they stay behind the walls of the Teorrain forever."

She throws the painting on the floor and practically sprints out of the room, stepping on it as she goes and leaving only the sound of her heels clicking down the staircase to keep me company. I don't give myself time to wallow in my misery or mourn my friendship with Ember like I typically would. Instead, the adrenaline rush compels me to pack a bag and run for my life. Setting the damaged painting of my angel on the table next to the untouched strawberry-flavored drinks, I take one last look before dashing out of my room. I'd be a fool to think Ember won't report me now.

My time is running out, and my only chance of survival is getting to Violetta—because if my theory proves correct again, we are both unquestionably doomed.

CHAPTER
22

Violetta

*N*ova throws her head back as she lets out a high-pitched laugh at my confession, and the rest of us simply observe this bizarre reaction. Santiago and Othello's expressions are closer to what I imagined, an even mixture of shock and disbelief. It seems as if they want to ask me a million questions, but they're halted from doing so by Nova's crazed laughter.

"Good one, but what's the real secret?" She slows down her giggles and looks back and forth between Santiago and I in a questioning manner. "Are you two dating?"

Santiago stares at me with sympathy, as if he wishes that her guess was correct. Sighing, I stand and weakly step closer to Nova, this way she will comprehend the gravity of my next statement. I only intend to say this once more to them, and I'll do it with all the confidence Hart would like to believe he holds.

"It's not a joke, Nova. I'm in love with a Pravi boy," I say firmly this time, and her eyes turn cold. She watches me in the same fashion she did right before I was knocked unconscious in the field.

"How did you even meet a Pravi?" She asks through gritted teeth, while pulling the bow from her hair.

"I can't tell you."

Revealing that information would result in the sealing of the entryway in the library at the very least. That would effectively stop me from ever seeing him again and that isn't a risk I'm willing to take.

"Is he a Grey Guard?" She presses, with steady fury in her eyes.

"He's just a regular guy," I say.

Chapter 22

"A regular guy? He's our enemy," Santiago pipes up for the first time since I told them about Hart, and I still don't understand why he looked baffled by my admission when he's the one who found me out.

"He's on our side! I had no intention of falling for him, but he's different from any man I've ever met." My pleas fall silent onto their uninterested ears. Not only are my words meaningless to them, but they're clearly hurting Santiago's feelings, as he avoids eye contact with me.

"I never thought you would lie to me," Nova says with a judgmental tone.

"That's rich, coming from the girl who attacked me after I happened upon her major secret. You've been a leader in the Vermillion for two years!" At my rage she is forced to back down a bit, because I have a valid point.

"I desperately wanted to tell you every day." She looks down to her feet.

"Then why didn't you?" I whisper, while ignoring Othello and Santiago as they watch us closely.

"I could ask you the same question, Violetta." She stares me down and we both stand there for a moment. Deep-seated aggravation shifts into a sort of understanding between us. Both our stances relax, as we realize we are both guilty of deceiving one another more than we should have.

Nova shakes her head and pierces the air between us. "Either way, I am a leader here because I'm passionate about fighting for our freedom. I can't be associated with someone who is in love with one of the monsters that put us here."

"Hart is not a monster! There are many of them who protest the Crossed laws; they want that freedom for us. You are dehumanizing them." I fight back with bated breath.

"Your boyfriend's name is ironic, considering the Pravis are heartless with how they treat us. I'm sure he's no exception. They all preach change, but they never actually do anything to help us," Othello says while his arm protectively snakes around Nova.

If I wasn't so head over heels for Hart, Othello might sway me. The way he speaks is entrancing and convincing in an authoritative way. I can clearly see why the Vermillion appointed him as their leader even at such a young age, but I won't let a smooth voice tell me I'm wrong. My knowledge is unshakable.

"He is putting his life on the line to love me, so please think twice before you speak about him," I say harshly to Othello, and Nova flinches. "I promise you'll regret it next time."

"I won't have you speak to my boyfriend like that, Violetta." Nova steps in front of him.

"But you can insult my boyfriend when he isn't even here to defend himself?" I ask with a snarl.

"It's not like he would have the courage to talk to us." Santiago rolls his eyes and I turn around to glare daggers at him. I can understand that he's upset, but he's taking it too far. All I can see is red—they won't stop criticizing Hart just because of his blood. Absolute hypocrites.

I step towards Santiago and he takes a step back in cowardice. "Leave your feelings about what happened between us out of this."

He becomes stiff and wide-eyed at my words. He crosses his arms and shifts his weight from his left foot to his right as he looks down again. After pushing up his glasses and clearing his throat he finally speaks.

"You led me to think that the only thing keeping us from being together was the law when you're somehow involved with a Pravi? Explain that, Violetta." He raises his voice at me, and the impenetrable Santiago is at last showing his true colors. A vein in his neck strains under his skin, and my temper lessens as I begin to feel guilt for causing him this much pain.

"I'm sorry that I didn't consider your feelings enough." I reach out and lay a hand on his forearm. As soon as my fingers touch his black sweater, he looks to me with anguished golden eyes. "It wasn't until Hart came into my life that I realized you and I were a different kind of soulmate."

"I don't know how to stop feeling this way about you." He says this so quietly that I barely hear him.

"This fondness will dissolve, and I have no doubt you'll find the fortunate girl who is waiting for you." I keep my hand on him, but turn my head towards Nova and Othello, who are gawking at us. "The person who's meant for me just happens to be on the other side of the wall."

"If you have such a desire to be on the other side of the wall, you should join us. We can make that happen," Othello says, bringing the subject back around to his agenda.

"I refuse to be part of a rebellion that can't believe in the good-hearted nature of many Pravi. How do you expect to integrate into society with that attitude?" I ask, and the room fills with stone-cold silence. It must not have been something they thought much about, how they would adjust to society once they were freed. This proves to me how little faith they truly have in getting this law abolished.

"I'm sorry Violetta, but we simply can't approve of this." Nova looks at me and says her words with a shaky voice despite her firm stance. The grey room feels as if it's closing in on me as she says this, because I never wanted to have to choose between my happiness and my home.

"Are you going to report me?" I ask the question that's been lingering in the back of my mind, not truly wanting to know the answer.

"I don't know," Nova says, while tying her red bandanna across the crown of her head, covering the spot where her simple yellow bow sat only minutes ago.

Santiago steps forward to stand in front of me now, and we are forced to pay attention to him. I look up at his profile and realize that his features have gone hard. His eyes are fixed on Nova, and his jaw is clenched. His hurt demeanor has been shed, and an untamed man I don't recognize stands before me.

"I won't allow you to turn her in." His voice gets lower than it already was, to illustrate how deadly serious he is. "If you report her, I'll report you."

Chapter 22

At this statement, Othello advances to get in Santiago's face and speaks loudly, trying to intimidate him. "Are you threatening your own leader for a girl, brother?"

"I'd sacrifice my life for her." He stands his ground and growls the last few words, which clearly shakes Othello. " If you force my hand, I'll sacrifice yours too."

Nova steps in between the men. Her small frame is disproportionate compared to the two towering figures, but she's able to easily push them away from each other.

"Fighting is not the answer to this situation! We need to come to a resolution with a calm state of mind." She looks between them with vicious eyes that causes them both to shrink away, though it doesn't stop Santiago from grabbing my hand and holding it securely in his.

"Give her a chance," Santiago says to Nova softly, and her tense body loosens a bit. "The Pravi at least deserves for us to hear him out, and we owe Violetta that much for all she's done in our lives."

They look at each other for a few moments with an intense stare that makes the tension grow tenfold in the room. I don't know what Nova and Santiago's friendship is like, but they must have a deep understanding of each other for her to seemingly be changed by just the look in his eyes. Even thinking of them as close friends has my mind staggering.

"Alright, let's talk to the Pravi then," she says, and Othello's mouth opens slightly as he looks at her with skepticism.

I must be dreaming. Only moments ago, I was saying my last prayers and preparing to be hunted down. Now she's giving me an opportunity to prove that he's everything good in the world.

"Thank you, Nova!" I let go of Santiago's hand and run to embrace her without thinking. She seems surprised by this reaction after our intense argument but hugs me back tightly anyway.

"I hope you're right about him," she murmurs, quietly enough that the boys can't hear, and I smile with the certainty that she will support us once she meets Hart.

Othello walks across the room to the exit and says something to the bodyguard who has been standing by the door. The bodyguard hands him a key, and Othello's scarred eyebrow raises as he looks at all of us expectantly.

"I never thought I'd say this, but how do we meet this Pravi?"

CHAPTER
23

Santiago

*J*t really is an odd feeling to be unlocking the door to my library in the dead of the night to see the hideout of the Pravi man who stole Violetta from me.

"Since it's a Sunday night, he won't be here. We only meet on Tuesdays and Fridays," Violetta reminds us.

My mouth turns downwards when I remember her eagerness to stay late at work, on those days specifically. If I wasn't so concerned with saving her life, I would be upstairs journaling pointlessly out of frustration.

I'll save that for later.

"We still want to see this tunnel for other purposes," Othello states unyieldingly in a hushed voice, and Nova looks at him with a query in her eyes.

Any ordinary observer could decode their reason for interest in the tunnel. This could be their way out of the Teorrain, but Violetta remains oblivious to this: her emotions have completely taken over and she's not observing their interactions. Her head is probably filled with fantasies of being with this Pravi. Why did empathy for her have to puncture my heart? I need to stop reading all these writings about lovers who are utterly infatuated with one another. They never favor characters like me.

I hold open the door for the three of them, and one by one they glance at me before entering my beloved library. This is probably the most people that have been here at one time. Once we are inside, Violetta is sure to waste no time whatsoever. Without a glance at us, she rushes towards the door leading to her office. Her curved figure descends the stairs, and I hear myself mindlessly telling Nova and Othello to be careful on the fourth step because it's wobbly—something Violetta forgets to inform them.

Most of the footsteps stop when we reach the hard cement ground of the basement. Only one pair of feet shuffles across the floor before light illuminates the room, giving it its trademark faint-orange glow.

"Show us where the tunnel is," Othello says impatiently.

Violetta flips her long locks behind her shoulder whilst hurrying across the room, and gestures to a seemingly normal wall. "This is it."

At this statement, we all look to one another with puzzled faces. There's no doubt that Violetta is in love with a man, I saw him with my own two eyes. But him actually being a Pravi is another level of lunacy. Her story about this tunnel leading to the outside world is also a bit far-fetched. She is my closest friend though, so my gut persuades me to trust her. I have faith in what she says, but that doesn't mean Othello does.

Othello sighs and runs a hand over the tight curls on his head. "This wall?"

"When the laws were first made, this wall opened up to a tunnel for the Grey Guards to bring donations into the Teorrain. They shut down the tunnel when they abandoned this building and built the updated Donation Center," she explains hastily, and I can tell she's nervous. "There's an invisible keypad that requires a secret code in order for the tunnel to open; they must've thought we'd never find it when this place became the library."

"Open it and prove yourself." Othello's tone grows more frustrated, and I see Nova give him a warning glance.

"I can't." Violetta looks down at the ground and scratches her arm lightly.

"Why can't you?" Nova asks gently before Othello can say anything aggressive.

"Only Hart knows the code. We will have to wait until Tuesday because I have no way of contacting him—"

Violetta is cut off by a knock coming from the other side of the basement wall. We all perk up and straighten our posture at the unfamiliar sound. The knocking continues in what I realize is a unique pattern for a few moments, and Violetta looks at the wall with wide eyes. "It's him! I don't know why, but he's here."

"Let him open it then!" I shout eagerly.

Violetta hesitantly looks at the wall as if she's trying to figure out if she should let us meet him, like she has a choice. She rubs her hands on her jeans for a moment and tucks a stray curl behind her ear as she taps her knuckles against the wall in response.

After what feels like ages of stillness, the wall begins to move. Very little sound is made as it slides out of the way and the wall is replaced with a dark opening, just like she claimed. I don't move a muscle—astonishment encapsulates my very being as the Pravi emerges from the tunnel. He was here, right under my office the whole time, whilst I was upstairs thinking about Violetta.

Before us now stands a tall man with pin-straight hair, striking features, and a concerned look in his dusky eyes. His lilac-colored suit is tailored superbly and must be worth more than a modest-sized house in London. He is the epitome of the Pravi ideals of beauty, and I couldn't be more envious of him.

The Adonis-like stranger breathes out in relief as he sees Violetta. Dropping the bag he was carrying, the Pravi runs towards her in a frantic manner. He grabs her before even speaking and pulls her small figure towards him. He holds her head against his chest and kisses it tenderly, not even noticing he has an audience.

"I was waiting in the tunnel for you half the night; I was so relieved when I heard your voice." He closes his eyes before painfully choking out his next words. "Ember found out about us. It's only a matter of time before she reports us, so I grabbed a bag of essentials from my place. There's enough money in here for us to hide out for a decent amount of time, but we need to run while we can." He says all of this in one breath, while squeezing her tight as if he's petrified of what will happen to her.

Before Violetta has the chance to tell the boy that they are on borrowed time anyway, Othello coughs to make him aware of our presence. This surprises the Pravi so much that he jumps back and away from Violetta. He looks quizzically from her to Othello and Nova before finally settling his gaze upon me.

"Sorry to interrupt your little star-crossed plan, Pravi." Othello steps towards him without fear and slowly drags his gaze up the man's body, examining him closely. "We need to have a talk with you."

The Pravi takes a defensive step back towards the tunnel and looks to Violetta before speaking again. "What's going on?"

"A lot has happened in the past few hours that I'll explain to you later, but right now I need you to convince these people that you're on our side." Violetta's request seems more like a demand as her violet eyes remain locked onto his face.

Othello stands with a wide stance and crossed arms, waiting for Hart to address him. Nova stands behind him, clearly tense as she runs a hand through her hair again. It seems part of her wants this Pravi to convince us. I think this because I feel the same way she does and would like to be completely swayed for Violetta's sake. While I'd like to do something to comfort Nova at this moment, I know it's not my place.

The Pravi man that stands before us stretches his arms and adjusts the collar of his white shirt, which appears to have pearls sewn into its crisp edges. He walks over to Othello and juts his hand out towards him in a friendly manner.

"I'm Hart. What's your name?" He speaks out in a calm voice that's clearly an act. If I wasn't as good at reading people, I might even think that he shed all of his fear in an instant.

"Othello. This is Nova, and Santiago." He doesn't shake Hart's hand, but instead gestures to his girlfriend and I, keeping his seemingly cool exterior. "We are members of the Vermillion, a rebel gang that represents freedom for the Crossed and opposes the Pravis' view of us." He stares down the Pravi in a way that could make anyone's blood turn to ice.

"I also oppose the way that Pravis view the Crossed." Hart moves towards Violetta and interlaces their fingers together as a way of demonstrating their unity. "I am one of many who protest the government and the laws that have you all trapped here."

"We don't need your pity. We need actual change, in ways that matter." Nova pushes past Othello, deciding it's her turn to inspect Hart.

"I'm just tired of being separated from wonderful people, simply because their blood varies from mine. This has nothing to do with pity." Hart swallows and sticks his chin out, gaining momentum as he continues to speak. "I should have the right to be with the girl beside me."

He looks so genuine while saying these things. I can feel my hopelessly romantic nature causing me to falter. Most of my passionate feelings have been geared towards Violetta for the past couple of years, but I'm beginning to rethink them. While the way that this man looks at her makes my stomach drop, the words that drip from his mouth have me hooked. My subconscious has started to root for them.

There is magic between them; anyone could see that. They're squeezing each other's hands, and it breaks my heart that they are this frightened. I should scream at him for taking her from me, but perhaps she was right about us being a different kind of soulmate. She has always been my best friend, though I found her beautiful. She has been a fantastic companion, but that doesn't mean a spark is there. I'm beginning to realize the purity of the connection between her and Hart: they have a bond like the couples in the Vermillion. The grey walls of the basement spin as I come to an important realization.

I am not in love with Violetta Akan the way that Hart is.

While I care for her deeply, I'm certain my life will go on with or without Violetta. This is not something I believe for Hart, however. Watching the way that they look at one another is like watching the sun come up over the horizon, and it seems as if their own happiness would mean nothing if it were to jeopardize the safety of the other. This is a truth I've never known. I can only hope to have that one day, but being behind these walls is going to limit my ability to find it. What if my true love is outside of here too, waiting for me?

"He's right. What if I'm destined to be with a Pravi, but I'll never know because we are writing all of them off?" I ask abruptly, and I can tell they are surprised to hear me speak up in defense of Hart.

"They put us here! Are we forgetting all of the suffering they've put us through?" Retorts Othello, who moves a skull ring around his index finger while flexing his hand.

"Did Hart specifically put us here? We can't ignore the fact that not all Pravis are the same," I say in the most persuading tone I can muster. "Othello, what ethnicity are your parents?"

A distant look clouds his eyes and his hard facial features seem to almost soften, before he lets out a sigh. "Santiago, please don't do this to me."

"Aren't both your parents Pravis?" I tilt my glasses and raise an eyebrow at him. He rolls his eyes in annoyance at the knowledge that he's about to be taken down a notch by a librarian.

"Yes, they are," he says while rubbing his temples.

"Don't you think what they did was brave? They loved each other even when they knew the world was conspiring against them. What a noble downfall to succumb to." Now that I've begun to speak with conviction uncharacteristic of me, the room has gone silent. "Those people that you revere were Pravis. If they loved you, why can't Hart love Violetta?"

The amount of strain in the enclosed space of the basement grows tenfold as I await a response. Othello and Nova are speechless. They know my argument makes more sense than any of theirs could. Hart and Violetta gawk at me with gratitude, and I nod at them with a sense of satisfaction. I'll have to journal about this later to figure out my feelings, but it feels good to do something just based on a gut feeling for once. Adrenaline is rushing through me while I wait for someone to say something. When it becomes clear that no one knows how to respond, I decide to take control again.

"Now, can we please help these poor souls? We could use all the support we can get from the other side of the wall," I state while gesturing to the couple, who are still slightly trembling.

"We can't argue with his logic, Othello." Nova steps over to my side, and it feels incredible to know she agrees with me.

Othello takes a deep breath and looks to the ceiling. He adjusts one of the black piercings in his ear—which only accentuates his power—and nods at us ever so slightly. Nova glances up at me with a slight smile playing on her lips. The corners of my mouth turn upwards too, and I know we are both thinking the same thing: we've saved Violetta's life. Just as I'm overwhelmed with relief, the sound of a phone rings out.

It's the landline upstairs: the phone that is only ever used to contact the authorities.

Rushing up the stairs without hesitation, I don't look back, though I can hear Nova's footsteps behind me. I'm trying to think of why they'd be calling me at this hour, but the phone doesn't ring unless there's a serious problem. I pray that they've found a new reason to call.

Pushing open the door to my office, I run across the room to pick up the phone, which almost slips out of my palm. I wrap the cord around my hand before speaking into the receiving end of the line.

"This is Santiago at the library. How can I help you?" I try to sound as formal and calm as humanly possible. My life may depend on it.

"Santiago, we couldn't reach you at your residence, so we called assuming you were here. We received a report that Violetta Jean Akan, who works at your establishment, has been directly involved in a crime. Would you happen to know anything about this?" A harsh tone questions over the phone and confirms my worst fears.

"I didn't know, but I am appalled! Is there anything I can do to help?" I lie through my teeth while silently praying again, asking God to protect Violetta.

"We will be coming to search your library as soon as possible, so stay where you are. If you hear anything from her, you are obligated to turn her in immediately or you will be arrested as well." He stops for a moment and I think he's done before he says, "This is your last chance, Santiago. If you know anything, tell us now."

I hesitate for a moment because I'm not the daring type. I have never been one to defy the law, to stand up for myself, or to even leave my office for long. I spent years sitting in this room reading and writing about a better life than this, one that I wanted back. Now is my chance to prove to myself that I am not a coward. I can be the type of man that a strong girl would be proud to love one day. I look to Nova, who is anxiously listening for what I am going to say next, and seeing her expression is all the motivation I need.

"I will be here when you arrive and help to the best of my abilities," I say, and Nova closes her eyes before hugging me while the phone is still next to my ear.

"We are on our way."

The line goes dead and I put the phone down quickly before I encircle my arms around Nova. It feels nice to have someone who cares about me like this. At least I got a good friend out of this situation.

"You all have to leave right now." I push her away from me lightly and lean forward. "Hide them and keep them safe. I will buy you time," I say in a whisper.

A mischievous smirk tugs at Nova's lips, and she walks quickly towards the door. She opens it and looks at me over her shoulder for a moment with a glint in her eyes.

"Get ready, Santiago. The fun is about to begin."

CHAPTER
24

Hart

I am almost positive that my life is nearing its end. Ember didn't give me much of a head start with my race against the authorities. Who would have guessed that all those years of friendship would be erased in the name of the law? I'd like to act surprised, but Ember is solely a product of her uptight and unfortunate upbringing.

I don't have the luxury of time to register the circumstances of my fugitive status, or the fact that my "best friend" is the one who put me in this situation. I'll just keep focusing on following the instructions of these strangers. I have faith that they aren't leading me into a trap, at least.

There's a solid chance that I'll never see the light of day again. I'm jeopardizing everything for a concept I was adamant didn't exist until a couple of months ago. I'm not sure who I've become and if I like him yet, but I do know that I love Violetta and she loves me, so I must be doing something right if she sees good in me.

Although the pitch black of the night only allows me to see her silhouette, there is an apprehensive aura that's emanating from her. It's my fault that we are in this situation. I'd apologize to her right at this moment, but Nova emphasized the importance of staying quiet as we sneak into the church.

We took questionable pathways from the library to the church and stayed as silent as possible. Nova didn't even have time to give us a plan. By the time she was done running down the stairs from Santiago's office, she only had time to tell us that the Grey Guards had found us out. I had an out of body experience when she said those words. As the governor's son, there was never a time I thought I'd be on the run from the law. Othello had looked to her as if the conversation that we were having wasn't totally resolved, but he didn't exactly have time to argue before Nova was dragging us out of the library.

As we reach a building that resembles a place of worship from long ago, Othello carefully unlocks its tall door. He raises one finger to his mouth, before shuffling into the building. Nova remains close to him as we walk in. There's a certain familiar feeling between them, and I wonder what their relationship is: if they have secret feelings for one another or if they're purely colleagues. One thing is certain though, Nova is nothing like what Violetta described. I pictured a soft-spoken, nice girl with ribbons in her hair. Instead, what I'm looking at is a domineering, opinionated girl with a red bandana wrapped around her head.

I'm just taking an educated guess, but I'm pretty sure Violetta didn't know that her roommate was part of the Vermillion. She wouldn't lie to me. Plus, she seemed pretty shaken up when I got to the basement. She must've only recently learned of Nova's involvement with the gang, and not had time to fill me in on her double life.

Santiago is almost exactly how I pictured him though—a black sweater and jeans can't cover up the fact that he's a gentleman. His glasses somehow accentuate his hauntingly golden eyes. Something about him is memorable, and it's not just the English accent that Violetta failed to mention.

Maybe it's because I've seen very few Crossed people, but so far, they are unique in a sophisticated way. Even Santiago would be considered exceptionally good looking in Geal. I wonder if one of the reasons for damning them all to live here was because Pravis are threatened by their intelligence and confidence.

Apparently, I've zoned out while walking through this empty building, because Violetta grabs my hand to lead me along. Nova sits down in a pew and stomps her feet in a rhythmic pattern, like the knock that Violetta and I share. A square gap appears on the floor, and she motions for us to follow her onto a ladder down into whatever awaits us below. I silently do as she asks without hesitation, and make sure to watch Violetta carefully so that she doesn't let one of her combat-boot-clad feet slip. Othello is the last to climb down the ladder, and there seems to be nothing but empty space around us.

"The Crossed will rise," Nova says into the darkness, and a light that wasn't present before appears.

I hear quiet footsteps while the light comes closer and becomes more defined. As it approaches, I can make out its source: a candle being held by a large figure.

"What are you doing here at this hour?" A man's hushed voice echoes throughout the unfamiliar space, and Violetta's soft hand finds mine.

"We have an issue," Othello says to the man in a kind voice. "We need to hide these two. They're fugitives, and dead if the Grey Guards find them."

I flinch at Othello's blunt wording. The man comes closer and raises his candle to look at Violetta's face and then mine. He lets out a small gasp as if he's looking at a ghost when the light illuminates my face. I should be the one who's surprised though, because his fearsome features and large eyebrows are enough to scare the living daylights out of any man.

"He looks strange." The man speaks with an uneven voice.

"That's probably because he's a Pravi," Othello says with a snort.

The man steps back, as if he's petrified by this fact. "Please tell me you're joking."

"He's a bit arrogant, but he won't hurt you. I'll tell you everything later, David. Trust your leaders and help us." The man doesn't look completely convinced by Othello's words and scrutinizes him. He probably shouldn't have led with insulting me.

Nova places her hands on the stranger's forearm, staring up at him with an affectionate look in her wide eyes. "Please help me protect my friends."

The large man suddenly goes weak at her expression and a wide grin, complete with dimples, crosses his face. It's almost as if he's completely forgotten that other people are here, and that we are very short on time.

"Anything for you Nova," he says with admiration dripping from his voice, and I roll my eyes at how easily a pretty face can sway a man's judgment.

Nova gives him a sweet squeeze on his arm before turning back to us with a grave declaration. "Here's the plan: I'm going home to change and then I'll clock in for work. When I'm inevitably questioned by the authorities, I'll claim that I haven't seen you all weekend. This should buy us some time until we can figure out our next move, and I'll come back when I feel it's safe. Othello and David live here so they will hide you. The Grey Guards have no idea this place exists under the church."

"Oh, the things I do for you," Othello pipes up, giving Nova an exasperated sigh.

She ignores him and walks to Violetta. "Stay safe. I love you, V."

"No matter what happens, I love you too." Violetta lets go of my hand and wraps her arms around Nova's small body. They hug for several moments before Nova finally breaks the embrace.

"You better take care of her till I get back, Pravi," Nova says to me, in a tone that should be lighthearted but instead feels deadly serious. I salute her since I'm not sure how to respond, and she stares at me with a puzzled face. I drop my hand gracelessly, and Nova steps over to Othello, who looks at her with his lips turned downward in a frown.

"We've trained for this. I will be fine, and back by your side in no time," she says softly, and he straightens up and gives her shoulders a quick squeeze.

"Come back to me in one piece," he says, and she reaches up to cup his face as he leans down to capture her lips in a kiss.

I guess that answers my questions about the nature of their relationship.

She walks away from Othello and mouths a quick thank you to the man, apparently named David. He waves to her like she's the Queen of England and he's but a loyal subject. She turns towards the ladder and climbs up with bravery that I could only hope to have. I suddenly feel a sinking feeling in my gut at how final that goodbye seemed. The Grey Guards must really love capital punishment.

Othello doesn't miss a beat though. The second that David pulls a lever which closes the opening, he is already walking away from us. David motions for us to follow him, and Violetta finds my hand again, which I'm thankful for. Although I'm being led down an ominous hallway, being able to hold her hand in mine is a good reminder of why I subject myself to this kind of activity early on a Monday morning.

"This is my room. You and Violetta can stay here for the time being, I'll be busy with David all day anyway." He opens a door and pulls a string that causes a small lightbulb above us to illuminate. The room before us is small, cold, and sad to say the least. It's about the size of my walk-in closet at home, and it hurts to know these are the conditions the Crossed people are used to. There's not even a mirror, and his bed is simply a cot with a knitted blanket that I doubt covers his whole body.

"Thank you so much, Othello." Violetta looks up at him with a grateful twinkle in her eye.

His rough stance loosens up and his mouth turns upwards the slightest bit as he nods at her. He then looks to me, and the semblance of a smile is ripped from his face as he cocks his head at me.

"Something needs to be done about your clothes, man," he says in a condescending tone, and I look down at the designer lavender suit I'm wearing.

Looking at his alternative style, I understand why he isn't a fan of my ensemble. I suppose the pearls on my collar alone wouldn't help me blend in. It's too bad I had no time to change before leaving my house.

He walks over to the pile of clothes in the corner of his room, and thoughtfully picks up a black short-sleeved shirt with jeans of the same color. "We look about the same size; put these on."

He shoves his clothes into my unwelcoming arms and then walks out of the door, closing it lightly behind him. I look to Violetta and her pink lips part as she flashes her teeth at me in a grin. "I think he's starting to like you."

"If this is how he shows that he likes someone, I'd hate to see what he's like when he isn't fond of somebody." I let out a sarcastic laugh and throw off my blazer. "Turn around, I'm going to change."

She spins towards a wall and starts talking while I begin unbuttoning my ivory dress shirt. "I'm so happy that we managed to convince them. Thank you for trusting me," she says, and I almost chuckle at this. Trusting her is just a natural response; it's not something I should be thanked for.

"Anytime, angel. I could use an explanation as to what exactly happened for them to have caught us like that though," I say while fastening the jeans and pulling the end of the shirt down to cover my waist. Othello's clothes do fit me, but they are fairly tight. I feel like I should be auditioning for an edgy boy band. "You can turn around now."

Violetta turns back around, and her eyes bug out momentarily before she drags her gaze from the top of my head all the way down to my feet. She looks as if she's holding back a laugh, and I feel ridiculous.

"No negative comments, please." I hold up a hand to her before she can say anything.

"You're striking in anything you wear, but those clothes make you look like the mysterious visitor of my dreams." She lets out an embarrassed giggle and a red tint rises to her cheeks. She wasn't going to make fun of me, she was just shy. If I had known that all I had to do was dress like this to get such a reaction from her, I would've thrown away my entire wardrobe for this one outfit long ago.

"Do I look like one of you now?" I spin around for her to see my full attire and she laughs even louder.

"You look like you could run the Vermillion." She walks over to me and wraps her arms around my neck before placing a peck on my cheek. I stare into her captivating eyes, and everything else falls away. There hasn't been a moment that I've wondered if all of this is worth it when she's in my arms like this. She's all I see, and all I'll ever need.

"I hate to end our fun, but can we discuss what is going on? Because I'm extremely confused," I say, and she releases a long breath before stepping over to Othello's cot. She sits down and wraps the blanket around her shoulders, gesturing for me to sit beside her.

"Where do I even begin?" She asks, while still trying to get comfortable on the cot.

"How about you start with your roommate, who is not at all how you described her." I sit on the cot and adjust the blanket over her shoulders so it doesn't slip.

Chapter 24

"This might take a while, my love," she says, and I lean back against the hard wall, because I know I'm in for a lengthy story.

CHAPTER
25

Violetta

*H*art's incredibly cute facial expressions were a major contributing factor among the reasons why I fell for him. It's tough for me to take him seriously sometimes. His reactions are so amusing when I talk to him, especially as I spew out an abridged account of what has happened in the past twenty-four hours. His jaw hangs open at the multiple revelations throughout my story. Specifically, Nova knocking me unconscious, her status as second-in-command, and Santiago being part of the Vermillion and threatening to turn them in if they turned us in.

Even though this tale is quite grim, I still find myself stifling a laugh when his face looks so adorably concerned. He's stayed completely quiet for the whole story, which only further displays how dissimilar we are. If he was telling me this, I would be interjecting with comments every twenty seconds.

After what feels like hours, I'm done with my explanation. He leans his head back against the wall and closes his eyes, while his jaw clenches in a frustration that I can empathize with.

"So, Nova's been in the Vermillion for over two years and you had no clue?" He asks, with his eyes still closed. He looks even more irritated than I was, although I suppose I didn't have much time to counter before I was being chastised for dating a Pravi.

"She didn't think she could tell me because I'm too much of a 'rule follower.'" I laugh at the irony of her presumptions, seeing as I'm now hiding in Vermillion headquarters with my Pravi boyfriend.

"She still should've told you; you're her best friend!" He opens his eyes.

"Ember is *your* best friend, and she just basically signed our lives away," I say, suddenly defensive of Nova.

"She *was* my best friend," he says bitterly, making it very evident he's hurt by her actions. "And it doesn't seem like the Vermillion does anything inherently bad, so I just don't comprehend why she couldn't explain herself."

There isn't anything to argue about with him, because it *was* wrong that she hid all of this from me. If she had explained to me what the Vermillion was doing and how she's involved, then maybe I would've even joined her.

"Well I can't be mad at her now, especially since I didn't tell her about you for months either." I shrug and the blanket slips off one of my shoulders.

"What about Santiago? The guy seemed too tame to be in a rebel gang." Hart sits straight up and places the blanket on my shoulder again.

"You should've seen him defend me." I think back to Santiago's unusually bold demeanor and his eyes, raging like a cyclone. "I was so certain of who my friends were, but it turns out I'm just getting to know them."

Hart reaches his hand out to rub my back in a comforting manner. "I'm sure you do know them, you're just learning there's another side to them."

"I just regret not telling them the truth sooner. We wouldn't be in this mess." I'm appreciative to have Hart here with me despite the state of affairs we are in.

"Everything happens for a reason; you taught me that." He gives me a soft smile and my heart melts. "This isn't great, but we have each other, and God is on our side."

Hart's changed so much in the time I've known him, but he's remained the same in all of the most enchanting ways. I hope that I live a long life with him by my side. This can't be the end of us; I won't let it be.

The door opens right after he says those words, and Othello walks in. "We need to talk, and you two need to eat. So, let's kill two birds with one stone." He looks at us expectantly and reaches out a hand to me, which I take willingly at the mention of food. The blanket puddles onto the floor as Hart and I stand to our feet.

Othello strides out of the room and we eagerly step after him. Othello is so far down the hallway already that I can barely make out the candle in his hand. We pick up our pace, so we don't lose him in the dim corridor. As we fall in line with him, there's a slight, smug shine in his eyes.

He opens the door into the large room where Nova dragged me earlier, and I shudder as the vivid recent memory comes to visit my mind. The bright lights of the room hit my eyes all at once and it takes them a moment to adjust. I instinctively wrap my arm around Hart's, and he props his elbow up like a true gentleman, washing away my distress like drops of summer rain.

"It's about time you two got something to eat," a throaty voice calls out from the opposite end of the room.

David sits at an old plastic table in a chair that's far too small to be holding a man of his stature. He waves us over with a grin stretching from ear to ear. For someone who looks so intimidating, he seems to be one of the most hospitable people I've come across. He must be the definition of a gentle giant.

We walk over to David, and plated before him is a display of fine-looking foods. The cuisine varies in color and smell, and it's all delectable. Beaming down at the food with wide eyes, I squeeze Hart's arm in excitement. He seems to be all too underwhelmed, though. This makes me wonder again what kind of food he's used to outside of the Teorrain.

"Don't be too nice to them, David," Othello says while he sits, maintaining his straight posture. "They're practically our prisoners after all."

"Says the man who cooked them all of this," David says in a teasing tone, and Othello quickly turns his head to shoot him a sharp look. This doesn't faze the large man though; he simply looks back to us with the same high-spirited smile. "Don't let him scare you, he's actually a really considerate guy."

Othello sighs in frustration. "Dig in, guys."

Hart reaches to make a plate for me, but I'm already piling it all onto the plate myself. I didn't grasp how hungry I was until the first bite of food touched my lips. My body relaxes as it becomes lost in the haze of this delightful gourmet feast. Hart chuckles at me softly, but I don't even look up when he sits next to me with his own plate.

"Othello, this is the best thing I've ever tasted in my life," I say, and he looks at me with surprise, probably because this is the first time I've complimented him.

"Nova gives us the best ingredients from the Donation Center, so you should thank her later," he says in between bites of saffron-colored rice. "Nothing will ever compare to her Sopa de Lima though."

My chewing comes to a halt for a moment as I take in what he just said. I shouldn't find it jarring that he's had that soup, since they've been dating for years. Still, it's a bit strange to hear; I've only just found out that she has this secret rebel boyfriend. There must be so much that she's shared with him. I wonder what he knows about me.

"Nothing can compare, but this is pretty close," I reply in a kind way, because I feel a sudden need to get along with this stranger. I should find common ground with the man that Nova loves, because if I survive this, he could be a part of my life for a long time.

"I appreciate that," he says as he wipes the corners of his mouth with a napkin. "I rarely get to entertain, so this is a special occasion for me."

"We are so grateful for your help and generosity," Hart says, and Othello eyes him again as if he still is wary of his motives. Instead of acknowledging Hart, he simply gets up and excuses himself to the restroom.

As soon as his footsteps are far enough that they fade from earshot, I let myself ease up a bit. Hart also seems to have let his body unwind as he eats less carefully than he did while Othello was present at the table.

"He's not usually this abrasive, I think he's just very conflicted by this situation," David says to make Hart feel better.

"I never really imagined Nova dating anyone, but he's the last kind of person I would've expected her to be with," I say bluntly, letting my guard down around this warm-hearted stranger.

"Agreed," Hart pipes up through the food he's wolfing down.

"They are a great couple. I never saw Othello be so tender until Nova came into his life… they complement each other quite well," David says before taking another bite of bread.

"I suppose there's no science behind attraction," Hart says and winks at me.

"Can I ask you a question unrelated to the current subject?" David puts his bread down and looks at Hart intently. "What's it like outside of the Teorrain?"

Hart places his fork down and taps on the table; he typically does this when he's thinking of how to describe something. I wait expectantly for his reply, because I love when he illustrates the world beyond this town.

"It's more polished than inside the Teorrain, and the people are always trying to stand out. For example, everyone out in society has dyed hair, as it became the standard decades ago. I've rarely seen someone with naturally-colored hair like Violetta," he says, and I think of his response before forming my own question.

"What's wrong with my hair?" I ask while twirling a thick curl around my finger.

He looks at me apologetically. "Nothing! How could I find fault in hair so heavenly?"

I breathe out a relieved sigh. "I was worried you didn't like it."

"I *love* absolutely every single thing about you." He reaches over to tuck a lock of hair behind my ear and my heart skips a beat. "Most of all, I love your heart."

David laughs and snaps us both out of our love-induced haze. "If I doubted your genuine love for Violetta before, I definitely don't now. You have my unbiased approval. I just hope the rest of the Vermillion feels the same way."

"The rest of the Vermillion?" I ask with bonafide confusion.

"That's what I wanted to talk with you about." We all jump as we realize Othello is standing behind us, and I'm curious as to how long he's been listening. Not curious enough to ask, of course. "We need to present this situation to the rest of the Vermillion as soon as possible, so I've called an emergency meeting tonight."

"Wait, why do we need to get the rest of your gang involved?" Hart puts his napkin down on the plastic table and stands from his chair.

"Because having an army of people on your side is the only real thing that could get you and your girlfriend to safety, genius," Othello says in a mocking tone, and that familiar feeling of dread washes over me again.

"Will they actually listen to us, or are they just going to try to kill Hart for being a Pravi?" I speak up and even David looks to Othello now, interested in how he will respond to my practical question.

Othello crosses the room to me and invades my personal space for the first time. I look up at him and notice every feature about him that might've been hazy before: his dark eyes, the scar on his eyebrow, and the well-trimmed curls on the top of his head that bear a resemblance to my own hair. He leans forward, and I feel Hart take a step towards him defensively.

He simply smirks at me and says in an unbothered voice, "That's what we're about to find out."

CHAPTER
26

Santiago

*T*he last piece of advice my parents passed on to me was to never lie. My mother's voice floats back to my mind, and the words are still in tune with what my father was saying alongside her. They stressed how even one white lie could spiral easily and become a web of deceit that's impossible to untangle. I kept this advice close to my heart and followed it at every turn in life. This being said, let the record show that I, Santiago Atticus Singh, am an honest man.

Except for this fleeting moment in time.

"When was the last time you saw Violetta Akan?" The Guard shines a bright light into my eyes, and I hesitate because of the unwelcome device shining into my sensitive corneas.

"Friday night when I left work," I say without a snag in my voice, almost as if I've been lying my whole life. "I haven't heard from her since."

The Grey Guard gives me a hard look out of the corner of his eye, as if he doesn't trust what I'm saying. He knows that Violetta has been my only employee for years, which makes this all the more suspicious. The Grey Guard and his team spent the better part of nearly two hours searching every corner of the library. They came in with grid detectors and contraptions I'd never heard of, even before I was placed in the Teorrain. Since they've forced me to wait in my office the whole time they've been searching, I'm convinced they must not trust me in the slightest.

A white uniform adorned with gold medals shines bright against the dark skin of this Grey Guard. He's balding and looks to be of South Asian heritage, like my father. What a lucky man. It must be a nice feeling to know that you're safe just because you're fully one race. I wonder if he takes it for granted.

"Do you have a close relationship with Ms. Akan?" He asks with a bad-tempered quality in his voice.

"She's my subordinate, nothing more than that," I say firmly, without so much as pausing to think.

"Are you sure about that?" He asks, looking at my right leg, which is involuntarily bouncing up and down under my desk.

This is a bad time for my nervous tick to reveal itself. I stop moving my leg and incline my head to show him the artificial sincerity on my face. If there's ever been a time that I needed my acting skills to kick in, it is right in this moment.

"Sir, I'm English. We practically invented boundaries," I say with an involuntary sneer.

He frowns. "Did she ever let on that she was in a romantic relationship? That's what she is wanted for."

"Never." He stares at me as if he wants me to elaborate, and so that's exactly what I will do. "She is quite private, which is why I hired her. I wasn't appointed to this job to make friends."

"It seems like it. Sloan just sent a message from the Donation Center and apparently the girl's own roommate had no idea. She was seemingly crushed by the news." Another Guard walks into the room with this statement and I've never felt so jubilant to hear a Grey Guard say anything in my life. This news means that they credited Nova's act. We truly could pull this off; I just need to make it through these questions.

"The roommate didn't know either?" The Guard who is interrogating me looks to the other Guard, who has been standing outside the door. She shakes her head at him in response to his question before looking at me and walking forward to approach my desk.

"Do you know Violetta's roommate?" She asks in a poisonous tone.

"No, I'm afraid not," I say casually back to her.

She cocks her head to the side and looks at me quizzically. "That's odd, the report stated that she claimed to know you."

This statement causes my mind to set ablaze in panic, and I bid a farewell to self-assured Santiago who I was so briefly acquainted with. I try to not let this emotion display itself on my exterior. If Nova and I had had enough time to sync our stories, then this wouldn't be a roadblock. I must think of something to rebut what she just said.

"Well, I know of her because of Violetta's stories. I'm sure she meant the same thing," I say, noting the calm tone of my voice is breaking slightly.

"You just said she is a private person," The other Guard pipes up, and I feel sweat forming at my brow. I am failing at this quite terribly.

"After two and a half years working together, we were bound to exchange a few more words past pleasantries. I know very little still, and positively nothing about her dating anyone." The Guards look at each other for a moment as if they are exchanging a silent conversation.

Suddenly, the second Grey Guard steps forward and I can see her in the light better. She has dark eyes that are almost black, and a much younger face than the other Guard. Her mouth is set in an intimidating scowl, and her black hair is securely tied on top of her head in a tight bun. She slams a drawing device on my desk, a piece of technology I've not seen in years.

I am puzzled by her actions, and cautiously glance down to view the picture on the screen she's placed before me. It doesn't take but a second to recognize the man in the photo, who stares forward with a straight face and is clad in a tuxedo. I try to hide the recollection on my face and force myself to appear to be perplexed.

"I'm sorry, but what is this?" I ask with an oblivious lift in my voice.

"Hart Jaehyung Kang. He's the person that your employee has run off with. You have no idea how imperative it is that we find him," she states, and before I can even wonder what that means, she brushes her hand over the gold gun at her side. "Have you ever come in contact with him? If you tell us the truth now, there will be no consequences for you."

At this very moment, I want to run away and never look back. I want to tell the truth and rid myself of all this madness. I don't want to be involved with a dilemma that could kill me, but no part of me wants my friend to perish. When they tell the story of how we saved Hart and Violetta, I want to be spoken of as someone who fearlessly aided them. I can't be a coward any longer. I find myself rising from my seat, much to the astonishment of the Guards, whilst fastening the highest button on my sweater.

"It's not in my nature to lie, and I'm appalled that an employee of mine would willingly tarnish the name of my establishment. I shall do anything to help you, and I detest what Violetta has done," I say, with my shoulders set straight back as I size them up: something I'm not used to at all. They both appear disappointed and clueless about what their next move should be. This must be working.

A huff comes from the male Guard. "We are going to search the library one more time and then we will be on our way. Report to us if you have any insight into where they are." He stands and leans so close to me that I can see every pore on his nose. "I truly hope that you're not lying. The governor is not a man you want to mess with."

I nod. The governor becoming involved in this matter seems extreme, but I don't understand a lot about American politics. The Guard leers at me one final time, before signaling for the female Guard to follow him as they leave my office.

A sense of awe sprints through me at seeing the door close behind them. It seems that I'm having some trouble convincing my own mind that I accomplished that. Sinking back into my chair, I write in my journal to seem as if I'm going about my normal activities, just in case they come back.

I've always held the firm belief that people don't change to their very core. Most people have a set personality, and it's just who they are. I've been the steady, timorous type. The chap who never gets mixed up in anything wild or senseless.

A substantial reason for my timid nature is that I'm trapped behind this vast wall, but would I have the bravery to act on my dreams if I were free? What if this city is my perfect excuse to remain a tranquil wave, while claiming to hold the courage of a mighty storm?

Despite all of this, I can't deny that my entire being has been refined in countless ways within the past months. This must be substantial evidence that my earlier hypothesis has been disproven. I've become stronger, braver, and more daring. I fight for what I know is right, even if it means tolerating the Vermillion's eerie fashion choices.

While sitting in my office for the day, I go about my usual routine and try to ignore the distinct lack of Violetta. I'm not supposed to leave the room until the Grey Guards give me the orders, but it seems they forgot about me. My legs are aching from the lack of blood flow, so they carry me to dust the bookshelves down the hall despite my better judgment. I straighten my collar and run a comb through my hair: just because I'm a criminal doesn't mean I have to look like one. I open the door and a Grey Guard is standing right outside, swiping his hand over his drawing device to make note of something.

"We are just about done here," he says, barely looking at me and scrunching his nose.

"Find anything?" I try not to sound annoyed that he should've been finished searching hours ago.

"No, but we have a few leads in the case." He looks at me with a smile that makes my head throb. "They can't hide for long."

"Good to hear," I say through clenched teeth, and then turn my back to him before walking towards my books. "I'll just be dusting my books; thank you for the visit." I gaze at the books all around and feel a sense of dread embrace me.

Violetta always made this room feel alive; she couldn't help but read to me while she was dusting. I used to chuckle at how preposterous she looked with a duster in one hand, and a book in the other. She had the most enthusiastic voice I'd ever heard. Now that she's gone, it's just become a dull room, filled to the brim with literature that is aching to be read.

As soon as I hear the door close behind the last Grey Guard, I set out to survey the whole library. I may be polite to Hart, but this does not imply I trust all Pravi folk, especially not Grey Guards. Scanning every inch of every room to see if they set up cameras or recording devices anywhere, my eyes are sharp and keen to their deceptive games. Sadly, the technology is such now that it would be almost impossible for me to detect a camera. I've heard they have small, translucent ones nowadays.

Placing my hands on my hips and observing the clock on the wall after I'm done searching the entirety of the library, I decide it's time to get ready. It's almost time to leave for the emergency Vermillion meeting that Nova told me would take place tonight.

After walking over to my desk, I pull out the black clothes that I keep for this specific reason. I shed my white button down for a black sweater that fits me well, before folding the nice slacks which had covered my legs. I slide the dark jeans on and grab the red bandana I've grown so attached to.

I look to the window, and I'm staggered by my likeness. The man staring back at me looks as relentless as a hurricane. He smirks at me as the storm surges.

A powerful expanse of adrenaline must have come over me, because before I know it, I'm already at the church again, knocking that same knock on the floor. I whisper out the Vermillion motto into the empty building, which seems quieter than usual. It's taking everything in me not to shiver at the cold feel of the place.

"Santiago, I'm glad to see you're okay." David approaches me once he hears our motto spoken to him.

"That makes two of us," I say, laughing slightly, and his happy face is illuminated by the candle he holds.

"We'd better get going; the meeting should be starting soon." His expression turns downcast quite abruptly as he starts to lead me down the hallway. "There's going to be a vote on what to do with Violetta and the Pravi."

I stop in my tracks. "A vote? Can't Othello just do whatever he pleases?"

"We are a democracy, brother. When a major issue arises, Othello has to present it to the family to decide on." He continues to walk toward the giant door that leads to the meeting room, while I stride after him.

"What happens if they don't approve of the situation?" The words almost get stuck in my throat because I'm afraid of the answer.

"Othello wouldn't tell me," he says, before opening the door for me into the bright room filled with brethren of the Vermillion. I look from him to the entryway and see Ryan waving me over to his side. I take one last glance at David, who's worried features don't comfort me, and trudge over to Ryan.

He talks to me about his wife for a bit, and then questions what this meeting could be about with a concerned frown. Pretending not to know, I tune him out. I can't focus on anything except what's about to happen. A slight pang of guilt hits me for being so distracted when talking to him; I'm sure he notices my eyes darting around the room, looking for something.

Finally, applause fills the room and Othello is entering with a calm face. He walks to the center of the room and gestures for the crowd to settle. Everyone sits down on the floor, including yours truly, taking a seat next to Ryan near the back of the room.

"I've called you all here today because we need to have an emergency vote." He speaks in his typical charming tone, but it doesn't stop the crowd from looking to one another quizzically.

The chatter grows louder as they discuss his words amongst themselves. While several of them are arguing about what they think could be happening, Violetta and Hart walk out from where Othello was and stand beside him. The ruckus is silenced as soon as they see the two, standing in unity next to our leader.

"This is Violetta Akan. She works at the library and is an upstanding citizen. A few months ago, she met and fell in love with this man. So she is now requesting our help with her situation." The crowd looks around with confusion still smeared on their faces. There's never been a need to take a vote on a couple being together, and they still haven't figured it out. "This is Hart..." he pauses.

"...a Pravi."

In the moments following those two words, the room sets off in an uproar. Some in the crowd are standing and screaming, questioning as to how Hart is even inside the Teorrain. Others simply sit with their mouths hanging open in utter shock. Many voices collide in a clash of disunity, yet not one person sounds like they are in support of helping them. Ryan's cheeks have flushed, and he's tightening his jaw in what seems to be rage. I can understand their reactions, because when I learned of this information, mine wasn't much better. Their response only appears to be worse because of the shrieking; the volume is outstanding compared to my own wrathful scribbling in an unwelcoming journal.

Through the frantic horde, Nova saunters up and stands in front of Violetta and Hart. She's wearing a tight black dress, making her appear all the more powerful and threatening. A red bandana is tied around her wrist, while her hair is secured in a ponytail atop her head. Daggers shoot out of her eyes at the members of her group as her dark red lips part.

"The Crossed will rise!" She screams, and the room quiets down at her boldness. They've become docile just from hearing her voice. "These words bind us together and give us hope for the future, do they not? We represent the generation that will have these walls taken down, but we also represent unity and respect. Othello brought this case to you all because he respects you. He wants your opinion on the matter, but you have to listen to the whole story."

Not one person in the room says a word, even the most opinionated members sit back down. They continue their silence as a way of showing her respect. Othello doesn't miss this opportunity to speak, as he gives Nova a thankful nod.

"I was only a young boy when my parents were arrested for hiding me on a farm. They were raised in America and knew full well what the laws were. They defied them anyway, accepting being thrown in jail rather than living their lives knowing that they'd met their soulmate and done nothing about it. They cherished me more than anything: a Crossed child, a menace to society at this point in history. I may not have known much about them before I was taken away, but I recognize two irrefutable true facts about them." He waits a moment to build up tension and get the full attention of his audience, like a true leader. "That they loved each other, and that they were Pravis."

The room stays silent as people realize what he's trying to get at. He searches the room until he finds my eyes, and when he does, I see a faint grin play at his lips. He's telling me he's grateful for the argument I gave to change his mind, and I nod at him because it's actually working. He steps towards Hart and Violetta before putting a hand on Hart's shoulder, a gesture that causes many people to gasp.

"I am certain that these two are in love. Hart is one of many Pravis that oppose the laws that keep us tied to this place, and their story shouldn't end in death." He looks to the crowd with a pleading expression. "To save them, we are going to need support on our side. What do you say?"

"Before you all make your decision, I beg of you to put yourselves in our situation," Violetta pipes up, which causes a few people to sit up straighter with interest. "I didn't want to love him, but that's the thing about love. It isn't biased; it doesn't see skin color or blood."

She stares at the troops, desperately searching their eyes, hoping to see some semblance of mercy in them. They all stay silent; I'm sure they have no clue what to say in this state of affairs. Most seem to have their eyes fixed on Hart, studying him. I take notice that his wardrobe has changed, and this has made all the difference. He looks somewhat brooding in the dark clothes that I'm assuming are Othello's. I wonder if that's helping with his case.

Hart grabs Violetta's hand, and their fingers intertwine. The distinct contrast between skin colors becomes even more apparent as I stare at their joined hands. I can't help but still feel a prick of envy, perhaps not because of them specifically, but for what they have together.

"Please just turn me in," Hart says steadily, and the whole room is shocked to hear the Pravi speak up. "Help Violetta, hide her, and get her to safety. She can join you and fight alongside the Vermillion."

At this statement, Violetta rips her hand from his and retorts, "Hart, what are you doing?!"

He shakes his head before taking her hand again and raising it to his lips, placing a delicate kiss on her palm. Releasing her hand, Hart steps forward so that he's nearer to the people, and even Othello looks to be completely flabbergasted at his actions. Anyone could tell that this certainly wasn't in their plan.

"While none of you know me, and are hesitant to believe me, please know that what I'm about to say is sincere." He looks back to Violetta with sorrow in his eyes as if he's apologizing before he speaks again. "The woman standing behind me is the most intelligent, and courageous person you'll ever meet. I have no earthly clue why she fell for someone like me, but she shouldn't be punished for my pursuit of her. Love is selfless, and this is why I have absolutely no issue with turning myself in. My death means nothing if she is able to live. Just please take care of her as it's my last request."

At this, there is continued quiet in the room, and all eyes are on Hart. Violetta looks as though she's about to collapse. Nova comes beside her and tries to hold her up, but Violetta doesn't even seem to notice. Her eyes are locked on her only love, who has just offered up his life for her. Her pink lips are parted in shock, and slight noises leave them as if she's trying to speak but is far too stunned.

Much to my own dismay, I'm standing up now. I've had quite enough of this.

"I stand with them," I say, and the whole room turns in my direction with wide eyes. "If we don't, then we are hypocrites. I will help them for my parents. For the Pravis that loved me."

My eyes are focused on Violetta and her tear-stained face. Her trembling lips mouth a thank you to me, and my heart swells with pride for doing the right thing.

"I also stand with them." Ryan stands to join me, and I give him a surprised glance, to which he only laughs under his breath.

Soon the entire room stands, one by one. They are soundless, but their movement echoes louder than a gong. I can't quite comprehend what I'm seeing, but it brings an extra bit of warmth to my heart knowing that even if this is in vain, the Vermillion was willing to help them. Violetta raises a hand to her mouth as she begins to cry joyful tears, and Nova hugs her tight, with a grin stretching across her face from ear to ear. Othello and Hart are still standing there, without movement, overwhelmed by the gesture of the people.

Julia, an assistant of Nova's, walks over to Othello and asks what we are all wondering now, "How do we help them?"

To this question, he looks up at the ceiling for a moment, and then to the crowd. He gives Nova a questioning look, and she lets go of Violetta before addressing Julia's query.

"I suppose we get them initiated into our family first," Nova shrugs at her, before glancing at Hart with a mischievous twinkle in her eyes. "Are you prepared to join a Crossed gang, Pravi?"

CHAPTER
27

Hart

I hate press conferences. Truth be told, I am uncomfortable being in the spotlight in any capacity, and that's a secret that's eaten away at me for years. I was fifteen years old when I first realized how rapidly my reputation could become something less than honorable. My father had just gone from being the mayor of our city, Briste, to the governor over all of Geal. His acceptance speech was one that will live through time, it was as moving as it was utterly fabricated. I sat through it like a champ, reacting to every part of it in the appropriate way and waving to the young girls who came to get my attention.

As the press conference came to a close, I confidently walked off stage. Sadly for the younger version of myself, I wasn't looking and tripped down the stairs that led backstage. Until that day, my image was that of a suave, handsome, intelligent teenager who was ready to support his father in any way. Ridicule from the public followed for months after, and the high definition clip of my fall was all over the country. People took immeasurable joy in the incident that resulted in a concussion and hurt pride.

My mother was incredibly disappointed in me for not watching my step. I had made the Kangs look foolish. After promising my parents that I'd work my hardest never to embarrass them again, I became overly aware of when people were watching me. I was determined to never become a laughingstock again, and worked tirelessly to regain my attractive, well-spoken standing with the country. If my father planned to become president, I had to act like the children of President Grey, faultless in all ways.

If only the people of Geal could see me now—Hart Kang, that careful and collected young man, standing beside his girlfriend after being initiated into a rebel gang. The entire country might have a simultaneous fainting spell upon witnessing this historic day. In fact, I'm sure they are already blowing up my disappearance on the news.

My only hope is that my father couldn't cover up what I've done. My goal is to have every reporter across the nation writing stories on my defiance. Maybe they will talk about my refusal to let the Crossed laws hinder me, and it will spark curiosity in the souls of those who support the laws. There's a sense of satisfaction that runs through me at the thought of generating widespread publicity for this issue. The shock my parents must feel knowing that they failed to silence me after years of success is only an added bonus.

A red bandana is now tied around my left thigh, and Violetta keeps hers secured about her wrist like Nova. She beams up at me with admiration and I feel my heart die unto itself all over again. Throwing away everything I've built my life on is far too easy when it means I'm fighting for people like her to be free.

"How does it feel to be the first Pravi to become a Vermillion member?" Asks a manly voice to my right, and I'm taken aback by the man's warm face, which is much less threatening than many of the others at this meeting.

"It feels like I'm the luckiest man alive," I say, because I'm still shocked that we survived that meeting. I will have to thank Santiago later for what he did. I feel like a stereotypical jealous boyfriend for being suspicious of him earlier.

"Well don't get too excited; we still have to figure out how to get you and your girl to safety," he says with some sort of remorse in his tone. I can tell he's not used to being serious. It's almost as if there's a permanent smile set on his face, and the wrinkles at the edges of his mouth confirm my hypothesis.

Santiago steps in and puts his arm around the man with a smile. "Give the bloke a moment to breathe, Ryan! He thought he was going to die mere hours ago; he needs rest."

"Santiago, can I speak to you in private for a moment?" I blurt out in an unintentionally somber tone.

"Of course," he says nervously, seemingly startled by my question.

Walking out of the crowded meeting area, I lead him several feet down the corridor into Othello's room. He turns the light on and waits for me to speak up.

"I just wanted to thank you privately for what you did back there," I say, and he lets out a breath that he's evidently been holding in.

"It was all for Violetta; she's told me how much she cares for you," he says casually, as he takes off his glasses for a moment to wipe the lens on his sweater. "She's convinced you've really fallen for her."

It's too difficult to not laugh slightly at his choice of words. "I never fell in love."

"You didn't?" He speaks louder, infuriated that I've confirmed his intuitions about me. "Then what are you doing with her?"

"Falling in love implies that I could simply fall out of it." A chuckle escapes me, thinking of the impossibility.

"What do you mean?" He's becoming exasperated at my answers.

"Every day in Briste was like walking at the edge of a cliff. One wrong step, and I'd be dropped down a long abyss of emptiness. Then I met her and came to see I'd been plummeting towards loneliness the entire time. Violetta became my friend and it felt like I was walking on solid ground." I think for a moment on how to finish describing the depth of our story. "I didn't *fall* in love, I was saved by it. Love stopped me from falling and allowed me to finally feel safe."

He puts his hands in his pockets. "You're quite the poet, Pravi."

I smile at the compliment, and decide to return the sentiment once more. "Taking a stand for us was bold, and I respect you a lot for that." I notice he's relaxing his posture, my flattery is making him more comfortable.

"I'd do anything for Violetta," he says.

"I will take good care of her wherever we end up," I say with sincerity, and he nods curtly. "That's all I wanted to say."

He nods again and turns to walk through the door. Stopping right outside the open door, he turns back around towards me and his right hand balls into a fist momentarily.

"I will accept you because she loves you. But, if a day should come that you hurt my best friend in any way, I guarantee you'll regret it," he says in a low voice that sends a slight shiver down my spine.

With that threatening comment, he leaves me in the room by myself to think on his words. There isn't a logical reason to worry, because I could never hurt Violetta, but somehow he still found a way to shake me up a bit. Sitting down on the cot, I barely have time to brush off his comment before there's a knock at the door.

"Violetta?" I call out in a hopeful tone.

"How'd you know?" I perk up at the purple eyes in the doorway. She canters over to me and sits beside me on the cot.

"Lucky guess," I respond to her with a quiet laugh. "How are you? That was a whirlwind, you must be exhausted."

"I'm definitely tired, but also relieved. If there was ever a doubt in my mind about your loyalty to me, it's completely gone." She reaches over to link her arm in mine before leaning her head on my relaxed shoulder.

"Never doubt my love for you; I would go to any lengths to secure your happiness," I whisper, and let my head fall gently on top of hers.

"Just stay alive then," she murmurs back, and I feel her grip on my arm tighten. "You are essential to my happiness."

We stay like this for what feels like the longest time, saying nothing to one another. There is a sense of peace between us, but this could just be because we are getting to relax a bit. My freedom has somehow just begun in a place where independence seems to be in limited supply, yet I can't help but feel more liberated here than outside of this boundary.

Violetta sits up as another pair of knuckles lightly tap on the door before it opens just a crack and Nova appears with a bright face. "I have fantastic news."

I stand up quickly from the cot. "What is it?"

"Othello got in contact with someone who may be able to help get you two to safety far from here," she squeals out in an excited whisper.

Safety. The thought of it is more than enough to keep me hopeful at this moment; if there is any possible way to leave here alive then I am willing to do whatever it takes.

"What? How?" I ask rapidly.

"There's a driver who drops donations off at the center and knew Othello's parents. He's scheduled to be at the center tomorrow, so Othello will see if they can make a deal regarding a safe passage out of the city," Nova says while bouncing up and down on the balls of her feet.

"I have a sizable amount of money that I was able to grab on the way out of my house, can it help us?" I ask without thinking, and Nova's eyes widen while Violetta's hand tightens around my arm again.

I'm sure later they are both going to want to know why I have access to so much money. I probably should tell my girlfriend about my identity in society before our possible deaths, but it's frightening when I know that she's going to ask what my parents' stances on the Crossed laws are.

"Possibly, but we will have to wait and see what Othello comes back with," she says, donning a tight smile fastened with unasked questions.

"Should we go with him?" Violetta's voice pipes up beside me. "It may help Othello to convince his contact to help us."

Nova reaches a hand up to her ponytail and spins it around her short fingers as she thinks about the idea. Violetta is right that it would help Othello to persuade this person to help us, but it also could be a big risk to leave this room in general. I'm sure Nova is thinking about this not only from a leader's standpoint, but from that of a close friend.

"That's far too dangerous; everyone is actively searching for you two. Othello is risking his neck even by going, but his chances are much better if he's alone," Nova says in a kind tone, as if she's rejecting Violetta.

"If we can do anything to help, please let us know," Violetta says, and Nova takes her hands in hers and gives them a reassuring squeeze.

"We are going to find a way to get you both out of here," she says to us in a reassuring voice. She lets go of Violetta and walks towards the door before turning around and locking eyes with me.

"Also, there's a bathroom across the hall if you'd like to wash up before bed." Her eyes glance over to Violetta before continuing. "V, you can follow me to a different bathroom near David's quarters."

"Thank you, I will take you up on that," I say, and the corners of her lips turn up once more. They walk out of the room and close the door behind them, leaving me to my thoughts again.

Touching my hair, I'm still somehow surprised to find that it's messy. I'm rather rumpled all around, so nothing sounds better than getting clean right now. As I walk out of Othello's room, the washroom greets me. Instantly, I notice how different it is from the layout at my home. The bathroom is not friendly to people who wrestle with claustrophobia. There's no glass showering place or marble bathtub like I'm accustomed to. Just a shower head, a sink, a toilet, and a ratty towel left for me on the toilet seat. I wonder how they even get water down here. That'll be something to ask about later.

Once it's on, the water comes out light and warm. I shed my clothing and hurry to stand underneath the stream. I allow the water to wash away all my thoughts and worries. For a moment it's like I'm still at home, rinsing off after a day of classes. I stay like this until the water turns cold, which doesn't seem to be long.

After drying off and pulling on a pair of my own pajamas, I walk into my room, where Violetta is drying her hair with a towel. She has such a focused look on her face, like making sure her hair is dry is the most tedious task ever given to her. I snicker at how cute she is before sitting down on the cot.

"What are you laughing at?" She turns and looks at me with strands of wet hair falling in front of her face.

"You're just really adorable sometimes, angel," I say while running my fingers through my own damp locks.

"We are running from the law, and you're thinking about how cute I am?" She says and whips the hair out of her face. "You need to get your priorities straight."

"I think my priorities are in the correct order, thank you very much." I stand up and put my arms around her waist.

Without hesitation, she drops the towel in her hand and places her palms on my shoulders. Her diamond-shaped face shines in the dim room, and I struggle to find breath just looking at her dynamic expressions.

"Can I ask you something?" She asks while trying to fix the black hair falling in my eyes.

"Anything."

She successfully moves my hair to one side of my face. "Is 'angel' a nickname you call girls that you find to be pretty?"

I shake my head. "I've never called anyone else by that name."

"Why have you called me that from the beginning, then?" She asks with a quirked eyebrow.

Now this is a question I don't mind answering. I'm grateful her inquiry wasn't about the money I brought up earlier.

"One of my favorite artists is Mikaela Merid, who painted many moving pieces long before the laws." I begin my story, and Violetta appears to be eager to see where it's going. "Her greatest inspiration throughout her career was her bodyguard, Jack, whom she loved dearly. She was unable to tell him that she had feelings for him because she was shy, so she found a different way to say it. She debuted her most famous painting, a portrait of him made with incredible detail, and called it 'Angel.'"

Violetta gasps. "Did he feel the same way?"

"He stared at the painting in awe for a few minutes, and then turned to her and pulled a piece of paper from his pocket. It was a letter confessing that he loved her, which he had planned to give her that very night." I stifle a chuckle at Violetta's grip on my shoulders and her wide eyes. "They lived happily ever after, and it ended up being a beautiful story. When interviewers asked Mikaela why she named the portrait 'Angel,' she would say that Jack shone brighter than anyone on this earth. She said his soul must've been made of something heavenly."

Violetta stares at me, still a bit perplexed. "That's a great story, but what does it have to do with me?"

"When I first laid eyes on you, I understood what Mikaela was talking about. You're unlike anyone else, and there isn't a more fitting word to describe you," I say before kissing her on the forehead.

She stares at me with all the love in the world, and I know it's a miracle that a girl like this could look at me the way she does. She places her head on my chest and hugs me tight, and I rest my cheek on her head.

"You're my angel, too." She says and my heart swells. "I just hope Othello can get us out of here."

"Even if he can't, we will figure this out." I tuck a drying lock of her hair behind her ear gently. "Our story won't end for a long time."

"How can you be so sure?" She mutters against my beating heart.

"Because we have a family now." I point to the red bandana wrapped securely around my thigh. She looks at it with a slight smile, but her eyes are still downcast as if it's hard for her to trust my affirmations. "I love you, and we are going to be just fine."

She snuggles closer into my chest, and I wonder how many times I'll have to say everything is going to be okay until it really is.

CHAPTER
28

Violetta

*B*eing woken up from a nightmare and realizing it was all real isn't exactly something I would consider pleasant, yet here I am. I try to focus on inhaling deeply, but then I hear a noise that calms me. Hart is on the floor next to my cot mumbling something incoherent. It takes everything in me not to laugh at the irony. He tries to act so imperturbable, but he can't control what he does in his sleep.

Moving the blanket away from myself, I sneak out of the room, being careful to close the door behind me lightly. I walk down the hallway trying to find the meeting room, in hopes of discovering a familiar face who can inform me of what time it is. That's the downside of being underground: no windows whatsoever.

I hear something move behind me and turn around quickly to see a faint light approaching me, which gives me a sense of relief.

"David, what time is it?" I call out to him kindly.

"It's almost two in the afternoon; you must've been extremely tired," David says, and I can almost hear him quietly laughing at me in the dark.

"Well, where is everyone then?"

"Nova is at work, and Othello is in the meeting room preparing to meet with his contact." The light is close enough now that David stops beside me before holding the candle outward to illuminate my face. "Follow me, I'll get you something to eat."

He continues walking down the hallway towards the door to the meeting room and my stomach must be grateful, because it begins to grumble a few steps in. He opens the door for me and walks in behind me before blowing the flame out.

"How about some cereal?" He asks, and I light up at the mention of the colorful preservative-laced food.

"I would love some!" My feet carry me to a seat at the plastic table that Othello set up the other day, and I wait for him as he walks into a back room. He quickly comes back with a box, milk, and a wooden bowl with the spoon attached. He sets all of them down on the table and sits in the seat across from me. Just as I'm excitedly pouring the cereal into the bowl, I hear footsteps approach us and I already know who it is without sending a glance his way.

"Look who actually decided to wake up and join us," Othello's voice rings out.

"I was seriously lacking sleep, okay?" I say in a defensive manner as Othello takes a seat across from me.

I nearly choke on my food as I lay my eyes on him, because he looks completely different. Not only have his piercings been removed, but he's colored in his eyebrow so it's hard to tell there's a scar there. He's styled in a way that makes him look mature, like he's not the leader of a gang. His typical dark apparel has been replaced with a white oxford button down and light jeans: no red bandana in sight.

"You can stop staring at me now, Violetta," he says with a smirk on his face. "I know I'm stunning, but I'm taken."

My eyes seem to have a mind of their own as they roll back into my head, and I scoff. "I was just in shock at seeing you dressed like an actual human."

"Your best friend picked out this outfit," he says nonchalantly.

"Why would she do that?" I ask, because Othello doesn't strike me as the type of person to ask for advice on outfit choices.

"I'm trying not to look like the leader of a rebellion for the afternoon, since I have to go to the Donation Center," he says slowly, as if I'm moronic for not guessing that in the first place. "Thankfully, the Grey Guards don't know what I look like, but I'm taking precautions to fit in."

Just then Hart walks into the room with rumpled hair, the same clothes as yesterday, and a confused look on his face. Othello snickers.

"What time is it?" He asks with a raspy voice as he takes a seat beside me at the table.

"Around two in the afternoon," I say, and he looks as if he doesn't believe me for a moment before his eyes look hungrily to my near-empty bowl. "Eat some cereal, you must be starving by now." He doesn't hesitate, taking a bowl from me, pouring cereal and milk into it, and beginning to eat.

"Othello was just talking about how he's going to meet up with his mystery contact soon." I try to catch Hart up on our conversation. He looks up and must notice Othello's appearance for the first time since he came into the room. He seems as taken aback as I was, but he refrains from saying anything about his new style.

"Do you have a reason to believe he will help you?" Hart asks between bites. Othello leans back a bit in his chair before answering. "He owes my parents a favor and has offered to try and help me escape before. I had someone ask if he'd be willing to meet me today, and he agreed. He has connections to Pravis that hide people like us."

I sit up straighter in my chair, and Hart drops the wooden spoon into his bowl. I didn't imagine Othello would actually have a favor to redeem from someone who could be of such help to us. Pravis who could hide us for a while until we figure out our next move? It almost sounds too good to be true. We could survive this with the help of people on the other side of the Teorrain.

"But, why wouldn't you take that offer?" I ask with intrigue.

Othello shakes his head. "I only want to be free from this place if we all are. I wouldn't leave the Vermillion."

"That's noble of you, Othello. I respect you for that," Hart says, and Othello looks at him with his eyebrows raised.

"You have very good character," I nod in agreement; Othello must be a reliable man if he would turn down that offer.

"It's just what any respectable leader would do." He hesitates before looking at Hart and speaking again. "You should know that firsthand, Kang"

Hart freezes up and his face goes pale as if he's seen a ghost. "What is that supposed to mean?"

"It just means that I have friends in high places, and they seem to know a lot about your family." Othello shrugs casually, but Hart's knuckles are turning white as he grips his spoon.

"Your friends know Hart's family?" I ask.

"She doesn't know about you, does she?" Othello doesn't even look at me when addressing Hart.

This back and forth is spiking my anxiety. "Know *what* about him, exactly?"

"She knows who I really am, and that's what matters," Hart says, setting his spoon back into the bowl.

"What is he talking about, Hart?" My voice pleads with him.

"Violetta, this isn't a big deal and we can talk privately later." Hart reaches out to tuck a strand of hair behind my ear like he does so often, but I don't appreciate it this time.

"If you don't tell her, then I'm going to." Othello looks to David, who just stares at me with sympathy. "She deserves to know."

Hart opens his mouth, and I roll my eyes. It seems he's just going to argue with Othello again. But instead of retorting, he nods and turns in his chair towards me. He takes my hands in his and lets out a long breath.

"Angel, the reason the Grey Guards are so unrelenting in their search for us is because my father is the governor of Geal." He says this and my mind goes completely blank, searching for ways to process that information. "I didn't tell you because I was afraid you would see me differently, like everyone else does, with their incorrect presumptions. You were the first person to see through the facade my family had forced on me from a young age. I was a coward for not telling you, and I can only hope you'll forgive me someday."

There are no words coming to mind, only various opposing emotions. I want to scream at him and leave this place. I want to hold him close and tell him I understand. How do you accept that your boyfriend kept such a secret from you about his identity? But, is the governor's son who he really is on the inside? Would I have loved him if I'd known?

While I remain silent in a state of disturbance, Hart's eyes are getting increasingly watery and his cheeks are flushed. His hands are shaking, and I pull mine back from him. He's terrified that he's lost me.

"You probably need time to figure out how you feel about me," he says as he stands and wipes the corners of his eyes. "I'll give you space, angel."

He starts to briskly walk toward the door, and my instincts finally kick in. My mind goes a million miles a minute and there's a lot to consider, but I can't let him think that he will lose me. I'm disappointed that he kept this from me, but if I'd known from the beginning, I might not have fallen for him at all. Everything happens for a reason, and there's a reason I love that Pravi boy for everything he is.

"Hart!" I yell while hastening my stride to catch up with him at the door on the other side of the room. He turns around with eyes red and wide. "I trusted you, and you withheld something so important from me. You hurt me, and I'm not exactly happy with you right now."

"I don't deserve you or your forgiveness." He looks at the ground, unable to meet my eyes. "I selfishly wanted to keep you in the dark so you'd love me back. Everyone thinks that my father and I are two of a kind."

"Tell me the truth, does your dad support the Crossed laws?" I ask him with bated breath and pray he will tell me otherwise "Is that what this is about?"

"Yes," Hart chokes out. "He does."

I flinch at his answer, but continue my line of questioning nonetheless. "Do you?"

"Of course not!" He snaps his head up quickly with disgust written on his face.

I step forward and place my palm on his right cheek. He leans into my touch and closes his eyes as his body begins to relax.

"You're nothing like him, then. That's all I need to know for now," I say, and his eyes open and tears are filling them again, this time with relief. "I love you for your soul, Hart Kang."

He lets out a breath, grabbing me and hurriedly pulling me against him. His heart is beating so rapidly, but his breathing has slowed to a calm. "I'm so sorry, Violetta. I will explain more later."

"Good, because you're not off the hook yet; I have a lot of questions," I say into his chest and he chuckles a little.

Othello lets out a short laugh from across the room and begins applauding us. "You know what, Pravi? I actually like you. That was quite the show, but you answered correctly on all accounts. You have guts, so I'm going to help you," he says before checking his watch and walking over to us. "Even though you are a Kang."

"Do you want me to accompany you, boss?" David asks, and Othello shakes his head immediately at the idea.

"It's better if I handle this alone; I'm not sure that I'll be able to make contact with him today. I need to draw as little attention as possible," Othello says, and David nods in agreement.

"I'll be back within the hour, you two have fun with David," he tells us, and opens the door before looking back at us briefly. "We have to do this whole 'dramatic reveal' thing more often, it was thrilling." He winks and rushes out the door before we can say anything.

David looks at us with a devilish grin at the same moment that the door clicks behind Othello. "Do you two like board games?"

"I don't know, I think Violetta might lose," Hart says in a joking manner, to which I punch him in the arm, and he recoils.

"Careful, my angel. You're skating on thin ice," I say while David rushes to the room in the back to bring out a board game for us to play.

We sit there together for the next few hours chatting, and it's not so bad. David is quite interesting and has some great ideas for fighting the government in the future. His wide nose scrunches up when he talks about the Grey Guards and the president. He talks about lighthearted things as well, like all the exciting times he's had with Nova and Othello. I'm completely captivated as he tells these stories; it gives me more insight as to what my best friend has been up to for the last couple of years.

He tells us about how he met Othello and became part of the Vermillion, how he felt as if it gave him a higher purpose. That's when I realize how wonderful this rebellion is. I used to believe it was just a hateful group of people trying to get themselves killed by defying the powers that keep us away from society. I couldn't have been more wrong. It's about lifting each other up. It's about the hope for a better tomorrow, trying to ensure a good future for the upcoming generations of Crossed people.

By the end of our conversation, I feel like we all have a much deeper understanding of each other. I'm actually starting to like Nova's formerly-secret boyfriend from these stories.

Hart buys a property in monopoly and then gasps, "I can't believe I forgot!"

He rushes out the door and returns within a minute to the meeting room. He drops on the floor where he was sitting previously with what looks like a thick, rectangular piece of glass, and I look at him with confusion.

"This is a drawing device," he says, holding it with caution. "I took out the tracker in it before I left, but it ensures that we can look up anything in the world. It's a smart device that could come in handy."

"I'm not sure what we would need to look up, but it's nice to know you have it for when we get to safety," I say, and he smiles at me before moving to turn the device on. A green light appears and scans his face. A blue light flashes twice, and then the glass lights up with so many different words I can barely keep track. David and I gaze at it, hypnotized by the numerous pictures.

Just as we are becoming entranced by this foreign object, we are knocked out of our daze when the door swings open. All of our heads turn around expecting to see Othello, but instead it's Nova who stands there in the doorway, with her face stained with tears. She drops to her knees and looks at us with the deepest form of fear in her eyes.

"Someone tipped off the Guards," she says in between strangled sobs. "They arrested Othello."

CHAPTER
29

Santiago

*O*rganizing the novels that came in today seems to have become a newfound form of agony for me when Violetta isn't here to cheer me up with her rosy comments. This cherished place is turning into a vacant nightmare made up of my former dreams.

I pick up the copy of *To Kill A Mockingbird* that I'd lent to Violetta and open it to a random page. The pages are worn down, and I smile at them. Seeing the pages of a book appear as though they've been read carefully many times lifts my spirits. It isn't the crisp new books that make me happy, it's the ones that have seen a thousand eyes. My father was always sure to remind me that books are merely words written on pages until someone begins to read them. It's only when the words jump off the page into the reader's imagination that a book becomes true literature.

It's easy for me to get wary of being in the library. It can feel cold and empty, but these books have always made me feel more alive than I ever could ask. I've lost count of how many I've read, everything from Homer to Hughes. Each unique story pulled me far from where my thoughts lay. If I'm grateful for anything, it's having the opportunity to run a place where I can easily access literature. My parents would've wanted that for me. Although I'm sure they wouldn't have wanted me to be in this situation in general.

As much as I think about my parents, I think about my aunt more. I wonder if she tried to save me from being taken to this place, if she knew that they were going to throw me in here. From what I can tell, it's more than illegal to condemn someone who isn't a U.S. citizen to a life behind these walls. She was supposed to meet me at the airport with my younger cousin. Everything was going to be alright, and now I'll never see my family again.

The Grey Guards have made sure we don't have any way of getting in contact with the outside world. They were sure to make internet access illegal when they built the Teorrains, and only give us landline phones that can call the authorities. Truthfully, I'd never seen a phone attached to a wire until I came here. They let us write letters and mail packages within the Teorrain, but all of these are opened and screened for possible criminal activity or harsh words against the government.

The red landline phone in my office usually only rings when fugitives are on the loose or they're informing me that they've caught them. That's why it's much to my surprise and chagrin when I hear the phone ringing down the hall.

I run sloppily to my office and stare at the phone for a moment before bringing myself to pick up the receiver.

"This is Santiago Singh; how may I be of assistance?" I ask and suck in a breath.

"We wanted to inform you that Othello, leader of the Vermillion, has been caught and will suffer a public trial this evening in the Marketplace Square," the gruff voice answers, and I almost drop the phone before I pull myself together to avoid suspicion.

"Thank you for keeping me updated. Have a nice day," I say and hang up, before dropping to my knees. I throw the glasses off my face and place my head in my hands, letting out a silent scream. My hands are trembling and fear is absorbing any other thoughts I'd had. How could this happen? What does this mean for the future of the Vermillion? What does this mean for Nova? They can't kill him! He's Othello, he's invincible. My racing mind won't put an end to these questions, though they can't possibly be answered by anything except time itself.

As I'm gripping the loose strands of my hair in frustration, I realize there's nothing else to do but run to the square. I need to know what's going to happen to him and be there for Nova. She must be petrified. I extend my arms out and pat around the cold floor until I find my spectacles. While putting them on quickly, I run a hand through my hair and try to smooth out my wrinkled button down.

Dashing out the door of the library, I fumble with the keys and lock it behind me. While I'm aware that it's almost imperative that I don't draw attention to myself, I still run towards the square with abandon. There's a dampness forming on my forehead. I'm not sure if it's the sweat from running or the scalding feeling of dread in the air. As I near the Marketplace Square, I notice a large crowd of people standing in front of a platform. It's in the middle of the shops, and the Grey Guards only use it for making a spectacle.

There are people pushing each other to get closer to the front. I hear someone whisper that they want to know what he looks like. They want to witness this historical moment, the trial of the faceless Vermillion leader who has been captured at last. The saddest part is that most of these people are probably going to be glad that he's been caught; they don't know who he truly is.

They only know the lies the Guards have told us, the rumors of his violence, and other tidbits that couldn't be more incorrect. They don't know his plans to march peacefully, to protest without harming anyone. They don't know he's just a visionary who dreams of a world where equality and love unify even the most dissimilar people.

I search around the crowd and my height allows me good access to the view of spectators. My eyes find Nova after several moments, standing close to the platform with a helpless look on her face. I've never seen her like this, so weak and frightened. There are too many people between us. Whilst I'm tempted to bulldoze through them to get to her, I find myself frozen where I stand as the crowd goes silent.

Suddenly we see several Grey Guards, all adorned in their usual ghostly-white uniforms. The two in the front are dragging a man I can only assume is Othello, with a black hood covering his head. My breathing becomes labored as they force him to kneel in front of us. One of the Guards moves to rip the fabric off his head, and I notice his face is littered with purple marks as if he's been thoroughly beaten. He's looking to the ground, refusing to make eye contact with the crowd, but the scar on his eyebrow leaves no question that this is our leader.

"Here kneels before you the notorious criminal, Kace Basri, who goes by the alias Othello," a Grey Guard's voice thunders through the square. "He's been charged with treason, a crime punishable to the highest degree. His fate has already been decided for him by order of the government."

A moment passes before he utters the one word that makes me feel like this can't be happening.

"Death."

The crowd begins to gasp collectively, and several people speak up and scream that he should be given a fair trial. Much to my surprise, many seem to wonder what he has done that warrants death. The female Grey Guard that helped interrogate me is standing behind Othello, and even she seems to flinch at the sentence. I put a hand over my own mouth to stop myself from screaming in terror. Nova simply stands there, staying silent and looking up at her boyfriend on the white platform, whose bottom lip is slightly quivering.

Witnessing his agony reminds me that we are the same age. He may seem invincible to the Vermillion, but he's still so young. He has so much life to live, and there's so much I wanted to learn about him. I didn't even know his real name until this moment. The Grey Guards wait less than a minute before pointing their guns towards the audience, and all commotion ceases.

"If anyone would like to join him, speak now and see what awaits you," a second Guard steps up and yells.

Othello slowly raises his head and his light green eyes immediately land on Nova's pained face. His lips form into a half smile as his eyes well up with tears. He mouths, "I love you." She mouths back the same thing, and she quickly wipes away a tear with the back of her hand. The Guard who had been speaking approaches Othello with a Scelus, a weapon containing a lethal poison—one that causes an instantaneous death once injected. The poison was discovered when I was young, and made illegal in most countries, including this one.

"Any last words, Othello?" The Grey Guard speaks out, pressing the silver injector to his neck.

Othello breathes in one last time before angrily screaming, "The Crossed Will Ri—"

He's cut off as the Guard presses down on the Scelus, and his body begins to shake while he coughs uncontrollably for a moment. Everything becomes hazy as I see Othello's eyes roll into the back of his head before he goes limp on the ground. It only took twelve seconds for the strongest man I'd ever met to leave the earth. Twelve seconds, and the world became abominable to me. The sun has gone down by now, leaving us in the dark to be confronted with the grim presence of death in the square. I stand there only for a moment before my adrenaline kicks in, and I'm pushing people away as fast as I can to grab Nova.

"Nova, we need to leave." I grab her arm and spin her towards me, and she looks up at me with tears running down her face faster than snow falls in the winter.

"I c-can't move," she stammers while struggling for breath. "He said he would be safe. He promised me."

There's nothing I can say, and nothing I could ever do to erase what she just saw. She begins to hyperventilate, and only seconds pass before her heavy breaths stop altogether and she faints. Thankfully, I am close enough to catch her in time. I throw her left arm around my neck before picking up her limp body. A few people try to stop me and ask me what's wrong, and if she's okay. I tell them she's just a friend who doesn't like executions, and while they continue to stare, I still leave with her in my arms. The lie leaves my lips without a second thought, and I quickly look up to the sky, asking my parents to forgive me.

Chapter 29

The adrenaline pumping through my veins must've increased, because I carry Nova as if she weighs nothing. Her right arm is hanging down and swaying from side to side with every step I take, and her combat boots' laces are untied.

My arms somehow don't become tired as I walk all the way to my apartment, where I lay her down on my bed and pull the warm blanket over her. My eyes stay on her face for what feels like a lifetime, as I'm lost in thought about what just happened. Images of Othello flash through my mind; the sight of his defeated form on that platform seemed like it was staged. Like the Grey Guards used his death for entertainment.

Eventually, I get up and walk to my kitchen before filling a pot with water and heating it on the old gas stove. Nova's going to need to drink some of my special chai when she wakes up; it'll make her body stronger. Although I don't know how it will help her broken heart.

The steam from the water reaches my face and I shudder from the warmth of it. Anytime something unpleasant has happened to me, I've found that a good cup of tea has done the trick to distract me momentarily. Yet, the once-powerful effects of tea have seemingly dissolved as I hear Othello's voice yelling out through the cinnamon aroma.

My hands go up to envelop my ears as an attempt to block out the sound coming from my own mind. Closing my eyes doesn't help either. I wonder if I'll ever forget the look he had when they announced his sentence or if his final words can be erased from my memory.

I put the last of the ingredients into the diffuser and sigh as the flavors flow into the water. The color gradually becomes darker until it becomes a perfect shade of caramel, something that would typically make me feel content. I pour the tea into my favorite teacup, which has pink flowers painted on the handle. The first thing she sees when she wakes up should be lovely; she deserves that at least.

I sit beside the bed with the cup in my hand and I realize her eyes are already open, staring at the ceiling without emotion.

"Drink this, you need to stay hydrated," I say, reaching out my hand to extend the warm tea to her. She avoids eye contact with me as she nods and sits up to take the teacup from me. We sit in the still room while she sips the tea, and I'm slightly surprised that she didn't put up a fight about it. I'm more stunned at how eerily calm she's being given what has just transpired.

When I learned of my parent's crash, I was anything but quiet. I screamed, cried, and begged the police to tell me that it wasn't true. My sorrow didn't seem to end for the months that followed when I stayed with my friend and his family in Kensington. I would cry myself to sleep and wake up with a heavy heart. Acceptance didn't come easily to me, yet here, Nova holds herself up with no strife crossing her face. I'll never quite figure her out; she's nothing like me.

If only I could get into her head right now and figure out what she's thinking. Part of me knows that wishing for that wouldn't help her at all. There isn't a right way to comfort someone, and every person deals with grief in their own way. Being empathetic like me is a bad trait to have in times like this. I need to be there for her, but at the same time I want to run back to the square and get revenge for my fallen leader.

Chapter 29

The last drop of tea makes its way down her throat as I see her force it down. She hands the teacup back to me before pulling her light-colored hair behind her and twisting it into a bun that sits low on her head.

"Santiago?" She asks, and my ears immediately perk up at the mention of my name.

"Yes, Nova?"

"Where am I?" She asks in a raspy voice, and I feel slightly relieved to hear her asking a question simply about her surroundings.

"In my apartment." She looks at me with her brows furrowed in confusion. "I didn't know where else to take you once you fainted."

"How did you get me here?"

"I carried you." I shrug as if it's nothing, as if I'm not incredibly impressed with myself as well. Her eyes get wide in astonishment, and I nod at her to confirm that this is bewildering.

"Are you okay? Do your arms hurt?" She asks, looking concerned. I wonder what I did to deserve a friend like her, who is worried about my arms when she's going through something so traumatic.

"You're as light as a feather, my dear. I didn't have any issues," I say, and she lets a relieved sigh escape from her lips.

"I shouldn't have fainted," she says, sitting up straighter, her voice cracking. "I promised him that if this ever happened. I would be strong."

"You can grieve for someone and still be strong." I reach my hand out to rest over hers, and her long eyelashes lift to reveal her familiar hazel eyes.

She lingers on my words, as if she's considering them and whether they're true. She looks down at our hands and a few tears fall from her eyes again. She raises her head and nods to me before letting her hair back down, as if unsatisfied with the bun she had it twisted into.

"I will mourn him later," she says as she throws the thick blanket off and stands up from the bed. She smooths out her light blue dress before she rushes over to the door of my apartment. "I won't be able to grieve properly until I do something."

"Where are you going?" I ask, and she turns towards me with determination in her eyes.

"I'm going to start a revolution." She reaches her hand out to me. "Care to join me?"

I stride towards her and take the outstretched hand in mine, squeezing it to show her support. Looking at Nova's trembling hand, untied shoelaces, and tear-stained cheeks, I've never been more sure that she's the only person who can take down the system. This is why there's no hesitation in my voice when I tell her, "Always."

CHAPTER
30

Hart

I've never been to a funeral before, not a real one anyway. I went to a memorial service once for my great aunt Hye-jin, and one of her last wishes was that everyone wear pink to celebrate her life instead of mourning her death. She lived a full life and died peacefully in her sleep. People did cry, but they also felt happy knowing she had spent a long time on earth. The current death I'm facing is absolutely nothing like that, and I'm not prepared for this funeral whatsoever.

David was the one to inform Violetta and me of Othello's passing. He tried to avoid telling us the details of his execution. He told us in broken sentences that Othello was brave up until the very end. Even with his last breath, he still tried to let the people of the Teorrain know that they would rise above. Each word that came out of David's mouth punctured a new hole in my chest, and I was left there with a hollow feeling in my heart when he stopped speaking.

Violetta fell against me as soon as she heard the news. Even I felt the breath stolen from my very being, knocked out by the invisible force named desolation. A man's life had just ended because he tried to help us. I feel like his blood is on my hands.

A Crossed man died trying to save me. He died trying to save a Pravi.

While I lay here in this cot almost an entire day later, I'm still not able to comprehend the reality around me. Violetta's head stays quivering against my chest as she weeps for the freedom Othello will never get to see. If there was any hope in my mind that they wouldn't kill Violetta when we are found, it was murdered in that square along with our great leader.

Sleep didn't hesitate to flee from me last night, and I spent the whole morning looking around Othello's room. I might not have known him long, but he had a huge impact on me. These last few days have felt like years, and Othello's impression on me can't be measured in time. He was upright and so sure of himself. Sure, he essentially forced me to tell Violetta about my identity, but I had that coming. He cared about people and fought for me to be part of the rebellion.

While wandering around his room, I found a notebook with the plans he had for the Vermillion, and most of them weren't even about starting a revolt just yet. He had planned to grow the gang and create a sense of hope within the community. He didn't want anyone to feel alone. Seeing this written out on paper only grows my sense of emptiness; now he will never be able to see this through.

I feel odd wearing his clothes now, but part of me feels like he would want me to keep them on, since he deeply hated my style. So, this morning I placed the red bandana under the hair that sweeps across my forehead and tied it tight at the back of my head. I will wear this from today on with pride, to show Othello the respect he deserves.

"It doesn't feel real," I hear Violetta's soft voice say to my right. "I keep thinking this is just some horrible nightmare."

"They say that denial is the first stage of grief." I say under my breath.

"We barely knew him, but somehow I feel as if a part of me died," she whispers.

"It's not the length of how long you knew someone, it's the impact they had on you." I try to validate her feelings; they remind me of my own. "He died while trying to help us, and he was the boyfriend of your best friend. He was important."

"I just wish he would've never gone."

"Thinking of 'what if' situations will be our eventual downfall. We have to grieve in a healthy way." I put an arm around her shoulders and pull her close to me. She cries into my chest again, and I feel her tears seep into my shirt. My hand goes up to her hair and I begin to stroke it lightly. Words aren't going to help her now, and I know because they won't even help me.

She stops crying after a while, and by then it's time to face the despair that awaits us in the meeting room. Violetta joins me in silence as we walk down the empty hall. There's an unfamiliar feeling to it, since a stranger is leading us down the hall instead of David. He has been busy arranging for this funeral since he learned the news himself. The man opens the door for us, and the usual bright lighting of the meeting room is replaced with a dim glow. To my astonishment, there are lit candles all around the room.

There's no picture of Othello, but every single member of the Vermillion is sitting in front of Nova, who stands there with her eyes closed. Her hands are wrapped around a red candle that slightly illuminates her exhausted features. The dark blonde locks which she usually tames in some way are completely free. Her hair hangs just above the black dress she's wearing, which flares out at her waist and cuts off just above the knee.

Violetta and I take a seat near the front of the room. We both want to be close to Nova to support her emotionally just in case she needs it. That may be a hopeful thought on our part, though. We have barely seen Violetta's roommate ever since she told us of his capture and quickly ran out of the church to watch his trial. She came back late last night, and immediately asked for David to help her with preparations for his funeral, which she wanted to have as soon as possible. She told us briefly that she doesn't blame us, and that she's going to be okay. I can't help but find her attitude odd, considering what she witnessed.

I'm wondering how she will choose to conduct this funeral. It could be in the way I've seen movies portray them, with all the emotional moments and testimonials. I'm not sure what I would say about him, or even if I should. After all, I'm the one at fault for his unfortunate demise.

Nova clears her throat before slowly opening her eyes and surveying the crowd sitting before her. She holds the candle in place close to her chest and grips it like she's holding on for dear life.

"Othello wasn't just a leader to us." She hesitates for a moment before continuing. "He was a friend, comrade, and head of our family. He would've done anything to protect us, and he did up until his death." She chokes on the word "death" as if it causes her physical pain. I see her eyes flick to the left of the room where Santiago is sitting, and he silently mouths something at her, to which she nods back at him.

"Othello's last words were: The Crossed Will Rise," Nova says after sucking in a breath and looking into the flame she holds. "He had so many ideas of how to gather our people and make us strong enough to defeat the unfair conditions we've succumbed to. He didn't do anything to hurt anyone; he only protested the government by having us rely on each other.

Did the mixed blood running through his veins mean that he deserved to die so young?"

Many shake their heads and a few people whisper, "No" under their breaths, but most in the room are keeping their heads down while they wipe the tears from their cheeks. Nova stays quiet for a moment, looking down at the candle in her hands like she's preparing for something.

"If we don't rise up now, they will think that they have scared us into staying down. We can't let this frighten us; it should motivate us instead. We need to revolt immediately, before they kill more of us," she says loudly, and people finally start talking amongst themselves. Voices all around me discuss the matter, and I overhear some arguing that we aren't in the right state of mind to be making any decisions like this. They become overwhelming, and the sound drowns out my own booming thoughts. I feel Violetta slip her hand in mine, as if she could feel me tensing up.

David then rises and walks from the back of the room to join Nova and stand before the people.

"We need to do something! They can't kill our leader and get away with it!" David's voice echoes like thunder. "This is the perfect time to take action—they won't be expecting it."

"If you think you're safe by not revolting, you're wrong. We are all sitting ducks," Nova says, and this seems to strike fear into the people's hearts. "If Othello was caught, then any of us could be next very soon. The Crossed are dying out, just like they want, and it's not long before we are an extinct people."

"We will continue to be killed by them, in one way or another, unless we decide to fight back for once. This is so much bigger than us. We must do this for the other Teorrains out there, and the future generations of Crossed who fear for their lives." Santiago speaks up now to support Nova, and she looks at him with gratefulness in her eyes.

I examine the diverse faces around me, and they've become captivated by the things being said. More of them begin to silently nod in agreement as the discussion continues. Nova knew exactly what to say to move them from feeling hesitant to being on board with her plans.

"Othello told me of the dreams he had, where the Crossed would be unified enough to march together beside the walls until the government was forced to give us better living conditions. He even thought we could end this," David says with watery eyes. "Let's take action instead of mourning. It's what Othello wanted for us, to live a better life than he did. Let's grieve his death properly once we are free."

"Let's allow them to hear our outrage!" Santiago rises too, and joins them to stand beside Nova, whose lips are now pressed together firmly.

"We will force them to notice us!" Nova yells, and the whole room begins to clap in agreement with her. Several people shout in support, hollering out hope for the future. This is not how I thought this funeral would go, but I know Othello is looking down on us with pride. Tears can only do so much. We can celebrate his life by fulfilling his only wish for the Crossed people.

Tears fill Nova's eyes as she lifts one fist in the air and screams, "For Othello!"

The people don't hesitate to join her, and we all punch a fist in the air to show solidarity. The commotion settles down after a few minutes, and many are still crying. I look over at Violetta, who is laughing through tears of her own at the beautiful sight of these people rallying together. It's truly empowering, and I'm in awe that I get to be a part of it.

"What do you all say we officially make Nova Alejo our new leader?" The room cheers in agreement with David's suggestion. Nova looks to Violetta with eyes that are filled with a mixture of pain and joy, and a smile forms on her face.

David walks to the back room and grabs a poorly-bound book before marching back to the front of the room where Nova stands. Everyone settles down as the room gets extremely serious, and all eyes are on Nova and David.

"Can all those appointed as officers please stand?" At these words, several people around the room, young and old, get up from their places and walk to the front of the room. One of them is a woman with grey hair whose clothes look torn and tattered. She takes the book from David in a polite manner before using both of her unstable hands to extend it out towards Nova. Her hands are still on the candle, but she eagerly places one of her palms flat on the book.

The woman smiles at her with sorrow before speaking. "Nova Esther Alejo, do you swear on the Vermillion Code of Unity that you'll do everything in your power to protect our lives?"

"I do," Nova says without hesitation, her voice ringing out loud and clear.

"Do you swear to never betray one of your own kind?" The woman speaks again. "Do you swear that you will lead us fearlessly and courageously?"

"I do." Nova's chest rises and falls slowly, as if with each breath she is reflecting on the seriousness of her commitment.

"And finally, do you swear to put the interests of the Vermillion above your own at any turn?"

"I do."

The woman looks at her with a nod and takes the book away. She passes it back to David carefully before he opens it and gives Nova a red pen. She switches her hands on the candle before confidently signing her name in the book, and then passing the pen around for all the Vermillion to sign. As soon as the last person finishes, David puts the book under his left arm, before using his right to take Nova's hand in his and raise it high above their heads.

"Brothers and sisters of the rebellion, I present to you, Nova Alejo." He looks at her with a wide smile and tears well up in his eyes. "Leader of the Vermillion!" He yells out the last statement, and the crowd cries out their approval. I don't even hear one whisper of disagreement with her new status. The people must know how capable she is, just like Othello did.

Nova leans down slightly to blow out her candle and look around the room one last time. "Get ready for a long night, people. We have a rebellion to plan!"

Several people rush to Nova at these words and embrace her. She welcomes them with open arms. I stand there taking it all in. I only wish I could freeze time in this moment when everyone is full of faith. If I've learned one thing from my studies, it's that the victor writes the history books, and the underdogs like us rarely win in the end.

I guess it's time to discover what side of history we are on, and I may have an idea that'll change the way our story gets told.

CHAPTER
31

Violetta

$\mathcal{N}$ova flips through the pages of Othello's notebook, stopping to touch each one and read it carefully. She's been doing this for several hours, while David has been leading the Vermillion meeting down the hall, allowing her a break. It's been a week since she was sworn in as leader. Since that moment, she's been tirelessly working to plan the perfect time to follow through with the march. Tomorrow is the big day, and she's barely had time to breathe this entire week. It took Hart and me until now to convince her to take some time for herself. Hart is at the meeting, relaying some information that Nova wanted the people to know on this evening, the night before everything changes.

Much to my surprise, she didn't want to spend her last unoccupied hours knitting like she would do back at home. Instead, she insisted on looking through Othello's things, despite my advice that it might only lead to pain. So, trying to be a supportive friend, I'm sitting here on my cot watching various emotions cross her face while she reads through his unfulfilled plans.

Asking about her past with Othello is a risky move, but I feel like there is some part of her that wants to talk about him. Maybe she'd like to speak about him in a way that isn't morbid, or for the sake of building up righteous anger. This man may have only been in my life for a short while, but he's been part of Nova's for years. I want to help her cope and learn more about him in the process. Not to mention, she's been silent for a long time and that can't be good.

"Nova, how'd you fall for Othello?" I muster up the courage to politely ask.

She glances up from the notebook but doesn't look towards me. A look of concentration fades from her face into one of peaceful recognition. There's a small smile that tugs at the corner of her mouth and she looks at me with wistfulness in her eyes: the kind only nostalgia can bring.

"A boy named Kace came into the Donation Center one day for a can of chickpeas. When I handed them to him, he told me that he liked my smile." Nova giggles a bit, closing the notebook in her hands and placing it on his makeshift desk. "After the fourth time he came in that week, he asked me if I'd like to be his friend. I said no."

"You said no?" I ask in surprise, and she nods at me.

"He said he would come in every day until I agreed to be his friend. Every time he came in, he would try to get to know me by asking questions about my life. After a few days, he had me convinced that he was the one for me. I agreed to being his friend, and more. I had no idea that he was Othello at the time." She sighs as she thinks about her clever boyfriend, and I find myself smiling. "Now, here I am, leader of the Vermillion. Who would've thought?"

"I would've." I mindlessly answer her rhetorical question.

"You could've guessed I'd be leading a gang one day?" She goes to Othello's rack of clothes and looks through it with her back turned towards me.

"Well, no. But, you're the only other person that could lead this rebellion." At this she scoffs, as if she doesn't believe my sincerity. "Nova, you're a natural-born leader. People don't just hear what you say, they really listen. They act on your words because they are powerful. *You* are powerful."

"I'm just the leader because my boyfriend made me second-in-command and then had the audacity to die." She laughs in a sardonic way that echoes painfully off the walls.

"He made you second-in-command *because* of who you are. He fell for you because you're a leader, and he could see that. I'm sure of it," I say, and her hand lingers on one of his jackets before she turns back towards me. "The Vermillion hasn't ever done anything like this, but the people are more than ready now. You did that, and no one else could've."

Maybe I've said too much and hurt her in some way, but I want to help her see herself the way I do. I'm not totally sure how to handle a situation like this; it's brand new to me. All I can do is silently pray for wisdom.

"I don't know how to do this without him," she whispers, looking down to her shoes and hanging her head.

"We were made to heal. You're already doing a great job, and you haven't even noticed," I say confidently.

"I don't want to forget him, Violetta. I don't want to forget how he made me feel or how his laugh sounded." Her sentence drifts off in a cloud of emotion.

"Healing doesn't mean forgetting. If you get cut by a knife, it'll heal over, but the scar will remain there as a reminder of what you went through. Time will ease the pain of this, but you'll always have that beautiful scar that you can look on fondly."

She raises her head to reveal glossy eyes and a smile on her face. "I hope my scar looks as cool as the one on Othello's eyebrow."

At that statement we stare at each other for a moment and then burst out laughing in unison. We never could take a situation seriously, and even though Nova is all for having deep talks on occasion, she likes to keep the humor alive. It's one of my favorite things about her; she's a girl that never lets anything truly hurt her. She's a warrior with armor made of silk and steel, so sweet yet so strong. I hope that one day I can be as unshakable as her, but for now, I'm still petrified about what tomorrow may bring.

"Alright, now that we have gotten the sad stuff out of the way, I have a real question," she says after our laughter dies down. "Why Hart? Even if you take away the fact that he's supposed to be our sworn enemy, he seems like the complete opposite of you."

"You can say that again." I chuckle under my breath and run a hand over my hair. "I was incredibly mad at myself when I started caring about him, but he proved to me that he was someone worth taking a chance on."

She crosses her arms and tilts her head. "How did he manage to do that?"

"Get comfortable, Nova." I pat the space on the cot next to me. "This could take a while."

We sit here for a long time as I tell her the long-overdue story of how one night, a couple of Pravis broke into the basement. I explain the momentary lapse in judgment that led to our months of lessons, and how I'd fallen for him without even having knowledge of it. She gasps when I tell her about our fight but smiles wide when I get to the part where he said he loved me. I end the story with a sigh, remembering how he held me like he was afraid I would evaporate into thin air any second.

"I wanted to tell you so badly; you have to believe me about that," I say.

"I kept a huge secret from you too, so I understand," she says and then chuckles a bit. "I still can't believe he's a Pravi."

"Love isn't biased, Nova. It doesn't see blood when it chooses someone." I pause and then decide to ask her the obvious question that's lingering in the room. "Are you still mad that I fell for a Pravi?"

"It's just hard for me to accept fully," she says, and my hopeful expression flickers into one of disappointment. "Until then, I'll just work to know him better, because your love story *is* really sweet."

I let out a relieved breath at her words and continue, "All these preconceived notions I had about him were completely false; he's really so loving. I just know that he was destined for me all along."

"What makes you so sure?" Nova asks out of curiosity.

"Before I even knew him, I would see flashes of these light brown eyes in my mind. I thought they were hallucinations haunting me, but it turns out it was just a sign of what to look out for." I reach over and squeeze her hand lightly. "I never believed in a destiny so lovely until I knew him."

Nova smiles back at me, but I can tell she's thinking about something worrisome.

"What is it?" I ask.

"Even though it's a peaceful march, they could kill you and Hart if they recognize you. Do you understand the gravity of that consequence?" She squeezes my hand back.

"I'm willing to take the risk for what I believe in. So is Hart," I say without hesitation in my voice, although I feel it slightly in my heart.

"You've changed a lot, Violetta," Nova says.

"What do you mean by that?"

"You're sure of yourself now, more firm in what you want, and braver than anyone I've ever seen." She lets go of my hand and stands up again, fixing the fabric at the end of her dress.

"Likewise," I say, smiling up at her.

Just then, Hart knocks lightly and opens the door to the room. His expression lights up at the sight of us, a stark contrast to the tired posture he stands with. He greets both of us before Nova looks down at her watch and shakes her head at how late it's gotten. She tells us she must return to her apartment so she doesn't raise suspicion, and that she will be back tomorrow for the march. We bid her goodbye and she rushes out in a hurry, forgetting to do much else other than nod at us. Hart comes to sit on the floor at my feet, looking at me with a raised eyebrow.

"So, what did you two discuss while I was gone?" He asks coyly.

"We were talking about you." I say, technically not lying, because we did indeed talk about him at one point.

He crosses his legs and sits up straighter. "What about me?"

"I was just telling Nova how annoying I found you when we first met," I say in a teasing tone.

"Annoying?" He asks with a hurt face, as he puts his hand on his chest in sarcastic bewilderment. "No, I refuse to believe that. You loved me at first sight."

"Maybe that's how it was for you, but I just found you conceited," I say, flicking my long curls behind my shoulder.

"At least now you know I'm not," he says.

"Do I?" I joke, and he narrows his eyes at me.

"You drive me crazy, Violetta," he says with a short, breathy laugh, and I reach my hand out for him to hold. He interlocks his fingers with mine, and his long sleeve slips back enough for me to notice something shiny peeking out from under it.

"Look at that!" I exclaim, and he looks at our wrists, which are adorned with matching silver bands. "It's so odd to think that our parents had identical bracelets and passed them down to us."

"I wonder how popular this style was, for them to both have had one." He examines our wrists closely and watches the bracelets shimmer. "There must be a bunch of people out there with the same accessory."

I shrug. "Maybe it's just us."

"Maybe it's just destiny." He glances up at me and runs a thumb over the back of my hand. "Like how I saw your eyes in my dreams before I even met you."

My mouth hangs open for a second. "The same thing happened to me! I thought I was losing my mind!"

"You saw me too?" He asks, getting up on his knees so our faces are closer, and I nod at him. "Then we truly must've been meant for one another."

"Not even the Teorrain could stop us," I whisper, and he smirks at me.

"It's lucky I'm the governor's son and could find a way in here."

"Speaking of that," I slowly let go of his hand and let it rest in my lap. "Why does your dad support the Crossed laws?"

Hart stares at the hand I took away. "He just wants an endorsement from the current president for when he runs for the same position. She's a believer in the Crossed laws, but there *are* lots of politicians who hate her for it. There's even talk that some are going to try to pass a bill soon that would revoke the laws."

I think about this momentarily before asking another question. "How do other countries feel about the Crossed laws?"

"It doesn't seem any of them particularly like it, but they are keeping to themselves because President Grey has made everyone believe you all live in a society equal to ours." His eyes fill with frustration and sorrow.

"I wish everyone knew the reality," I say, and he moves up onto the cot next to me. He grabs my hand again and lightly kisses me on the cheek.

"They will one day." He pulls away from me and returns to the floor, where he lays down on a blanket. "Let's get some sleep, we have a long day tomorrow."

I go to turn off the light and then lean down onto my pillow. I can already hear Hart's breathing become slow, and I myself am so close to letting my eyes close for several hours. Before I do, though, I think about what will happen tomorrow. My heart races as I consider the large possibility that we will never come back from this march. The last thought that crosses my mind before slumber is something I hadn't realized before, but also something that makes this all worth it, and puts my heart to rest.

I crave freedom more than I fear death.

CHAPTER
32

Santiago

*T*he day that will go down in infamy has come, and I am not boding well with its arrival. I've spent the last week completely certain of myself and my decision to back Nova in her plans. There was seldom a moment of doubt in my mind. Yet, as I stand here in the meeting room with the rest of the Vermillion on this dreadful morning, I question myself. Was my decision completely based on the rush of adrenaline I felt after seeing my friend killed?

Glancing down at the wine-colored chambray shirt I was told to wear, I cringe inwardly. *Am I going to die in this?* The faces around me seem to be determined and confident, so unlike myself in this moment. There's an image in my head of us all meeting death in a hail of gunfire from the Grey Guards. It makes my blood run cold.

Although I *would* very much like to live, I don't necessarily fear death for myself. My true hesitation is brought on by the thought of those around me getting hurt. I can't imagine a worse fate than watching more of my friends die. I'd be left forever isolated within these walls, with the knowledge that I supported the efforts which sealed their fate.

Whilst my mind races with one daunting thought after the other, I catch Nova eyeing me from across the room. She's walking towards me with a piece of cardboard in her leather-glove-clad hands that has the words, "The Crossed Will Rise" splayed across it in giant red letters.

"Are you alright? You look pale," she says as she approaches me, her words almost drowning in the noise of the crowd around us.

I clear my throat and try to relax my features. "How can that be? I'm rather tan, actually," I say, trying to make light of it. Judging by Nova's solemn expression, my joke isn't well received.

A panicked laugh escapes me as she grabs my forearm, dragging me all the way out of the meeting room. I blindly allow her to lead me, as there's no sense in arguing with her. She opens a door, shoving me inside an awfully cramped room. As she pulls the string above her head, a tiny light bulb illuminates the space around us. There are boxes of gauze, latex gloves, protective face masks, and various medical tools in here. I wasn't aware the Vermillion or the church even had access to supplies like these.

"Nova, I feel very uncomfortable in this enclosed space," I whine as she closes the door, shutting us both into this suffocating, clinical closet.

"Good!" She whirls around towards me with defiance. "We aren't leaving until you tell me what's wrong with you."

"Nothing is the matter with me. Go back out there, we need to leave within the hour." I test out my most convincing voice, but she crosses her arms.

"You're a terrible liar, Santi," Nova says to me, and it's become apparent that confessing is the only option if I want out of this dreaded closet.

"Alright, I'm scared," I say, and her expression softens.

"Of dying?"

"I'm scared of *you* dying," I whisper into the space between us. She breathes out and takes my hand in both of hers, squeezing it tight before speaking.

"I need to do this," she says earnestly, and her hazel eyes glimmer under the light. "But, if something does happen to me, you must carry on. I'm convinced that not even death itself can stop us from meeting again, my friend."

"I'll march by your side until I collapse. But, please don't die," I find myself pleading with her, my voice cracking on the last word.

"I can't make any promises about what's to come." She gives me a response that only a leader would give, not the reassuring one I desired. There's nothing left to say, because I know none of my words could ever sway her to back down from this.

Standing here under the dull glow of the light bulb, we don't speak for several moments. She eventually sighs and releases my hand. "Now that we are alone, I have to ask, are you still upset about Violetta and the Pravi?"

I'm aware Nova is simply trying to steer the conversation away from the rebellion, but she is skilled at the art of distracting me. Moreover, this is one of those times I'm willing to be distracted. My eyebrow raises as I meet her eyes. "Why do you ask?"

"We just haven't had a chance to talk about your feelings since everything happened so quickly." She shrugs, and somehow I find it ludicrous that she cares about my mental state when she is about to lead a revolt.

"I was gutted for a bit, there's no denying that," I say with a small chuckle, and Nova seems to be holding back a laugh as well. "But I've come to realize that it was simply the idea of love that was driving me mad. Violetta is a wonderful friend whom I care for, but she's not the girl that's meant for me."

She eyes me suspiciously as if she doesn't entirely trust my statement. "How can you be so sure?"

"Your roommate walked into my library at a time in my life when I felt hopelessly alone. It was easy to become infatuated with her since we had so much in common." I look down to my shoes and shake my head. "Choosing to be with Violetta wasn't convenient for that Pravi. Still, he gave up everything he's ever known for her because their love runs so deep. My feelings were miniscule in comparison. I'd like to believe that when I truly do fall in love with someone, it'll be with the same might as the love that Hart has for her."

Nova's expression brightens, and she seems impressed by my thoughtful answer. She's not aware that it's only so eloquent because I wrote those exact words in my journal earlier, but I'll let her think I came up with it on the spot.

She crosses her arms. "You're pretty smart for your age; most boys wouldn't be able to figure that out."

"The Teorrain must've forced me to mature faster," I say absentmindedly.

"I don't think these walls had a hand in it. You're just a caring friend, and you see that Hart makes her happy." I smile at her, grateful for the compliment.

"You must see it, too," I say while pulling my left sleeve down a bit.

"I think they're both crazy." She puts her hands on her hips as she exhales before continuing. "But then again, so am I."

"Aren't we all?" I ask, and we both begin to laugh.

"At least we are the brave kind of crazy," she says with a lighthearted air in her voice, but I flinch as I'm reminded of what we are about to do. She sees my reaction and steps towards me with sympathetic eyes. "We are going to live to see those walls come down, Santiago."

"Let's march then," I say, with doubt still brewing in my gut.

Her eyes swell with pride and she reaches a firm hand out to me. I straighten in slight surprise at the gesture but extend mine in the same way. We shake hands in solidarity before she pulls on the string once again to turn the light off. Opening the door to the hallway, she strides out first with confidence in her step. Once again, I don't delay falling in step behind my valiant leader.

The walk to the meeting room is silent. When we reach our destination, she turns to reveal that friendly smile that I've grown so fond of. I pray she never stops smiling, and that nothing takes her strength. I smile back at her, and then she turns to the room of Vermillion members, who wait expectantly for her to speak.

"My brothers and sisters, today we take fate into our own hands. It's now or never!" She exclaims. Everyone begins hollering with enthusiasm. In case it's my last chance, I look around to savor this moment. The faces of these people are determined and filled with faith in this rebellion.

Hart, Violetta, and David rush forward to where Nova stands by the door. Hart and Violetta's hands seem almost glued together, and David holds a sign in his hand similar to many of the Vermillion's. We glance at one another warmly as Nova opens the door and leads the entirety of her rebellion down the hallway.

Once we reach the stairs, she steps back and gestures for me to lead the way. I climb the ladder, noticing Hart is not far behind me. The panel at the top opens and the director of the church is there to help me up. After safely emerging, I turn to reach for Hart's arm and safely pull him up as well.

One by one, the people of the Vermillion crawl out after us while the director stands as a lookout by the door. Violetta lingers near Hart, anxiously waiting for her best friend to join her. Nova climbs the ladder last, and I reach my arm out for her. She gladly accepts, and her hand lingers in mine once she is standing. I nod to her supportively.

Nova takes her place at the front of the crowd and begins to lead the Vermillion as we follow her out of the church—all sixty-five of us wearing our finest red and black clothing. Several of the people we pass as we make our way to the main road holler after us anxiously, asking where we came from and what we are doing. Someone even threatens to call the authorities. Nova doesn't look back at them, so neither do we.

The early-morning sunlight hits our eyes, and we officially begin our march. The whispering and gawking of our people was expected, but at least we haven't been spotted by the Grey Guards just yet. None of us let out a peep; we aren't here to yell or scream, we are only here to silently protest our harsh treatment. Throughout history, I know there have been few wars won with peace, but Nova isn't the type to condone violence. It would prove to them that we are the savages they think we are.

I hear many voices as we continue to march, those of concerned people begging us to retreat for our lives, and those who are spurring us on in support. An old man walks over and joins the back of the group and a girl hands him the other side of her sign, so they can hold it together.

The day wears on like this and we march along the walls for hours. Many people join us, and many come to gawk. Sweat drips down the side of my face, and Nova's exhaustion begins to show through her determined expression. Hart and Violetta have yet to let go of each other's hands, but I'm fearful of what will happen to them specifically when this all goes downhill.

The sun is blazing bright as we enter the afternoon, and I'm quite surprised by how many have joined us. We never even had to say anything, they just fell in line and continue to do so. There must be at least a couple hundred of us presently. As I inspect the faces behind me, it's becoming difficult to find my friends in the growing multitude. On our fourth time around the Teorrain, Nova stops abruptly. She's holding a hand up, signaling for the people to listen.

"I propose we go into the marketplace before circling again." Her voice rings out loud and clear.

"No need for that, Miss Alejo," says a loud voice, and the group collectively turns toward the sound to see a handful of Grey Guards watching us, each one fully armed. The voice came from the woman standing at the front, and I recognize her as the Grey Guard who questioned me last week in the library. She eyes me with a knowing stare before turning her attention back to Nova. "We have come to make a deal with you." The officer speaking is wearing several silver medals, unlike the other Grey Guards, leaving me to believe she holds the highest rank among them. Her lips are pressed against a handheld, circular device that amplifies her voice. The crowd stays quiet, watching Nova and waiting for her response.

"What kind of deal?"

"The entire Vermillion will be granted immunity for their reckless behavior today, no harm coming to any of you." The Grey Guard's eyes, which oddly resemble Nova's own hazel irises, search the crowd until they land on two people in particular. "But, Hart Kang and Violetta Akan must be surrendered to us."

A chill runs down my spine, but the gasps which I expect to come from the crowd never meet my ears. Dead silence resumes, and Nova turns to Hart and Violetta, who wordlessly plead with her. She shifts towards the Grey Guard again. "We are marching for justice, not to be granted immunity from crimes we did not commit. You will not take any Vermillion members while I still breathe, whether they be Pravi or Crossed."

The officer's features relax momentarily, almost like she's relieved by Nova's opposition. Perhaps she has been waiting to attack us, and Nova just gave her a fantastic reason. She speaks into the small disc again. "Miss Alejo, this is the best offer you will receive. Are you sure of your decision?"

"I won't let them see the same fate as Othello." Nova grabs one of my hands and another Vermillion member grabs the other. I notice Ryan urging people to stand in front of Hart and Violetta, like a shield. Soon all of us are standing before the Grey Guards, hands interlocked together in resistance. "Do your worst."

The Guards begin to raise their weapons at us, and I look to Nova one last time. She stares at her people with a tight-lipped smile, trying to memorize the beauty of their resistance. I gaze up at the sky and it's strikingly blue, without a cloud in sight. It's too beautiful of a day to die. I continue to peer upwards, awaiting the sound of war. It doesn't come.

Instead, when I hesitantly open my eyes to peek at the scene before me, the Grey Guard at the front is raising her palm to the Guards behind her. "Hold your fire."

"Captain Katerina, what are you doing?" A Grey Guard to the right of her asks.

"I must consult the governor before we proceed with any plans," she says hesitantly, her voice sounding less aggressive than earlier.

She nods to the Guards and they fall back in line, parading away reluctantly. Captain Katerina trails behind them, glancing over her shoulder at us briefly with a ghostly smile that makes me feel that this is far from over. We stay in place, holding hands until they are out of our eyesight. Nova stands before the crowd with a comically big grin that is completely unexpected coming from someone who almost died a few minutes ago.

She addresses us happily. "They are scared! We are close to getting what we want, brothers and sisters. Let us continue in our march until they have no choice but to give into our demands."

The people in the crowd shout in agreement, and I follow her lead as she turns back around. As my feet carry on through the forming blisters, I feel my soul cry out in thankfulness that we are alive. There is much to worry about, but it's thrilling that we've made it this far. The Crossed are joining us by the dozens as we circle the wall again, singing an anthem of those longing for deliverance. The Grey Guards are so frightened by us that they are going to consult the governor of Geal about the matter. I don't know anything about the governor, but I pray he has mercy on us when they tell him of our bravery.

The light of day is slowly fading to the west, and the Grey Guards haven't come to arrest us yet. We have persevered. At the head of the pack, I've stayed in step with Nova so she has support should she require it. Hart and Violetta have stayed near the back of the group, welcoming new Crossed into the protest. As Julia offers me water from her bag, I notice Hart is carrying on his back a young boy with no shoes. The boy speaks to Hart, making him laugh, and the sight dares me to have hope for a new world.

Though the exhaustion of walking all through the day has caused several of us to become a bit somber, we continue to heed Nova's orders. She has halted several times to rally more citizens with her commanding speeches in the Marketplace Square. The Grey Guards still do not intervene. They have simply observed as she single-handedly rallies hundreds.

The night has met us and Hart trudges to the front next to me. He turns on a light on his watch that shines brightly and gives it to Nova. She briefly thanks him and uses it to guide us on the correct path. This is our seventh time circling the wall, and when the Grey Guard tower comes into view at the entrance, I'm nearly ready to collapse. In my state of exhaustion, it takes me too long to notice Nova has stopped in her tracks. I'm not comforted by the sharp intake of breath that comes from her, and reluctantly I take the wire-framed glasses from my pocket. Placing them on my face, I can clearly see the reason we aren't moving forward towards the entrance.

Dozens of white uniforms are standing in lines, forming an army large enough to rival our own. However, they carry weapons, whilst we are armed only with cardboard signs. Fretful whispers from the Vermillion flood my ears, but only a handful run in the opposite direction. Nova keeps her head high, but she knows the truth.

We marched ourselves right into their elaborate trap.

CHAPTER
33

Hart

I'm not sure how I didn't see this one coming. The Grey Guards stand with their guns pointed towards us, their faces emotionless as they stare us down. It reminds me of one of those old movies about the Wild West that my history professor made us watch last semester. Usually the person who drew their gun first was deemed the winner, because they were the only survivor. If this is a similar situation, we don't have a fair chance to draw our gun. We don't even have guns.

The boy I've been carrying on my back, Russell, has been insistently asking me why we've stopped. I place him on the dirt below us, urging him to run without looking back. He seems suspicious, but nods in understanding once Violetta whispers something in his ear. With a quick hug, Russell sprints off to the darkness far from here.

We stand there observing the Guards who threaten our lives, and they make no move towards us. Bright lights from the tower abruptly shine down on us and the entire area around them. Every detail of their blinding uniforms is illuminated. Our own tired faces and worn out clothes are visible to them, too. The lights have made it plain to see that they have killer machines, while we have only our determination. On a positive note, I can now see that we outnumber them. They survey us from only a few yards away, and instead of drawing their weapons first, they step back methodically. They are creating a path for someone to walk to the front of the wall of Guards.

A figure comes into view and advances toward us. Her hair is colored silver and pinned back into a low bun that sits just above her shoulders. Her pantsuit is white and gold pinstriped, the signature colors of this spring season. The wrinkles on her skin are nowhere near her eyes or mouth. She looks as though she's never smiled a day in her life. As surprised as I was by this outrageous display of officers, settling my gaze upon her face sends me into shock.

President Grey.

When she ran for president her platform included many enticing things, which is why she won by a landslide—the most promising of which was her vow to make sure the Crossed people were comfortable in the Teorrain and treated just the same as us. She eased the people's minds by ensuring that she would personally see The Crossed were given equal opportunities. Her way of speaking is like Othello or my father, a rhythm that spellbinds voters.

Seeing her here sends a desolate feeling to the pit of my stomach. I've had few interactions with the woman, and while they have been cordial, they were enough to tell me that she is a fraud. President Grey puts on a face for the public and hides who she truly is. Anyone who would let this type of injustice occur is not trustworthy. Nonetheless, her presence means that the government views the Vermillion as a real threat. We have them right where we want them.

The wretched sound of President Grey's heels are in earshot now as she approaches. A small unit of Grey Guards like the one we encountered earlier in the day stand behind her. Her stare is fixed on Nova, who stands in front of us with Santiago beside her. She sizes up both of them and peers at the group with displeased eyes. While these people may not know who my father is, they surely know that this is their current primary oppressor. Several cower in fear, but Nova keeps a calm exterior.

"People of Teorrain #14, can I ask why exactly you're out here marching all day?" President Grey loudly addresses everyone, though she keeps her glare locked on Nova in particular.

Nova nods and firmly states, "We are peacefully protesting our conditions and treatment."

"I can assure you that there's nothing to protest, sweetie," she says in a tone that drips like poisonous nectar. "You are being treated the same way as the citizens outside of the walls. Separate but equal, remember?"

"I was born outside of these walls, and we both know the Crossed are not being treated equally. Our leader, Othello, was ruthlessly murdered just last week without a fair trial. The death penalty hasn't existed since 2043 in any state in America, so why does it in the Teorrain? Because we have equal rights?"

Nova holds her ground with the cold hard facts, and my heart swells with pride when President Grey's face seems to falter a bit at her words. She didn't expect such boldness, but that's what you get when you mess with the leader of the Vermillion.

"You are talking about Kace Basri, the *criminal*, I assume?" President Grey asks confidently, and her eyes narrow at Nova, as if she knows all about their relationship.

"Criminal or not, he did not deserve to die!" Nova is getting louder, and President Grey smirks, knowing she's found a sore spot for her. "Othello only gave us hope."

President Grey crosses her arms over her chest and practically rolls her eyes at Nova's spirit. I can feel my fury getting hotter by the second as the façade our president has kept up for the masses fades away right before my eyes. My grip on Violetta's hand becomes harsh, and she grips mine back just as tightly. I'm convinced that nothing could break our hands apart at this moment.

"Hope of what?" President Grey snarls towards the crowd.

"Hope of being given the same rights as everyone else," Nova says confidently as she continues to keep a safe hold of my watch. "Hope of being free from the Teorrain."

President Grey looks blankly at her for a moment before a low, sickly laugh emerges from her gold-painted lips. The wicked chuckle continues and my arm sneaks around Violetta when I notice she's trembling. She gratefully steps closer to me as we wait for the president to compose herself. She eventually smooths a flyaway hair back into the stiff pile behind her head and shakes her head at Nova.

"While I was on my way over here, I had some time to look into your file. Learning about you made me realize that we aren't so different. Your father is from Puebla City in Mexico, just like my ancestors. It's quite the coincidence, really. But there's one monumental difference between us." President Grey steps towards Nova again, and her Guards follow close behind. "My heritage hasn't been polluted, like yours." At this she smiles again, like she's complimenting herself. The president is met with a stunned silence from Nova for only a beat before she retorts with all her might.

"I'd rather live out my days in this unjust city behind a wall than give up any part of who I am." Nova stands her ground without delay, and places my watch on her wrist before tightening it. "Madam President, you are highly mistaken. The true difference between us is that I am a *real* leader, not a coward who hides behind an abominable law. I will fight for freedom until we are let back into the world."

"That's never going to happen," she says with no remorse, although it's clear from the way her lip twitches that she is agitated by Nova. "You aren't allowed in society for a reason; we can't have you all tainting the rest of America. The people wouldn't stand for it."

"If we just had a chance to prove that the mixing of cultures isn't corrupting them, then—"

Nova is silenced by President Grey holding her hand up in objection, and her eyeline shifts towards me. She stares me straight in the eyes as she walks past Nova, pushing through the crowd until her entire security team is mere feet from us. I've been caught. Before she says anything, her eyes dart between Violetta and me, looking distressed.

"Ah, the infamous Hart Kang. We meet again," she remarks with a trace of frustration in her voice, and almost the whole crowd looks at me perplexed. Specifically, Santiago is gaping at me, while Nova whispers something in his ear. She must've forgotten to tell him, along with the rest of the Vermillion, the news of my status in Geal.

I pull Violetta in closer to me, protectively. "It seems unfortunate circumstances would have it so."

"You've been causing me a lot of trouble. Did you know that?" She asks while wagging a finger at me, and I feel an immense amount of irritation replace my fear as she carefully speaks her next words. "Your father has been so disappointed."

"I could care less about his opinion of me, or yours for that matter." I blurt out my true feelings without filtering them whatsoever; it's my first time letting this happen in front of someone of her status. It feels sensational.

"You pulled quite the stunt, young man." She lets out a defeated breath, as if she is lecturing her own son for a minimal act of disobedience. "Because of you, protesters have been rallying around the nation and causing big trouble. There's even a bill being drawn up to revoke the Crossed laws entirely."

"That is an incredible honor." Squeezing Violetta's shoulder and trying not to look into the bright light, I continue to let myself speak unfiltered. "I'm humbled to hear the people were so moved by our story." Taking a page from my father's book, I don't compromise my ethics, and avoid conflicting tones. President Grey and her Guards see right through my civil performance and appear to be slightly taken aback.

"Hart Kang, I hereby order you to come with me and publicly read the speech my team has prepared at a press conference tomorrow." Grey crosses her arms tightly and I notice the veins in her neck bulging; she's nervous. "You will assure the country that you simply ran away to escape the spotlight for a while, and the rumors started by Ember Choi about your alliance with the Crossed are false."

It just had to be another press conference. The audacity of Grey is far too much to handle, even for me. I sneak a look at Violetta, and she is staring up at me with steady resolve as if she's sure I'll do the right thing. After giving her a quick squeeze, I square my shoulders, turning my eyes back on the deplorable ruler before me. "Never."

Grey appears stupefied by this dishonorable response. "I always assumed you to be an intelligent young man, but I was wrong. You jeopardized the future of your country for an escapade." She sneers at Violetta, and in my peripherals, I notice Nova being physically held back by Santiago.

"I won't lie to my country about this outdated, vicious system." I spit out the last two words.

A sigh leaves President Grey as her expression turns into a disappointed scowl. "If you won't listen to me, perhaps you'll listen to someone more persuasive."

Sweat drips down the side of my face now, and the tone in her voice tells me she's brought the one person that can hurt me. I begin to silently beg that it won't be him, but this wishful thinking gets me nowhere, as the crowd of Guards parts again. My father is walking towards me with a cold expression on his features. He's wearing a black suit and his hair is crisply combed. The wrinkles and dark spots on his face are only barely noticeable under the scorching light, so it's clear his flaws have been covered by our styling team. He must not be too upset with my defiance, since he was well enough to have a fresh powder before confronting me.

He progresses forward and stops beside President Grey, whom he briefly shakes hands with out of courtesy. You'd think they were meeting for a luncheon with this behavior. He doesn't even bother to examine Violetta as President Grey did. Instead, he stares at me with a blank look as though I am not his son, but a man whom he's never encountered. Actually, he would have more warmth for a stranger than he does for me. At least a stranger is a possible vote for him.

"What have you done, my son?" His voice is more brittle than angry, and it throws my mind into a state of perplexity. "Your ancestors worked and sacrificed their whole lives so that you could fulfil your destiny to become a great leader. Yet, you jeopardize it all with this scandal. Does this young lady even know who you are?"

Though I swore to never waver from my new friends, my father's convincing words cause a pain in my chest that makes me feel like I should be apologizing to him. No matter how much my brain tries to tell my heart that it shouldn't care what this man thinks, there's a clear disconnect. My ancestors did fight for years to uphold the Kang legacy, and its ruin will forever be on my hands. But my ancestors did not fight their way to the top in this country for evil to prevail. I believe they'd be proud of me. Even if my father's guilt-ridden lecture causes me pain, it'd be worse pain to turn my back on justice.

Before I can think up a counter response, Violetta moves in front of me and appalls my father with her own reply. "I am aware of who he is, and I love him for all that he *isn't*," she says, and both crowds remain wordless while an air of bewilderment crosses their faces. "He isn't cruel, he isn't cowardly, and he isn't sitting idly by while an entire group of people are locked away without a voice." She takes a pace back so she is right by my side again, and her hand remains in mine. "Frankly sir, he isn't anything like you."

This situation feels like an absolute dream. To hear the most intelligent and good-natured person I've met stand up for me like this is filling me with faith that we can shake them. My father almost stumbles backwards at these words, and President Grey's left eye twitches at Violetta's audacity.

Dad pleads with me in a way I haven't heard since childhood. "Hart, leave with us now. We can cover up this mess and fix the state of the nation. You will learn to love again, son."

"I'm not just doing this for love, Dad." I gesture to all the Vermillion who took me in as their own, watching their fatigued faces stare at me with an abundance of pride. "I'm doing this because I want justice for The Crossed. Even if Violetta left me, I'd still be fighting for their rights. This is my family now, and I won't leave this place until they are free." The crowd behind me applauds and whistles with the little strength they have, while Father stares at me with sorrow in his eyes.

"I hope you know that you've basically just coaxed him into ruining his life, Crossed girl." President Grey moves towards Violetta and bends down slightly to examine her closely.

I defensively step in front of her. "I'd appreciate it if you didn't make accusatory statements towards my girlfriend."

"My *name* is Violetta Akan," she says assertively to me and President Grey. "And I didn't coax him into anything. He saw that you were lying to your country about what happens behind these walls and joined a peaceful protest. What exactly is our crime here?"

President Grey chuckles at Violetta before gesturing to the hundreds of Vermillion members. "Where do I begin? You are part of a rebel group conspiring against the government, you smuggled a notable young man into the Teorrain, and you are shamelessly engaged in an illegal relationship with him! Call me the bad guy all you want, but I'm just following the law," she says with a snort, while my dad stares at the ground, refusing to make eye contact with anyone. Our friends are only feet away, gawking. Santiago has repeatedly been fixing his hair and straightening his shirt while Nova stands still, clutching my watch as if it's her life source. I can't imagine how upsetting it is to hear their president say these things about them.

"If you are truly following the law, then when is my fair trial for these offenses?" Violetta counters, bringing it back to the main reason we are marching in the first place. "I didn't see Othello get one."

"Oh sweetie, life isn't fair." She bends down and gets in Violetta's face, but my girl doesn't budge. "You think I got where I am by going against these laws? No, my biggest funding comes from wealthy people who want the Crossed to become a distant memory. As long as the Crossed disobey me, I have the right to waive a fair trial and give them punishment as I see fit. Every time one of you breaks the law, I am that much closer to getting rid of your kind. Your lack of discipline only benefits me and my investors."

At this statement, the whole crowd begins to gasp and cry out for justice. My father appears devastated, as he focuses on President Grey with wide eyes. *Did he not know about any of this?*

I peek over at my friends, whose faces are flushed with rage. This information we've just heard changes everything. It wasn't just the Grey Guards being brutal, it was the leader of the entire country abusing her power.

The people of the Vermillion are getting louder now, and President Grey holds up four fingers in the air. The Grey

Guards behind her cock their guns in response. The sound is enough to bring everyone into a forced hush. No one makes a single sound or movement, but I refuse to hold it in any longer. "How did you fool an entire country into thinking that you haven't been mistreating anyone in the Teorrains? This can't go on forever; someone is going to expose you for your crimes."

"Who's going to get the word out about their conditions, Hart?" She clicks her tongue and smirks in my direction. "You're coming with us and speaking at the press conference, or your 'family' dies here."

My stomach drops and I look to my father in panic. He is still staring at Grey, absolutely baffled. As much as I was my father's puppet, he is such to the president, and there is nothing he can do. Although this is the end of the story, I'm glad we tried.

Nodding at President Grey hastily, I speak without thinking. "I will do as you say, but you must promise not to hurt any of them for as long as they live."

"I can agree to that." Grey straightens the collar of her suit casually. "It'd be a lot of work to get rid of all these people anyway."

This statement causes Dad's eyeline to shift from Grey to Violetta like he's trying to remember something he has long forgotten. Even the Guard who spoke to us earlier appears to be shaken by the piercing words as she lowers her gun. Violetta is grabbing my arm, though I try to walk forward, preparing myself to leave this place behind. "Please, don't do this," she begs me as our hands separate.

"You're going to do amazing things, Violetta." I barely get the words out before Santiago steps in front of me, putting his hands on my shoulders in a rough manner.

"Hart, if you go along with her plan, all of this would've been for nothing! We will find another way to get around this. Think of the people in the other fourteen Teorrains across the country. The Crossed are so close to being freed!" Santiago shouts at me while shaking my shoulders desperately. His voice is cracking and his glasses are slipping off his face. David is moving toward him, presumably to pull him off me, and though I ask Santiago to step away, he keeps saying things that wound my soul. While he continues to plead with me, in the corner of my eye I catch sight of Grey holding up four fingers to the Grey Guard who had lowered her weapon only moments ago. Glancing over my shoulder, I watch helplessly as she raises her gun once again.

Without thinking, I forcefully push him away from me with all my strength. His face is filled with a quintessential mix of shock and confusion. There's no time to explain what's happening. He can't see what I'm seeing: the gun pointed at his back. Everything happens too fast and too slow all at once. Santiago falls to the ground near David a few feet away from me at the same time as I hear the gunshot. An indescribable force sends me flying backwards, and the lights shining from the Guards' tower burn my eyes.

As I fall to the ground, Violetta rushes to place her hands over my wound. There's terror written on her face, and my blood covers her hands. My father is screaming somewhere in the distance. Pain overwhelms me when I try to steal a glance at the dark red substance staining my shirt, and it crushes all other senses. I try to reach for Violetta, but my arms aren't cooperating with my brain. She's frantically saying something to me, tears streaming down her cheeks, but I can't hear it through the ringing in my ears.

If I had the strength to tell her everything I'd like to, she would know that my heart will forever and always belong to her. She'd be certain that I had no regrets, and I'd do it all over again. She wouldn't be afraid because she'd realize that the Crossed are going to be free from this place.

"I love you, angel," is all I manage to choke out before my vision begins to fade.

She holds me as my body slumps, and I can feel her pressing something to my wound as she cries out. The last thing I see before the world turns white are the hundreds of Crossed people around me rushing forward towards the Grey Guards, and the muted sound of bullets being fired.

Godspeed, Vermillion.

CHAPTER
34

Violetta

A couple of years ago, Nova and I were on a walk back from the marketplace when I tripped and fell onto the rough pavement. My knees and hands were scraped so badly that my skin tore. Nova panicked and dropped the bags she was holding to help me. It took me a while to assure her that I was alright, but she was still worried. Though I acted brave, it still hurt.

When I reached our place, I frantically tried to wash away the sticky blood. It was exasperating, as it seemed that nothing I did could slow the bleeding. It's possible that my mind exaggerated the memory, but it felt like I'd watched myself bleed for hours. I thought I'd never see more blood in my life, but it turns out I was wrong.

I've just learned that a gunshot wound undeniably produces more blood than a few scrapes ever could. Hart's eyes close, and I realize I've got to pull myself together and do something. I wipe away my tears with the back of my blood-stained hand and scream out for David. As I yell out his name into the crowd rushing around me, I check to make certain that Hart is still breathing, continuing to press my hand against his wound. I've read enough medical books to know that I need to stop him from losing more blood.

Please survive this.

"Violetta!" David screams for me and pushes through the people running past us. I motion him over and he looks down at Hart's almost-lifeless body miserably. Hart's father is kneeling on the ground beside me, repeatedly calling his son's name.

"David, help me please," I beg, and he doesn't hesitate to pick Hart up like he weighs nothing.

"We have medical supplies in the church; it's our best shot." He looks to Hart's dad and back to me before turning to run against the crowd. Without hesitation, I run after him like it's my own life on the line.

"Wait!" The governor screams at me over the noise, and I turn with a fierce scowl. "Please let me come with you."

"Why should I trust you?" I scream back furiously.

His eyes are so full of helplessness that I almost feel sorry for him. "They've just shot my *son*. I need to be with him." His voice is unsteady, and his hands are shaking. It's at this point in time that I realize that no matter how terrible his dad might be, he's still Hart's own flesh and blood, and he is as petrified for his life as I am.

"Keep your head down." He nods to me, thanking me with his eyes, which resemble Hart's.

Governor Kang stays at my heels as I rush out from the square. Being aware that there are medical supplies in the church, and possibly someone who knows how to treat Hart, gives me the faintest amount of hope to cling to. The biggest problem is that the church is now miles away from us. As strong as David is, it's going to be a trying task to run the entire way with a full-grown man in his arms. My own lungs are beginning to feel strained from sprinting on this humid night. Time feels as if it's working against us, but if we can push on, Hart has a greater chance of making it.

Just as the hope in my heart is fighting to remain steady, bright lights draw close behind me, casting my shadow's outline onto the pavement. Turning my head while continuing to run, I see a Grey Guard vehicle approaching, and Governor

Kang nowhere to be found. Without thinking, I feel my feet pick up speed, but my pace is no match for the machine. Instead of running me over though, it pulls up next to me with a rolled-down window. The officer who shot Hart and the governor are in the front seats.

"Get in! We are here to help," the officer shouts at me while training her eyes on the road ahead.

"You're the one who shot him!" I scream at her while a feeling of lightheadedness enters my body.

"There's no time to explain, but she's going to help us," Governor Kang shouts back at me with panic filling his voice. "We don't have another option."
He's right that there is no time, and I have no other options. I could continue to run and pray that David makes it to the church, or I could get in this vehicle with my enemies, who might be tricking me. Neither seem like great options, but the latter leaves Hart with the best odds of living.

Reluctantly, I slow down and yell out to David who turns around. He runs towards me without question and helps me gently ease Hart's limp body into the vehicle. We sit in the seats behind him, where I can see Hart's chest steadily rising and falling still. David has yet to say a word, although he appears to be just as baffled as I am.

"Now that we have a minute, can one of you please explain what is happening?" My tone comes out harsher than intended, but it's hard to find the willpower to hold back my frustration.

The Grey Guard glances at me in her mirror. "My name is Katerina Sloan. I'm a friend of Othello's," she says, while reaching up and tucking a flyaway piece of auburn hair behind her ear. "My sister and her husband are in prison because of the Crossed laws, while my nephew was placed in this Teorrain. I spent the past decade working my way up through the Grey Guard program to protect and watch over him. Othello was instrumental in helping me spend time with my nephew, and in return, I gave him information. I only wish I could've prevented his sentence." Her solemn voice comes out with sincerity as she peeks in the mirror again apologetically.

David's mouth is slightly parted in surprise, but I am filled with nothing but rage. She was on our side the entire time, but still shot Hart? This doesn't make any sense. "Why would you try to kill Hart, then?"

"President Grey gave me the order to shoot the Crossed man who was stopping Hart from coming with us, but I was never going to kill him. I purposefully shot towards your friend's side so the bullet would merely scrape him, but when Hart pushed him out of the way, it grazed him instead." Katerina explains, rushing her words. The governor sits up straighter to look at her.

"So he's going to be alright?" Governor Kang stares back at his son now, whose eyes have yet to open.

Katerina nods at him. "I can patch him up with some of the medical supplies in the church. I've been smuggling them in there for years. The Grey Guard program includes necessary wound repair training in case someone is hurt. Seems ironic, given their moral standards," she scoffs.

She finishes speaking just as we pull up in front of the deserted church and parks the vehicle. We exit hastily, and the governor and Katerina rush inside. Following after them,

I keep the door open while David carries Hart from the backseat into the church. The church director is already helping Katerina down into the basement to get the supplies she'll need.

"Here, lay the young man down on the stage; it's carpeted," the director says to David, pointing to the platform where he would normally conduct a service. I sprint up the steps and kneel to aid my friend in gently laying Hart down near the podium stand. David's hands and shirt are stained with blood, but he remains calm, untying the red Vermillion bandana from his head before pressing it against Hart's wound as we wait for instructions.

"Governor Kang and Violetta, go sit in the pews during the procedure." Katerina steps towards us with a large medical bag and a white cloth in hand. "David, hold up this sheet for privacy, and Pastor Evans, aid in handing me tools as I need them," she says in a haste as she hands the sheet to David. I stand and open my mouth to protest—I can't stand the thought of sitting in the pews while she works, but she holds a finger up to me. "Don't argue with me, I need to concentrate, and you will only distract me. This will be very quick if you don't interfere."

Arguments are stuck in my throat while my feet carry me backwards and away from my boyfriend. I stare at Hart as long as possible before David holds the sheet up and he's no longer visible. As much as I want to be by Hart's side, it's obvious that watching the procedure wouldn't help the situation. If I'm genuinely thinking about what Hart would want, I don't think it would be to watch him while he bleeds on the ground. He has far too much pride for that.

Taking a seat in the nearest pew, my eyes continue to fixate on the white sheet and Pastor Evans, who is digging through the medical bag. Katerina said he would be alright, but anxious thoughts are getting the better of me. When I left the scene, hundreds of Crossed people were charging towards the president and the Grey Guards. I don't know what's happened to them. There's no certainty that any of them are alright, including Nova and Santiago. The Grey Guards could even be on their way here to arrest us.

As I bow my head to pray, there's a rustle to the right of me. I glance over and see that Hart's father has a similar look of anguish written across his features as he sits down in the same pew beside me. I'd like to ignore him and pray, but I feel his disoriented stare on me.

"Is there something you need?" I turn to face him with an edge to my question.

He continues to study me. "What did you say your full name was again?"

"Violetta Akan," I say with a raised eyebrow, while placing my hands on my knees to steady myself. The governor's eyes widen with a shudder before his gaze follows my movement and lingers on my wrist.

He reaches a hand over his mouth, looking dismayed. "Can I see your bracelet?"

I'm a bit taken back by his question. This man's son is undergoing a procedure only mere feet away, and he's interested in an accessory? Despite my better judgment, I stretch out my arm. I'm far too tired to argue with this man, who then examines my bracelet for what seems to be an eternity. When he finally looks back up at me, his eyes are wet with tears, and my confusion has reached its pinnacle.

"Your parents... are their names Clara and Kit by any chance?" He asks with a twinge of something like optimism in his voice. A blank stare is the best response I can muster, because I don't understand how Hart's father could possibly know who my parents are. He is running for president next year and my parents were modest farm workers. Has he been investigating my family?

"How do you know their names?" I ask, desperately awaiting a reply.

He ignores my question by asking his own. "Are they safe?"

"They are in prison as far as I know," I say, and he looks away from me for a moment, wiping his cheeks with the back of his hand. "I was taken from them as a small child."

"I'm so sorry to hear that." He speaks with a grief-stricken voice, continuing to gape at my bracelet. "They were close friends of mine; your parents are very good people."

"Wait, you were friends with my parents?" My voice feels somewhere far away, and my brain is struggling to take in this information, on top of everything else that has happened tonight. "Is this why Hart and I have these matching bracelets?"

"The other one was a gift to me from your mother. We were best friends growing up, until she ran away with Kit. I never saw either of them after that," he recounts while I put puzzle pieces together in my mind. There truly aren't words to describe the feeling that's come over me. It's one of both newfound clarity and absolute confoundment.

Hart and I really were destined from the start, just as I'd earlier hypothesized. There really was a reason we'd been seeing visions of each other. History, time, fate, and faith were conspiring to bring us together. My soul was made to find his and correct the mistakes of the past.

Hart's father clears his throat again. "I'm sorry for not supporting you and your people. I was bitter when your parents ran away. I couldn't understand why they would leave me alone with no one, and it caused me to turn away from my beliefs in anger. Blindly, I followed in my own father's footsteps and supported the laws that keep you here." He continues to speak with dread, and his head hangs down in shame. "I wasn't aware of the atrocities President Grey was committing, but this does not excuse my behavior. From now on, I will do everything in my power to bring these walls down."

I think for a long moment and close my eyes. Forgiveness is easier said than done, and it's hard to ignore what Hart's father has been supporting. It could be because I'm not in my right mind, or because he loved my parents, but for some inexplicable reason, I find myself forgiving him. "Promise me to admit to the country that you were wrong, and that you'll never turn your back on us again."

His eyes broaden, and he nods earnestly, without hesitation. He seems to be genuinely thankful that I am willing to move forward. This man could help me see my parents again, and that is worth swallowing any feelings of resentment for now— and Hart will be happy to hear that his father has changed his tune.

"I've finished, and he's waking up!" Katerina calls, before David folds up the sheet in his hands. Pastor Evans is helping

Hart swallow a small cup of water, while Katerina wipes her arms off with a dark cloth.

Governor Kang and I rush to the stage, where we sit beside Hart on the carpet. "Hart, can you hear me?" I ask, trying to see if he is fully aware. I remember some of the books I've read, in which the main character's love interest ends up developing amnesia from an injury. If Hart didn't remember me, I'd be beside myself.

He says nothing as he finishes drinking the water being given to him before he allows himself to fall back against the carpet again.

"Are we in the church?" He groans with a hoarse voice, observing the stained glass windows above him.

I grab his hand before answering, "Yes, and you're going to be okay; the bullet only grazed your side." His eye twitches as he's reminded of the pain, and he looks down to the medical gauze wrapped carefully around his body.

"I must've fainted when I saw the blood," he says weakly, and I push his hair back, placing a kiss on his forehead. He squeezes my hand with what little strength he has. "How did we get here?"

"Your father and a Grey Guard drove us here to help you," I say, and Hart looks away from me finally to see his father and Katerina watching him closely. He doesn't speak, but instead looks back to me with panic.

There is a quiet tension in the room before his dad begins to talk. "I'm so sorry for what I've done, and I'm going to spend the rest of my life trying to make it up to you, Hart. Even if it costs me everything."

Hart flinches in surprise at his father's bold statement, before immediately howling, as he realizes how much pain he is still in. "I'm speechless," he says after a moment, attempting a small smile at his dad, who lets out a sigh of relief. "How long was I out, again?"

At this, I start to laugh, which I didn't know was possible in the current circumstance. My body is sore and weary, my mind even more so. Yet somehow, I join in as everyone indulges in a small chuckle at Hart.

"We have a lot to tell you," I say, with a smile at David. He reciprocates with a warm grin, and Governor Kang reaches into his blazer and pulls out a small triangular device, which is lit up on one side.

His brows furrow at the device. "I've gotten thousands of messages and missed calls within the last hour." Apologetically excusing himself, he walks off the stage with the device pressed against his ear.

Just then, Nova bursts into the church with Santiago behind her. "They retreated!" She screams out in triumph and runs to the stage with sweat dripping down her neck. "Our plan worked! The livestream was successful."

Hart begins to laugh mischievously. "I knew it! Thank you for trusting me," he says to Nova as she hands him back the watch he'd loaned her earlier.

"Wait," I say, looking back and forth between them and their ridiculously large grins. "What is going on?"

Santiago catches up to her and looks at me. "Nova filmed the entire interaction with President Grey through the camera on Hart's watch, and had it broadcast through Governor

Kang's website. They just exposed the truth to the entire world," he says, through heavy breathing and foggy glasses. "Everyone beyond the walls just witnessed our rebellion."

My gaze quickly turns to Hart, who is laying on the carpet with his hand in mine, with the broadest smile I've ever seen on his face. The questions in my head won't stop piling up, because I can hardly comprehend anything that is happening. Looking at each person in this room, whose faces reflect the same delighted revelation, I let my own mouth hang open in surprise. Does this mean... we won?

Hart peers into my eyes with enthusiasm. "It seems I have a lot to tell you, too."

EPILOGUE

Hart

"*A*ll of this is making me feel quite uncomfortable, Hart," Santiago says to me as my hair stylist puts her finishing touches on his newly-trimmed hair. I roll my eyes at him, because it's the fourth time he's made a comment like this today. It took weeks of convincing to get him here. "I'm not used to this level of pampering."

"It was Violetta's wish that I personally style you for her party." That isn't exactly what she said, but she *did* mention that Santiago needed to loosen up.

He hesitates, before nodding and allowing my stylist to blow dry his hair. Watching from across the room, I don't see him relax much. Santiago is the only one of our friends who has yet to adapt to life outside the Teorrain.

It's been three months since our rebellion turned the world upside-down. That means that since their release, Santiago, Nova, Violetta, and David have had two months and twenty-four days to become well acquainted with their new home outside the walls. The government worked quickly to free the Crossed once everyone saw the livestream of the rebellion. People flooded the streets in protest, and the demand for justice across the world became too much for the oppressors to ignore.

A law was passed to abolish the Crossed laws once and for all within days of the Vermillion's march. My father became instrumental in implementing a nationwide plan to assimilate the Crossed people into our cities. His large budget went towards finding them homes, releasing convicted interracial couples from prison, and finding them jobs. President Grey was rightfully dethroned, and my father will be running for her position in the upcoming election. For once, I actually think this could be a good thing.

My parents were quick to agree that my friends and their families could stay with us for as long as they'd like. Our large estate with its several guest houses came in handy. Things have been going great, and I've felt joyful to show my friends the world they'd been deprived of. We have been trying different cuisines, going out to explore the city, and meeting up every evening to watch movies together. Besides Santiago, they've all settled in nicely.

My nervous British friend, who chose to reside in the small room down the hall from me, is stuck in his ways. He has kept his old clothes, and has not budged whatsoever on the routine he kept in the Teorrain. Things must change, though, because he's been accepted to study at my university in the fall and Violetta fears he won't fit in if he doesn't come out of his shell.

Violetta's birthday party tonight was the perfect excuse to clean him up and prove to him that being given nice things won't change his character. I've spent the day putting him through the works. My styling team gave him a fresh shave, haircut, and even buffed his nails. He's been flustered by the attention, but I had my staff keep him well equipped with turmeric tea to ease his nerves.

My stylist spins him towards a mirror before placing his glasses back on his face so he can see the transformation. "What do you think?"

He stares at his reflection and seems to be at a loss for words. I told the stylists to just spiff him up, and not to change how he looks too much. While I barely see a difference in his appearance, he seems to be shaken at the sight of his slightly shorter hair and powdered skin. "I look so posh!" He says with a grin, and the hairdresser looks at me, slightly confused by his reaction. I give her a thumbs up and she smiles back at my affirmation.

"See? Not all change is bad." I cross the room to him and face my styling team. "Thank you for your hard work. Please do grab a complimentary snack on the way out for your travels home."

The team leaves us with their cheery goodbyes as they hurry out of my room. Santiago is still marveling at himself in the large mirror when I address him. "Are you ready to see what I had custom made for you to wear?"

He turns and eyes me suspiciously. "As grateful as I am for this transformation, perhaps I should wear one of my own blazers. A custom-made suit seems a bit too much."

"Who said it was a suit?" I motion for him to follow me into my large closet, though he audibly sighs. We've gotten close these past few months, but somehow, he also has yet to adjust to my antics.

Placing my hand on the scanner in the middle of the room, I speak to my virtual assistant. "Vara, please get me item number seven on rack number four." Immediately, the fourth rack of clothing spins and slides out Santiago's outfit for the evening, which was freshly pressed this morning. I gently pick it up and hold it out for him. "Nova gave me the idea."

Santiago carefully takes the traditional Indian kurta from my hands and examines it closely. The deep blue fabric has been embroidered with a pattern of white flowers around the collar and wrists. I had it made almost identical to his father's, which his aunt showed me a picture of a few weeks ago. I knew Santiago would feel uneasy about changing his style completely, even for a night, but Nova convinced me that he would appreciate this.

"It's just like Appa's favorite kurta." He looks at me with appreciation, and I lean in to hear comments of gratitude from my friend. "I'll have to thank Nova for doing this," Santiago says, and my face turns into a frown as he throws his head back in laughter. "I'm only kidding, mate. Thank you, I'll wear it with pride."

I begin to chuckle along with him. "You're welcome, Santiago. Now go back to your room, get dressed, and meet me in the hallway in twenty minutes."

He smiles one last time before rushing out with his kurta. I turn and place my hand over the scanner once again, asking Vara for my own suit this time. The black tux appears before me in no time, but it takes the whole twenty minutes before I feel ready for this event. Placing rings on my fingers and fixing my bowtie is easy, but planning this party was not. I'm not sure why this nervous buzz in my head persists. Assuring myself that everything will be fine, I walk out into the hallway where Santiago waits.

"Are you ready?" I call out to him, careful to not fix my collar for the hundredth time.

"Absolutely!" Says a different voice from the opposite end of the hall. Nova and her brother, Graham, are waiting for us near the elevator. I start towards them and Santiago follows in my steps quickly. The glass elevator dings and opens for us to step in.

"You clean up nicely, Santiago. I'm happy to see you wearing the kurta," Nova says, and Santiago smiles down at her widely. She then looks to me and seems taken aback by my outfit. "Only a simple black tux, Hart? Are you toning things down so you don't outshine Violetta?"

I shake my head. "You know it's impossible for me to outshine her."

Santiago, Graham, and Nova all make the same groaning noise. "While I agree with you, please save the charming lines for her," Nova says, and we all laugh for a few moments before the elevator announces we are on the courtyard level. The doors open, and Nova tells Santiago and Graham to go ahead of us. She loops her arm around mine like she often does with Violetta and whispers to me, "Why did you invite Ember tonight?"

I keep my stare focused straight ahead as we walk towards the open courtyard where the party awaits us. "She apologized profusely, and her father even got David a job on their family's security team. I figured it's only fair to try and cordially move forward."

Nova huffs out a breath. "She turned you and Violetta into the authorities."

"If she hadn't done that, we wouldn't be here today." My voice stays low, and we are now standing in front of the entrance to the courtyard. There are lights glistening everywhere and music flows in when I halt and turn to face her.

"Nova, everyone deserves a second chance. You taught me that."

She raises an eyebrow at me before releasing her arm from mine. "Alright, I'll be nice." Nova sucks in a breath and her white, high-heeled shoes carry her into the party, where everyone awaits our presence.

Though I planned this entire thing, I'm still shocked at how stunning the scenery is. There are walls of flowers, soft lighting in the trees, a band playing from the gazebo, and at least a hundred people scattered around the large, open area. Scanning the gardens, it takes a moment for my eyes to find Violetta's parents standing by one of the hors d'oeuvre tables. As I walk toward them, I can vaguely make out the frame of Violetta, who is speaking with them with her back turned to me.

"Violetta!" My voice rings out clear above the loud sounds of chatter around me.

She spins around to face me, and the air is completely taken from my lungs, just as I'd expected. Her hair is falling down her back in a braid, and a flower crown made of lavender sits atop her head. The dress she wears heavily resembles the one she wore for my birthday picnic, except it's golden. She's as radiant as she was that night, but perhaps slightly more so, because tonight she looks jubilant beyond compare. Before I can continue to make a fool of myself by just standing here open mouthed, she hurries towards me and embraces me.

"This party is too much, angel," she says in my ear while hugging me, and I bring my arms up to hold her. "But I love it."

"Happy Birthday," I whisper as my nerves begin to dissipate, and she pulls away from me before taking my hand in hers. We walk over to her parents who are watching us while they sip their drinks. "Mr. and Mrs. Akan, how are you this evening?"

"We are fantastic, Hart. Thank you for arranging this magnificent party for Violetta's birthday." Mrs. Akan makes the same face that Violetta does when she's overjoyed, so I know her words are genuine.

"Turning nineteen calls for a great celebration!" Mr. Akan agrees with a bellowing voice and pats me on the shoulder happily.

"It surely does, Kit!" My father makes his way into the conversation and greets his old friends with a hug. They chat for a moment about the party before my father decides to help me by stealing Violetta's parents away. "Have you two met our pastry chef? You must try his chocolate eclairs." They both follow my father towards the pastry table on the other side of the lawn, leaving Violetta and I alone.

"So, may I have this dance?" I put on my most charming smile and extend my other hand out to her.

"I suppose I can grant you one for your hard work." She accepts with a shrug, and we make our way towards the dance floor in front of the band.

Reaching her arms up, she intertwines them around my neck as my hands land on her waist. The rhythm is slow and enticing as we sway together, with broad smiles adorning our faces. I take notice that she's wearing her silver locket with my initials on it and decide to tease her. "I see you ignored my advice and decided to wear that locket, even when it clashes with your golden birthday theme."

"You never change, do you? Somehow, through everything, you're still that same suave, blond boy from the basement." She scrunches her nose, teasing me right back.

"How could you say that nothing has changed?" I say, trying to act completely appalled by the accusation, and she holds back a laugh. "My hair is black now." I wink, and she can't help but let out a giggle. I'm certain there are many watching us, but it's impossible for me to look anywhere else when her eyes are on mine.

"These last few months with you have felt like a dream that I never want to be awakened from," she says, glancing around the courtyard at the splendor of the evening.

"Then you'll stay asleep, because this is only the beginning for us." I stop dancing and lean down to capture her lips in a soft kiss. Her hands make their way into my hair and my arms wrap tightly around her waist. "I'm going to marry you one day, Violetta Akan," I whisper before pulling away, and she stares at me with a mischievous glint in her eyes.

"Marriage would definitely break my rule, Hart." She shakes her head at me, smirking all the while.

While I'm thinking up a witty retort, my father coughs behind us, seemingly as loud as he possibly can, until we acknowledge him. "Yes, Dad?" It takes everything in me to mask the irritation in my voice.

"I hate to interrupt, but the band has been waiting for you to play your song for Violetta," he says, and I remember why I was nervous in the first place. I was so caught up in our dance that I completely forgot. She'd insisted that the party wouldn't be complete without it. After parting from Violetta with a kiss to her hand, I walk up onto the gazebo stage and stand in front of the microphone.

"Hi everyone, thank you for coming to this party to celebrate my enchanting girlfriend, Violetta." I gesture towards Violetta, and she blushes as the entire courtyard cheers for her. "I wrote this song for her a while back and she asked that I perform it for all of you tonight." More applause greets me as I back away from the mic and go to sit on the piano bench.

From this seat, I can see all the faces gathered around the gazebo to hear me play. My father and mother are with Violetta's parents by the pastry table, and Nova and her family are standing with Santiago, who gives me a thumbs up. Even Ember and David are shooting me warm looks from where they sit at one of the banquet tables. Still, somehow none of their reassuring faces are helping my pesky nerves.

Then I look at Violetta, who is touching her locket, and everything feels right. The first time I played this song for her with my violin in that worn-down basement, I was nervous because I wasn't sure how she would react. Now, I'm certain that she will be pleased even if I mess up. There is no reason to feel unsure anymore. She's standing there beaming up at me. She ignites me. Placing my fingers on the shining keys, I take one last peek at my angel for inspiration and close my eyes to find the right tune.

And then, the music begins.

Authors Note

Dear Reader,

I must convey my most sincere thanks to you. You spent time exploring *The Crossed* world and that means a lot to me. Violetta, Hart, Santiago, Nova, and every single character in the book are dear to my heart. Thank you for loving them like I do.

While this is a fictional story, it is also a call to action for my brothers and sisters of every race. Almost two years ago, I watched as a photo of a mixed family was belittled by millions on social media. There was mention from one particularly vitriolic account of putting mixed children behind a wall and making interracial marriage illegal in the U.S. once again.

I wrote this story as a response and warning to those that praised the account for the spiteful comment. This cautionary tale was born to show the oppressors how horrid the world would be if their notions came true. Thankfully, no matter how hard hate tries: Love always wins.

I implore you to reflect on how you've viewed mixed families until now, and if it's been a view that is clouded by stereotypes. You may not have even been aware of the racial injustices multiracial Americans and interracial couples face when you picked up this book. Either way, it's never too late to learn, grow, and become an ally, just like Hart did.

Additionally, I wrote this because I rarely read of characters that look like me. Mixed people are seldom depicted in the media. When we have the rare opportunity to be represented, they often portray us as weak, malicious, or unsure. Most often, they force us to choose a side.

This book above all is for my fellow multicultural people who are everything I know them to be and more: Strong, Unbreakable, Confident, Compassionate, and proudly Crossed.

Acknowledgments

First and foremost, I'd like to thank my parents, who defied social norms in the name of love and raised me to be proud of who I am. Mom, you're the strongest person I've ever known and I strive to be more like you. Appa, it is unfair that you are as kind, funny, and intelligent as you are because you make me look bad. I love you both more than mere words can say.

Thank you to my Irish-American and Indian families that have shaped who I am and made me confident in representing both cultures. Special shout-out to my grand-parents in India for always making me smile. Also, an honorable mention to my foster grand-parents, Bruce and Jackie Redmond, for treating me as their own and uplifting me in Christ.

Though they are not technically my blood relatives, I'd like to show my sincerest gratitude to the Benedict family, who have consistently made me feel special and taught me to trust God in all things. Especially Dave and Danielle, who let me stay at their house for prolonged periods of time even though I was an annoying teenager. There is no way I'd be as "normal-ish" as I am without their constant guidance.

My sincerest thanks to those who stood by me and supported me through every step of the way. Each of these people listened to me for hours on end as I struggled through certain chapters and lamented being at the coffee shop for hours writing. I wouldn't be the person or writer I am without any of these lovely souls: Savannah Jean, Torin Lucas, Drew Vojslavek, Jillian Hersh, Isaiah Alejo, Ashton Whitney, Adam David, Madison Stanley, Tristan Johnson, Stacy Gregory, Matthew Welcome, Leah Pontigo, Elizabeth and Ryan Joslyn, Stephen Alford, Hannah Moore, Michayela Perry, Hannah

Beatty, Grace Bowan, Stephanie Evans, Denise Meisburg,
Kathryn Dyer, Rykley Cooper, Kori Zamora, Hallie Shrader,
Abi and Max Sloan, and Tom Woods.

The entire team of people who worked on this book were
all strong women who spent long nights ensuring this novel
would be the absolute best it could be. I would be a mess without them, but I have to give special thanks to Kate Porch in
particular, who dedicated almost an entire year to the editing
process. Not only did she care immensely for the characters,
but she is a brilliant social justice warrior who inspires me
daily. The rest of my team are also incredible dreamers whom
I adore: Julia Parsons, Esther Legiste, Eliza James, Faith Lane,
and Amanda Crosby.

I would be remiss if I didn't mention those who came into
my life and provided motivation and hope for the future in
times when I needed it most. From teachers to roommates,
you all made a significant impact on my life even if you
didn't know it. So, I thank those who always believed in me:
The Casey family, the Lard family, the Shinkre family, The
Vaith family, The David family, Robert and Heidi Manzone,
Victoria Parnell, Brigilda Lleshi, Susan Freese, Brooke Mc-
Cabe, Natalie and Alexis Gettemy, Melissa and Taylor Mintz,
Marianne Dyer, Christine DeCastro, Larissa Hamblin, Han-
nah O'Donnell, Laura Fleck, Michael Gray, Roxana Lemus,
Sanghyun Lee, Matt Lee, Fernanda Arnay, Alicia and Josh
Brittain, Jackie Pacheco, Anna Reilly, Bryce Goodson, Katie
Iley, Melanie and Abi Stewart, Bene Singh, Charis Horner,
Lauren Ligeti-Juenger, Sue Rausch, Bill and Toni Gellerstedt,
Shawnna and Mishell Larmond, Jim Radloff, Zachary Sahni,
Hitha and Khushi Chandrashekar, Sandy Vargo, Steve Calla-
han, Catalina and Monica Reusche, Jonathan Janvier, Angela

LoRusso-Mack, Debbie Sanders, Joseph Ng, Claudia Ragosta, Tina and Derek Sloan, Ryan Pratt, Josh Portillo, Christian De Padua, the Pontigo family, Amelia Alamdar, Lily Bateh, Rachel Richardson, and the Crosby family.

Writing a book isn't the easiest with chronic pain, but it's somehow incredibly simple when you have a support team like mine. Thank you to all the followers of the Chronic Migraine Association of America for writing, calling, and texting to show your love and support. You kept me going. The best part of my week is chatting with you all and I can't show enough thanks for the strength you've given me.

It might seem odd to include this section of gratitude, but I want to thank the people I've never met who inspired me to follow my dreams like author Jenny Han, who wrote the first mixed race character I ever read in a book, or Avan Jogia, who gathered multiracial people together to write an epic collection of poems that represent us in a truthful and raw way. Even musicians like Jae Park of Day6, who encouraged me to give the glory to God in my work and whose music helped me through those torturous nights of brainstorming. Countless others like Harper Lee, Langston Hughes, and Bill Withers contributed to this book by becoming my muses. Art inspires art.

Lastly, I must tell you about a boy who was the first person I ever met that made me realize how special and wonderful of a thing it is to be mixed. Indo-Irish people are rare to come by, and I'm convinced he was by far the most special of all. This book is for every shining star like him who shared their light to those who were in the dark and helped other multiracial people understand their value. His legacy will live on. Thank you to the true protagonist, Jackson Vaith.

Sincerely,

TJ Rao

Made in the USA
Columbia, SC
28 August 2020